The Prairie Schooner
BOOK PRIZE

The Prairie Schooner

BOOK
PRIZE

TENTH ANNIVERSARY READER

EDITED BY *James Engelhardt* AND *Marianne Kunkel*

FOREWORD BY *Hilda Raz*

UNIVERSITY OF NEBRASKA PRESS | LINCOLN AND LONDON

© 2013 by the Board of Regents
of the University of Nebraska

Acknowledgments for the use of
copyrighted material appear on
pages 255–56, which constitute an
extension of the copyright page.

Library of Congress
Cataloging-in-Publication Data
The Prairie Schooner Book Prize:
tenth anniversary reader / edited by
James Engelhardt and Marianne Kunkel;
foreword by Hilda Raz.
p. cm.
ISBN 978-0-8032-4043-8 (pbk.: alk. paper)
1. American literature. 2. United States—
Literary collections. I. Engelhardt, James.
II. Kunkel, Marianne.
PS507.P73 2013
810.8—dc23   2012037697

Set in Janson by Laura Wellington.

Contents

Foreword by Hilda Raz *vii*

2003

Cortney Davis
"Leopold's Maneuvers" *3*
"March 28, 2001 /
March 28, 1945" 5

K. L. Cook
"Last Call" 7

2004

Rynn Williams
"The Sample Makers" *33*
"Big Yard" *35*

Brock Clarke
"The Fund-Raiser's
Dance Card" *36*

2005

Kathleen Flenniken
"Preservation" *59*
"Murder Mystery" *61*

John Keeble
"The Cross" *62*

2006

Paul Guest
"Elba" *79*
"These Arms of Mine" *80*

Jesse Lee Kercheval
"Beasts" *82*

2007

Mari L'Esperance
"Pantoum of the Blind
Cambodian Women"   *107*
"Finding My Mother"   *108*

Katherine Vaz
"Lisbon Story"   *110*

2008

Kara Candito
"Self-Portrait with an
Ice Pick"   *147*
"Carnivale, 1934"   *149*

Anne Finger
"Vincent"   *150*

2009

Shane Book
"Dust"   *171*

Ted Gilley
"Physical Wisdom"   *176*

2010

James Crews
"Paradoxical
Undressing"   *195*
"Metacognition"   *197*
"The Bees Have Not
Yet Left Us"   *199*

Greg Hrbek
"Sagittarius"   *200*

2011

Susan Blackwell Ramsey
"Boliche"   *217*
"Knitting Lace"   *219*

Karen Brown
"Little Sinners"   *221*

2012

Orlando Ricardo Menes
"Elegy for Great-Uncle
Julio, Cane Cutter"   *237*
"Television, a Patient
Teacher"   *239*

Xhenet Aliu
"Flipping Property"   *240*

Source
Acknowledgments   *255*

Contributors   *257*

Foreword

The anthology you're reading now is filled with stories and poems from the first decade of the Prairie Schooner Book Prizes, two manuscripts published annually by the University of Nebraska Press, selected by the editor of *Prairie Schooner* in an open competition. We've chosen one manuscript of poetry and one manuscript of short fiction each year since 2003, with a prize of $3,000 and a standard publication contract from the press for each writer. This introduction is a brief history of the series. In many cases, I remember the exact moments of first reading these selections and they continue to give me pleasure. And I remember the story of starting the Book Prize series.

I've long thought that one purpose of art is to extend human experience; so it has been for me. Over ten years we've chosen stories and poems about family, parents, and children as well as lovers of all genders and preferences; accounts of civil and civic catastrophe; diverse voices praising and lamenting urban life; revisionist texts and tales; documents of the disappeared; ecofiction; and lyrics and narratives about human genius, disability, poverty, and some actions that try to save the world.

These prize-winning selections reflect and respond to our times. Writers of debut books as well as more experienced writers were chosen anonymously each year. We've seen superb manuscripts withdrawn by agents to be published by commercial presses and reputations made and increased by winning a Prairie Schooner Book Prize. And we've seen the contest continue for ten years and longer with the promise that it will go on. Not many magazines endure for nearly ninety years of continuous publication as *Prairie Schooner* has. We aspire to the same for the Prairie Schooner Book Prizes.

Don't we all like to read, listen to, and tell stories? "The universe is made of stories, not atoms," wrote poet Muriel Rukeyser. Stories make order of the apparent chaos of our lives. These days, poets and writers and their audiences depend on an array of conduits to reach one another. *Prairie Schooner*, begun in 1927, is one of these conduits. This story about another kind of conduit, the Prairie Schooner Book Prizes, grew from the success of the journal.

Most writers want to publish. Why? Here's an old joke. A writer dies and goes to heaven. She's been good, won the major prizes, so St. Peter gives her the choice between heaven or hell. They go on the tour. In heaven the writer sees people chained to trees with their fingers moving fast over laptops. St. Peter snaps his fingers, and they're in hell. The writer sees people chained to trees with their fingers moving fast over laptops. "Oh," says the writer, who is wringing her hands. "What's the difference between heaven and hell?" "Well," says St. Peter with an angelic smile, "in heaven, you get published."

Journals publish. They serve writers and readers. Journal editors graft their visions, ambitions, opportunities, and passions onto the successes of their predecessors. When I became the fifth editor of *Prairie Schooner* in 1970, I knew my debt to founding editor Lowry Wimberly; second editor, Pulitzer Prize–winning poet Karl Shapiro; third editor, John Keats and Willa Cather Scholar Bernice Slote; and the fourth editor, the William Blake and A. R. Ammons Scholar Hugh Luke.

I also understood that the magazine owed a debt to the University of Nebraska, no metaphor. The budget was all red ink. The English Department harbored an inventory of magazines in a basement room, and our national distributor had discarded *Prairie Schooner* because we couldn't get to press on time. My first ambition was to retire the debt. I also meant to establish a publishing schedule, increase our circulation, and reinvigorate the journal's tradition of excellence.

Our assets were these: we'd published without interruption since 1927; we had a long list of successful contributors and the active support of the University of Nebraska, where we were part of the Department of English; and the University of Nebraska Press, one of the best presses in the country, was our publisher.

In 1927 *Prairie Schooner* was a regional magazine. Our local writers traveled east and west, north and south, with copies of the magazine in their pockets. Soon the journal and its writers were winning national prizes and our demographics changed. We grew beyond our territory.

When I was a new—and young—editor in the 1970s, the colleagueship of editors of major magazines, especially George Core at *Sewanee Review* and Stanley Lindberg at *Georgia Review*, helped us. I don't know why they took the time to answer their telephones to tell me how to make a magazine work, but they did. Before long, with their advice, *Prairie Schooner* managed and then retired the debt, hired a new printer, and found a new distributor. The University of Nebraska Press loaned us the services of a professional copyeditor and a copyright manager. We began to publish portfolios of international writing in translation, and these portfolios helped to expand our mission in a time of growing internationalism. Individual issues sold instead of going to basement storage. Special issues were reprinted as books and they did well. The magazine's size grew as our income did, from eighty pages to two hundred pages and more. We hired Dika Eckersley as our designer; we began to print four-color covers with bar codes. We joined the Association for Writers and Writing Programs, the disciplinary organization for writers who teach in the academy. Our various managing editors took the magazine to book fairs. And, as the editor, I became a participant in conferences, at annual meetings, and on panels, giving papers and eventually serving on the board of directors and then as president of AWP.

Prairie Schooner's opportunities grew fast. Our writers won prizes and published good books with commercial and university presses.

We were on lists and in illustrations: as the foundational roots of the tree of literary culture in *Esquire* magazine, for example, and in all of the prize anthologies. *Prairie Schooner*, always known for its support of beginning poets and writers, was called prophetic—we seemed to attract the best and the brightest writers at the start of their careers: Cyrus Colter, Marilyn Nelson, and Alberto Rios as well as Willa Cather and Eudora Welty. In 2001 *Prairie Schooner* celebrated seventy-five years of continuous publication with a conference at the University of Nebraska; Joyce Carol Oates was keynote speaker. One of her first stories and later ones were published in *Prairie Schooner*. Over one thousand people registered for that conference, planned for mid-September 2001. Then, with the rest of the country, we watched the World Trade Center towers come down. In shock after 9/11, we wondered who would come to our conference? Who would enter air space by choice? We knew: nobody. We were mistaken. Oates arrived along with every reader and every panelist on the schedule, and so did international scholars who came to discuss Oates's writing; other *Prairie Schooner* writers came to read and discuss their work and the state of the world. At the Seventy-Fifth Anniversary Conference, panels of poets, creative nonfiction and fiction writers, scholars and critics, and large and vocal audiences refused to leave rooms scheduled for other panels. They joined together. Few people left the building; instead they stayed to read and talk about writing and to discuss the place of the arts in an uncertain future. Then we had a party.

In the hubbub, California poet, publisher, and philanthropist Glenna Luschei climbed on a chair, raised her arms for quiet, and told us that she had endowed *Prairie Schooner* and its editorship, in perpetuity, through the University of Nebraska Foundation. From the highest levels of the administration and the foundation, which had supported and attended the conference, to the writers who had come far in interesting times and local supporters and readers and friends, we were surprised. Linda Pratt (the chair of the English Department) and I met in an alcove to dance our pleasure in a time of grief. The next week, a senior member of the administration asked what might the magazine do next?

We knew: poetry and short stories are difficult to publish. We wanted a book prize series. The University of Nebraska Press asked for a proposal. Reviewers were enthusiastic. They recommended the Prairie Schooner Book Prizes for annual publication in two volumes, one of poetry and one of short stories. We would have a national literary board to offer the editor advice about the finalist manuscripts, and the editor would choose both winners. The seed money for the prize was deposited in our accounts. And so we began.

Our First Crisis and Heroes: Forming the Prize

The book prize proposal to the University of Nebraska Press projected five hundred manuscript submissions after the first two years. The first year, twelve hundred paper manuscripts overflowed the departmental mailroom, stymied the staff, and shut down the front office. Who could open the envelopes in a timely manner? Who would administer the contest and oversee the ethical separation of screeners from judges from manuscripts? Who was going to remove author names from the books and assign numbers? Which computer could we use to create a spreadsheet? We'd believed that we could handle the mail. The journal received over five hundred manuscript submissions each month. We'd managed. But the piles of manuscript entries stood well over eight feet tall. We couldn't manage.

Many stories have heroes. Peggy Shumaker, a poet and contributor, had become a friend and colleague on the AWP board. And she, with others, knew how to get things done.

Peggy and her husband, businessman Joe Usibelli, had met with us at AWP meetings to talk about literary publishing. With Joe's keen questions and Peggy's suggestions we first began to imagine the Prairie Schooner Book Prize. If we had the experience, we also had the most important component for this new series: a collaborative team with university support. The outstanding PhD program in creative writing in the English Department at the University of Nebraska could provide screeners, readers, and staff for the project. The University of Nebraska Press, one of the best in the country, might support it. But we didn't have the start-up money to pay for what Peggy and Joe thought necessary: two large prizes. We decided that we'd have to wait. But as friends, we stayed in touch.

Now we had the money, the approved proposal, and the pure hubris. We went ahead with our plans. We also had eight-foot stacks of manuscript submissions we hadn't planned for. Are you surprised to read that I picked up the telephone? Peggy and Joe answered their phone. They gave advice: hire a book prize coordinator; find a separate office and a new computer. Then they sent a check to implement their suggestions and later promised an annual donation to keep the series alive.

After a rocky start that included the urgent need to draft an ethics statement for the series, we continued with our plans. All manuscripts were sent to an office removed from the journal offices by a floor. A responsible coordinator was hired. Our ethics statement served as a model for other contests (see the journal website: *Prairie Schooner* now uses CLMP's statement, which originally was based on the journal's), and we worked and we worked and we worked. I remember June and July of 2003 as weeks on a couch, an Oblamov in the Middle West where I lay covered by paper. Then as now we had no idea whose work we were reading. At the end of July, the first winners were announced: Cortney Davis, a poet and nurse practitioner, was selected for *Leopold's Maneuvers*, a book whose poems refuse to "brush off horror like salt" as they provide witness to birth and crisis, and K. L. Cook for *Last Call*, a book of short fiction. Cook's next book, *The Girl from Chamelle*, was published by Harper Collins. Each of the winners received a prize check along with a publishing. UNP took over all publishing, publicity, and distribution of the prize books.

By 2004 at *Prairie Schooner* we had all systems running. The winners were Rynn Williams for her astonishing and shocking *Adonis*

Garage and Brock Clarke for *Carrying the Torch* (he'd won a Mary McCarthy Prize already). His next book was *An Arsonist's Guide to Writers' Homes in New England*, one of the most widely reviewed books of 2007. Williams was moving from her upper West side NYC apartment with her children when I called to tell her about her prize. She sat on a packing box to talk. Her premature death five years later brought silence to that loud and compelling voice but her book continues to be read and taught. The next year, 2005, winner Kathleen Flenniken's poetry book, *Famous*, now in its third printing, was chosen by the American Library Association as one of ten Notable Books of the year, in all genres.

The fiction winner for 2005 was John Keeble, a novelist, nonfiction writer and farmer, and subsequent winner of a Guggenheim Fellowship. He described the landscape of his title story, "Nocturnal America," and the predations of human behavior on the land: "As we drove we gazed at the forestland, which in the watersheds grew so deep as to blot out the sun. In other places the clear-cuts opened gloomy vistas of stumpage and barrens backed by beetle kills." We know nothing good can happen here; this prose description isn't metaphor. Humans prey on the land. But human action also can "make an adjustment to the landscape": a huge iron cross, emblem of fascist fundamentalism, set up mysteriously on the steep sides of the "K____ Dam, a tributary of the great Columbia River" is brought down by the action of two men in "The Cross," reprinted here. Language restores meaning as action will. We'd chosen a book of ecofiction.

The next year brought Paul Guest's *Notes for My Body Double* to us. His poems speak of body and mind fused in remarkable ways. Whether the poet spoke as a persona or whether he was a quadriplegic we couldn't know. The poems were radiant and still are. Guest's prizes since include the Whiting Writers' Award, a Guggenheim Fellowship in poetry, and many more. His memoir and subsequent books of poetry have made a stir with readers and reviewers.

Jesse Lee Kercheval's ten linked Alice stories illustrate the formal connection between short fiction and the novel. Its narrative surprises are vivid, as seemingly impossible as life. *The Alice Stories* stayed with us, a family's stand against death. Kercheval's publishing credits in all genres were extensive and her reputation established when this book was selected. We couldn't know. We didn't care. The book was superb, surprising, original, and everyone who read it in manuscript recommended it for the prize. In "Beast," reprinted here, Alice is a model for her photographer husband: ". . . when my mouth was a weary smear, my eyes were narrowed, my neck bent with fatigue into a slightly odd and painful angle, then voila! there was tension and a hint of a story that would forever remain tantalizing and unknowable. There was art."

In 2007 we gave recognition and publication to reenactments of war, displacement, and redemption: Mari L'Esperance's prize-winning poems invoke silence at the heart of a daughter's longing for her disappeared mother. And Katherine Vaz's AIDS-affected story "Lisbon" here represents her collection of Portuguese American stories where grief and death may not prevail over a dying father's memory of the stems of unsold flowers stuffed into guns, a gesture of defiance during the 1974 Carnation War.

In 2008 Kara Candito was a PhD student in poetry and literary theory and Anne Finger was a well-known writer and disability studies scholar when each won the Book Prize, the former with her vivid debut collection set in the world of travel, filled with violence, sex, and cultural dysphoria, the latter for her brilliant revisions of familiar texts. Here, Finger retells the story of artist Vincent Van Gogh, this time in contemporary New York without his brother's support to buy paints, dying of poverty with scores of other homeless people, waiting for social security to provide enough money for food, never mind art supplies: no masterpieces for us to buy, cherish, display, or reproduce.

The 2009 prizes went to two debut collections, Shane Book's in poetry, *Ceiling of Sticks*, and Ted Gilley's short fiction, *Bliss*. Boundaries seem to dissolve in these books, between events, people, and even earth and sky as the landscape shifts under pressure; a boy grows up, a Cambodian lover meets an American ex-husband, memories of bathing merge woman and grandfather into one experience of loss. The effects of global politics press on individual lives. Filled with experiences of Africa and Latin America, California and the Caribbean, family and lost love, these separate books show the talent of their authors. Book was a Cave Canem scholar and a *New York Times* fellow; Gilley won the 2008 Alehouse Press National Poetry Competition.

The 2010 prizes are *The Book of What Stays*, James Crews's poetry which demonstrates how to live to write love poems, and Greg Hrbek's *Destroy All Monsters*, from which the amazing "Sagittarius," a myth about difference, admonishes us to cherish monsters; they are us.

In 2011, poet, teacher, and bookseller Susan Blackwell Ramsey's *A Mind Like This* reminds us that difference lives in language—Spanish "was a different building, not just repainted English" in a high school class where learning was "a first attempt to fit our thinking / in another's, like empathy." Karen Brown, a winner of the Grace Paley Prize for her first collection of short stories, won the Prairie Schooner Book Prize in short fiction for her next collection, *Leaf House*, represented here by "Little Sinners." Let Brown's words sound: "we are all alone with the stories we have never told." Secrets, told, become art.

The 2012 prize in poetry went to well-published writer Orlando Ricardo Menes for his collection, *Fetish*. Born in Lima, Peru, to Cuban parents, he has lived most of his life in the United States where he directs the creative writing program at the University of Notre Dame and is the author of *Furia* and *Rumba atop the Stones* and editor of *Renaming Ecstasy: Latino Writings on the Sacred and The Open Light: Poets from Notre Dame, 1991–2008*. He also has published translations of Spanish poetry, including *My Heart Flooded with Water: Selected Poems by Alfonsina Storni*, and he is the recipient of a NEA Fellowship. The poems in *Fetish* are set in Cuba, Miami,

Panama, Peru, Bolivia, and elsewhere. They are political and satiric, funny, smart, and represented here by "Elegy for Great-Uncle Julio, Cane Cutter" and "Television, a Patient Teacher."

Xhenet Aliu is the fiction winner for her debut collection, *Domesticated Wild Things*. "There is a sophisticated brand of humor in Aliu's fiction—her stories will make you laugh out loud," says current Prairie Schooner editor in chief, Kwame Dawes. "These are entertaining and insightful stories full of surprises and revelations." A former secretary, waitress, entertainment journalist, and private investigator, Aliu lives in Athens, Georgia, after recent stints in Brooklyn, Montana, and Utah.

In 2010 I proffered my resignation and began to leave the *Prairie Schooner* offices to imagine a new life. We moved to New Mexico in 2011, where I became the director of the Mary Burritt Christiansen Poetry Series for the University of New Mexico Press and the poetry editor for a small magazine, *Bosque*. *Prairie Schooner* and her Book Prizes continue under the visionary direction of poet and writer Kwame Dawes, who has invited me to become part of the journal's National Literary Board.

Why did we want to start a book prize in the first place? Readers, look here to find out.

Hilda Raz
Placitas, New Mexico

The Prairie Schooner

BOOK PRIZE

2003

Cortney Davis

Leopold's Maneuvers

*The four maneuvers used by an examiner to
determine the lie of an unborn child*

The belly an albino bowl
suddenly come to life, my hands
ready in the four positions
like the four witches in Oz
or the four winds that breathe,
all of us diviners. First
I cup the belly's pregnant curve
high under blue-veined breasts,
brim the slope and wiggle where an unborn
human head is round and hard,
the breech irregular. Second maneuver
and my palms embrace her sides, swelling
woman and curled child, where is your
back? Where are your small parts?
Third maneuver, my right hand grasps
the pubic hollow, fingers open
and close around the round ball
of a head, head ball, chin down, breech
balled at the fundus under
blue breasts, oblivious. And last,
great mother, as if compelled
toward the face of miracles,
my hands plunge the gutters

of a pelvic inlet I can only imagine,
feeling for the brow, the flexed
crown, the direction this child will take
emerging into light, our world,
the earth from its watery heaven
into its own brief span and back again,
   my hands
waving hello, good-bye, hello, good-bye.

March 28, 2001 / March 28, 1945

I'm in my basement exercising when
the radio announcer says that on this
day in 1945, it was an unprecedented
eighty degrees. It takes me a moment
to realize that, fifty-five years ago,
my mother was twelve weeks pregnant
with me. Maybe she didn't know or
maybe she blamed the heat, oppressive
at the Maryland shore where she walked
with friends along the water's edge
trying to forget the war; my mother—
thin legs, flat breasts, brown hair,
blue eyes. Pausing now in my
basement, I feel her slight nausea, how
sweat trickles between her breasts
and dampens the underside of her hair.
My father's in Italy, every day he writes
her love letters from the Po Valley,
unaware that I have stolen part of them
both and come to life, a gelatinous fish-
like curl in her uterus, a foreign body
that primes her ovaries, her estrogen,
progesterone, prolactin, the hormones
that make her, this very day, feel slightly
faint. She wades into the still-cold waves
and sits down there, splashing herself
with one hand, acclimating her skin
to the sudden chill. In Italy, my sun-
burned father sweeps land mines from
green depressions between the Apennines.

At night, he drinks wine and writes letters
before his turn at watch. This is the day
after his battalion entered Tezze,
triumphant, months before he'll win the
bronze star and come home half crazy.
Mother can't know that soon my body
will tear itself from hers and she'll birth
me at midnight, lightning stuttering the
labor room windows, an odd beginning
to the odd ending neither of us expects
when, at last no longer knowing who
I am, she will refuse my hand. When
she leaves the shore, suit damp to her
belly, when she hurries home to write
my father about how it was eighty
degrees so she went to the beach,
is she already unhappy or have I been,
all this time, mistaken? If only I could
ask what she hopes for, what she will
expect of me, and if she thinks, in any
way or at any time, I might ever please her.

K. L. Cook

Last Call

1978

Last call had been made over the intercom, and I began to scrub the stockpile of cocktail and beer glasses on the three-pronged bristles, rinsing them quickly in standing water, a glass in each hand. Enrico and Boozer stood at the far end of the counter, splitting what we'd made for the night, even though not all the customers had left. I was only the bar-back, their gopher, but they were good about dividing the money equally, giving me a full third. I doubt they would have been so generous if we worked at some little dive, but the Texas Moon was a big place—it used to be a roller skating rink—and when I worked there, it was full most every night. We made well over a hundred dollars regularly, so the split was usually good. Plus Boozer and Enrico knew I worked for my money, sweating like a frothy dog, changing the liquor and soda guns, hauling fifty, sixty cases of beer a night from the walk-in, and washing so many glasses that my back hurt from bending over, and my hands were permanently pink and wrinkly with flaky white circles all over my palms.

Arlene set her empty glasses on the counter and smiled at me. She'd been working at the Texas Moon for about a week, tall and slender and blonde, almost twenty. She wore loose-fitting shirts because her breasts were large, and I admired her modesty. We'd been winking at each other since her first day, accidentally bumping together near the walk-in. Earlier that night she let me chew a lime slice off the plastic sword she was holding.

I was examining her walk-away when somebody leaned over the counter and poked his finger in my chest. It was an older man in a cheap straw cowboy hat, creased at the top and banded with a little brown feather stuck in the side.

"How old are you?" he asked me. His voice was gravelly, like he had ice chunks caught in his throat. It reminded me, oddly, of my father's voice.

"Old enough," I said, guarding. For all I knew, he could have been with the Texas Liquor Commission. I tried to judge whether or not I should say anything else. If I made a mistake, the Texas Moon might have shut down since I was not, at seventeen, legally old enough to work there. My mother got me the job. She liked to know where I was (not in any trouble that she wasn't supervising), and if men started hitting on her, which they sometimes did, she could point to me and that usually got rid of them.

"That waitress over there," he said, looking at the pool tables, "claims you're her son. Is that true?"

Boozer leaned over the counter beside me. "Which waitress you talking about?"

The man sized Boozer up, not a hard task. Boozer was short, brawny, about ten years older than me. He had to stand on his tiptoes to lean over the counter. The man pointed at my mother, bent over a table, waiting for the two men there to pay their tabs.

"That good-looking blonde over there," the man said.

"That's *my* mother," Boozer said.

"I just want to know if she's *his* mother," the man said, trying again to poke me in the chest. I jumped back, and a little soapy water splashed on the counter. A couple of drops landed on the man's arm above a red tattoo of a fish.

"Sorry," I said. He scowled at me and wiped his arm.

"What's the problem, Travis?" Enrico called to me from the other end of the bar. I laughed, as I did whenever I looked at him suddenly. He was about fifty, at least six-foot-eight, bone thin, big marbly eyes, with a long neck and shaved head, only a few gray prickles around his ears and along the back of his skull. An ostrich's head.

"Well, are you or aren't you?" the man demanded.

"That's not his mother," Enrico said, deadpan. "That's *my* mother."

"Fuckin' bartenders!" the man said and waddled off toward the bathroom.

"Hey, Mother!" Boozer bellowed so loudly everybody still at the tables on our side of the Texas Moon stared at us. When she turned, we all waved. Then Enrico counted one, two, three, and we yelled, "Who loves you, baby?"

"My boys," my mother called back, laughing, her teeth flashing like neon in the half-dark. She turned back to her table, but that laugh stayed with me. My father used to say she had a laugh that "could melt butter and make invalids dance." And drunkards tip, I could easily add. At thirty-eight, she was good looking with silvery-blonde hair that kinked sometimes on the ends. She had high cheekbones and girlish dimples etched around the corners of her mouth and, to me, the saddest blue-green eyes, flecked with white, like a choppy wave in the sunlight. She had, too, what she called a "bump" on her nose, her only unattractive feature. I knew she got it from my father, though exactly how and when and why, I never discovered; they never told us kids, and we understood that we weren't to bring the subject up, that it was somehow a private symbol of an earlier, more desperate time in their marriage.

Our landing the jobs at the Texas Moon several months prior was the luckiest thing to happen to us since the accident. My father hadn't had any life insurance. My mother hired a lawyer, Raymond, to sue the trucking company and the driver who hit the car my father and my brother Carroll were in, but the whole process had seemed so long and drawn out, with them making an offer, then us, then the string of nasty letters, the threats and counterthreats, the delays. My mother finally just told Raymond not to tell her any news that wasn't good, and she more or less resigned herself to getting nothing. The Texas Moon was the first real money we'd pocketed. She seemed calmer now, more relaxed than I'd seen her in the past year.

Yet, it wasn't just the money that made the Texas Moon important to us. Part of it was being around Boozer and Enrico. They were a strange pair. Boozer had an ex-wife and a three-year-old boy named Cody in Brownsville. Enrico, I'd heard, served a couple of years in prison in El Paso, for what I didn't know. One waitress told me assault and battery (which I didn't believe) and another said he'd been a spy (which I wanted to believe). Enrico was old enough to be Boozer's father, but they weren't related. They had bartended together for several years, at the big clubs all around the state, some country and western, some rock, even some punk and gay bars. I didn't know if they were fired from all those places or if they were on a bartending circuit. I figured a circuit, if there was one, since I couldn't see why any manager would want to lose them. They were masters on the liquor and soda guns, lifting them high in the air, like six-shooters, creating carbonated waterfalls that threatened to, but never did, splash all over the counter and rubber drink strips.

Every evening, around six o'clock, before the band showed up and after I prepped, I flipped through *Hoyle's Bartender's Guide* and called out a drink—starting with something easy like a Hurricane, say, or a Long Island Tea, then moving on to the trickier drinks like Mau-Maus and Siberian Russians—and they alternated back and forth explaining how to make it. They played the game strictly, too, at twenty bucks a miss. "Verbatim," they'd shout at each other, angry sometimes, laughing mostly, hitting the counter with their fists. Since I'd become their bar-back for the summer, I was the official referee and score keeper, which was easy until they got bored with *Hoyle* and started in on the regional drinks only they'd heard of: Gooseberry Fizzles, Papa John Goolagongs, Laredo Spritzers. I didn't plan to make a career out of bartending, but it didn't seem like a bad life if you could manage it like Enrico and Boozer, working the big-money bars with a sense of humor and style. It was easy for my mother and me to forget ourselves in their routines and in the drum-thumping nights at the Texas Moon.

"Fix us up, Booz," Enrico said.

Boozer poured tequila shots. After Enrico finished splitting the money, he called us over. I rinsed two more glasses, so as not to seem too eager or greedy, and wiped my hands on the towel tucked in the front of my blue jeans. Enrico shoved my stack of bills and change over to me. It looked like a lot, maybe fifty bucks.

"Big night," he said. I never counted the money in front of them, just stuck it in my pocket.

"We busted our butts," I said.

Enrico elbowed me. "You want a chance to lose some of that?"

"Huh?"

"You play poker, don't you?"

Carroll and I used to play in family games. I was pretty good too. Better than Carroll, at least, who could never bluff. In that respect he was like my mother. He'd get a good hand, three of a kind, for example, and he'd start chewing on his upper lip, or his knee would bob up and down like a jack hammer, or he'd rub his cards so hard my father would have to replace the deck. I could have a full house, though, aces over kings, and wouldn't show it. Or sometimes I'd purposely start imitating Carroll when I had nothing, and then I'd bid like I held a royal flush. Three-quarters of the time my uncles would fold, and I'd rake in the kitty. My Uncle Gene refused to play with me; he hated losing to a kid.

"Yeah," I said to Enrico. "I play."

"Come over after we finish," he said. "We're having a party. You and your mammy can take our money from us."

"I don't know," I said.

"Stakes aren't that high."

I wanted to say yes, but I couldn't. My older sister, Julie, was in labor down in Beaumont, had been all day. She'd had complications, toxemia, and been bedridden for three months. The doctors said not to worry, but my mother had the same thing when she was pregnant with me, and my father's mother had died when she was pregnant with her third baby. My mother and I had bought an answering machine on sale at Radio Shack so we wouldn't miss any updates from Julie's husband, Bub, while we were at work.

"I really don't think we can," I said. "We're going to Beaumont tomorrow. Maybe some other night."

"Suit yourself, but I warn you. You don't have your fun early, you wind up cruel and cynical with premature wrinkles and gray stubbles." He patted his head and smiled, then went back to work.

I would have liked to play. But I'd learned from my father that you shouldn't press your luck. If you felt it coming on—and I could always feel it like a cool space around me, a clear-eyed alertness—you should channel it into one thing and one thing only. I wanted to give the luck to Julie, if that was possible. When I was younger, she let Carroll and me smoke in her car, and every weekend she'd take us to the caves in Palo Duro Canyon. She and Bub had been trying to get pregnant for four years. My mother was excited. Ever since we heard the news, she had been sending gifts: baby clothes, bottles, packages of disposable diapers, a playpen, a Johnny Jump-Up. And we had more things at home that we were going to take down that weekend.

"You boys thirsty?" Boozer asked, stuffing his bills in his shirt pocket and his change in his slacks. He had a stack of lemons and the salt shaker and a small Coke chaser (for me) lined up by three shot glasses of Cuervo.

My mother whizzed over, dropped off a tray full of empties, and handed a check and some cash to Boozer, who put it all in the till. She noticed the shot glasses.

"You two wouldn't corrupt my son, would you now?"

"Don't worry, Mom," Boozer said. "I'm already corrupted."

She laughed, then said to him, "You fix me up."

"Yes, ma'am."

Enrico leaned over the bar and put his head down. My mother

took her towel and buffed his knob of a skull. Then she wrapped the towel around her own head, turban style, and ran her palms over his gray prickles like it was a crystal ball. They did this every night, their closing-time ritual.

"Have you called yet?" I asked her.

"Not yet, Travis," she said. "I'll check the machine in a little bit. Quit worrying. That's my job. Everything's going to be fine." She picked up her tray and said to Boozer, "Don't start without me."

I put away most of the glasses, mopped, and eyeballed Arlene as she bent over to wipe off a chair.

A few days earlier we had climbed onto the roof of the Texas Moon during our break. It was cool up there, the air curling in from the east. I drank a Coke while she smoked a cigarette. She asked how my mother and I got the job at the Texas Moon, and I told her, though I didn't get into the details about Carroll or my father since I figured she had already heard from Boozer or Enrico.

I was suddenly nervous talking about myself with her, afraid she would peg me for who I was: a kid. But either she didn't notice or it didn't matter, and that fact tickled something inside my chest, made me bold and giddy. "How about you?" I asked. "What's your story?"

She told me about North Carolina, where she grew up, and where there were tall pines and oaks and an ocean. A man from Kansas brought her to Texas. He knew how to operate a cultipacker, and when he'd come to the Texas plains for the haying season, she tagged along. He began working in Midland-Odessa in March and had planned to work his way up to Canada. Arlene stayed behind in Amarillo, and she figured he was somewhere near Minnesota by now. She hadn't heard from him since he left, didn't expect to. I didn't say much in response, but I felt privileged that she had confided in me.

From her table Arlene suddenly turned and caught me staring, raised her eyebrows, and smiled before coming over to the bar.

"What do you need, honey?" I asked.

She lifted her hair off the back of her neck. Perspiration lined the top of her forehead and beaded above her lip.

"A big glass of soda water with lime and another rag."

"Is that all?"

"For now," she said and seemed to blush. I squirted up a soda water from the gun and gave her a towel, my last one.

"God, it's hot in here," she said.

"It's just me," I said. I took a napkin off the counter. "Lean over."

"Why?"

"Just lean over and close your eyes," I said.

I dabbed the little sweat mustache off her lip. She opened her eyes and smiled, then leaned back and drank all of her soda water in one long gulp. She took the lime slice out of her glass, bit the pulp, and plopped the thin rind back in the ice. She wiped her lips with a napkin, tossed it over my head, basketball style, into the trashcan behind me, then headed to her waitress station.

My mother alcoholed her tables and napkined the ashtrays, then came over to the bar. I asked her if she had called home to check the tape machine yet, and she said she would in a little bit. She wanted to rest her feet. When Boozer and Enrico returned, Enrico pulled out a deck of cards, shuffled them a couple of times, then slapped down two cards in front of my mother: a three and a ten. There was a gap between them.

"You ever played Between?" Boozer asked my mother.

"Plenty of times." She waited a perfect beat. "How do you think Travis was conceived?" Enrico laughed; his Adam's apple, as big as a cue ball, bobbed on his skinny neck. I didn't laugh, but I was proud and a little shocked by her timing. She used to hate off-color jokes. She'd leave the room when my father and brother started in on them.

Boozer said, "We're not talking Between the Sheets."

"I'm so happy," she said. "Because you're much too young for me."

"It's a poker game," Enrico interrupted. "Everybody take out ten dollars."

My mother said, "We can't play in front of the customers."

"It's a quick game. We'll play on this side of the register. Come on."

The dealer put down two cards and the person betting wagered if he thought the third card would fall between the other two. Boozer and I got bad splits to start with, a nine and a six, and a ten and a jack, so we passed. Enrico slapped down an ace for my mother and said, "Call it. High or low."

My mother looked puzzled.

"Low," I advised.

Her next card was a queen. "What should I do?" she asked.

"Bet the pot," I told her.

"No coaching," Enrico said.

"Bet the pot, Mom."

She did. Enrico slapped down a king. He cackled. "You should get yourself a new coach."

My mother pushed her money toward the center and patted my head. "I'll keep this one, thank you."

I told her to play my hand while I went back to the office to get more towels. When I returned she was telling Enrico and Boozer and Arlene, who'd joined them, about the time she saved my life when I was six years old. The money was gone and the deck of cards was by Enrico's elbow.

"It was just a regular hamburger," she said. "The kind you get at old drive-in restaurants. Anyway, it looked fine to me, so I gave it to him."

I knew this story, heard it a million times. I was accident prone as a child, and my mother enjoyed recalling her moments of motherly heroism. She used to tell this story to friends and relatives at Christmas and Thanksgiving, birthdays and summer campouts at Lake Meredith, but this was the first time I'd heard her tell it since my father and Carroll's accident.

"Who won the game?" I interrupted.

"Your mother won it on your go round," Enrico said.

She winked at me. "You'll get your split later."

Boozer said, "She's ratting on you now."

"Go on," Arlene said. She had put her hair up in a ponytail. She looked more girlish, and for a second I wondered just how old she was.

"I went into the kitchen for a second," my mother continued, "just a second, mind you, and when I came back, there he was, poor baby, on his back, scooting across the floor, gasping for air, his eyes rolled back in his head like he was having a seizure. I thought I would die myself. I rushed over and straddled him to hold him down. He thrashed and squirmed and, my God, I was so certain that he'd swallowed poison."

"Were you poisoned?" Arlene asked me.

"Just listen," I told her. She rested her elbow against the counter and brushed against me. I leaned forward a couple of inches from her ponytail and examined the back of her neck where there was a little V-shaped pattern of black hairs leading down to her top vertebra.

"I pried his mouth open," my mother said, demonstrating the maneuver with her fingers. "When I looked inside, what did I see?" She held a moment for suspense. This was my favorite part of the story. "A toothpick sticking in the back of his throat."

"Oh, gross!" Arlene shivered.

Boozer mimicked, "Oh, gross," and clutched his throat.

"What did you do?" Enrico asked, grimacing.

"I reached back there as delicately as I could and tried to pull it out. But I couldn't get all of it since it was splintered. Part of it had lodged in the back of his throat. I thought for sure it had pierced that little thing that hangs down. What's it called, Travis?"

This was my part of the story. "The uvula," I said.

"Did you call an ambulance?" Enrico asked.

"I didn't think I had time. I was in such a state. My adrenaline must have been high because I carried him all the way to the car and rushed him to the hospital, bleating the horn the whole way. A policeman clocked me going a hundred and nine. And I had to stand in the emergency room, trying to hold Travis still, as the doctors tweezed the rest of that toothpick out."

"Yuck," Arlene said.

"It had broken in two and punctured the side of his throat."

"You poor baby," Enrico said.

"I have a little hole in the back of my throat," I said proudly. Enrico got a flashlight, and they all took turns looking. My jaw hurt from opening my mouth for so long, and when Arlene scrunched her eyes to search for the hole, I was suddenly convinced that the inside of a person's mouth was his least attractive anatomical feature.

"So what's the moral?" Enrico asked my mother, putting away the flashlight and deck of cards.

My mother said, "I don't know. I haven't considered the moral. Watch your kids all the time, I guess."

"Check your hamburgers for toothpicks," I said.

Arlene laughed.

My mother followed me back to the walk-in freezer, where I stacked the dolly with another load of beer, my last for the night. She took out a wad of bills from her apron and pockets. I took out my money, and we counted it.

This was a good place to count money. The cool air made our breaths steam and chilled the sweat on our bodies. It smelled good in there with the cardboard cases of lemons and limes and oranges and the malty smell of the beer kegs. I felt closer to her there than I often did at home, where the absence of my father and brother—practical jokers and talkative punsters both of them—made easy banter somehow wrong.

I counted fifty-six dollars and some leftover change for myself, the most money I'd made since I'd been working at the Texas Moon. My mother wound up with over a hundred, which was pretty good for her. Plus sixteen more from the Between game. She handed her money to me, and I uncrinkled the corners and stacked each bill face up in the same direction. I folded it in half and slid the wad in my back pocket.

"Nothing new from Bub?" I asked.

"Oh, I forgot. I'll call in a minute." She started for the door.

"Bet you ten it's twins," I said.

"There aren't any twins in our family." Her breath misted in front of her. "Or Bub's."

"I've got a hunch."

"That's a sucker bet," she said.

"There's got to be two or three kids in there," I said. In the bleached Polaroid they sent us, Julie's belly pooched out like a medicine ball. "I think it's twins."

"No, that's just the way we carry children, honey. When I was pregnant with Carroll, your father thought the same thing, was sure I was gonna have quadruplets. He'd never seen anything so big. He'd thump my stomach, say I was as ripe as a watermelon." She paused, smiled, and fingered the bump on her nose. "And I was. I was ready to bust, I tell you, couldn't wait to get the pregnancy part past me. All that waiting and worrying and feeling like you're not yourself."

She reached into the ice chest by the lemons, pulled out a couple of ice cubes, and threw one to me. While we ran them over our necks, the water dripping through our fingers, I thought about how little she'd mentioned my father or my brother since we started working at the Texas Moon.

For the first few months after the accident, she couldn't do much of anything. It had been snowing heavily when the policeman knocked on our door. My mother answered and I heard some muffled noises, and when I rounded the corner to the den I saw my mother leaning against the door frame, her face in her hands, her slender little-girl's back moving in spasms. The policeman had his head down, and when I saw him he looked, strangely, like a polar bear, draped in a white fur of snow. He started to speak to me, but my mother turned at that moment, her face creased. "Oh, Travis," she said and then, "Oh, God." She turned back to the wall, and I went to her. She tried to stop herself from crying, from making a scene, but she couldn't. The policeman stood there, dumbly, and said, "I'm sorry." The only thing I could think of then was how terrible his job was, how I'd never want one like that. He looked so pathetic, his eyes down, embarrassed, the snow spitting at his back.

The doctor gave my mother Valium. She would sleep all day and when she woke, she would sit in front of the fire in the living room, draped in one of my father's old air force sweatshirts, looking through family albums. Or sometimes she would write long letters to Carroll or my father, as if they were on a trip and she expected them back soon. My uncles helped and Julie came to stay with us for a couple of weeks, but after that I took care of us. I made most of the meals. I did the laundry and grocery shopping. I had to coax her out of bed in the mornings, force her to go to movies and play Scrabble with me. She liked to tell the toothpick story, how she had rescued me, but I knew, firsthand, how fragile she was.

She took another ice cube and put it in her mouth, crunched, swallowed. "Anyway," she went on, "it's not going to be twins. I promise you that."

"Bet me," I said.

"I can't just take your money like that."

"I'd take yours."

"True," she said. "But I'm not as selfish or as greedy as you." We both laughed.

"Okay, then, I bet you it's a boy."

She thought about it for a second before saying, "Okay. That's fair." Air misted from her lips again as if we were outside after a January snow. I noticed her eyes were a little red, probably from the tequila.

"Well, go call," I said, nudging her shoulder.

"I'm going, I'm going. You're worse than a nervous father."

She opened the door, and it was like walking into a furnace after the chill of the walk-in.

Enrico handed me a few more dollars, my share from the last customers. I reloaded the cooler and then washed the rest of the glasses while Boozer wiped his cash register and Enrico refilled the margarita and daiquiri mixes. A couple of pot-bellied bouncers gabbed at the front door, and I saw one of them usher out the man who had poked his finger in my chest earlier. He staggered, and I wondered if the Texas Moon was the only place he had to go at night.

Arlene was cleaning the sawdust from the carpet with the big clumsy vacuum cleaner, the crap job given to new waitresses. I watched her right hand bear down on the long hose as she moved it back and forth, her left hand at her hip holding the cord up and back so that it didn't get tangled. Already she was an expert. She maneuvered that thing all over, fast and thorough.

Most of the musicians had left, but the manager talked to one of the roadies by the stage, haggling over something. My mother'd been in the office on the phone for nearly ten minutes before she finally emerged, slowly, her face pale. A couple of the other waitresses went up to her, but she just waved them off.

Boozer tapped my shoulder. "What's wrong with your mother?"

She sat down on a stool at the bar. I recall very clearly lifting my shriveled hands out of the water and wiping them on my towel. Enrico didn't set the mixers down, but he watched her. She didn't say anything, just stared at the wall behind us. Her eyes were swimming, and I saw her throat tighten, the muscle thickening right under her chin.

"What's the matter, Gloria?" Boozer asked.

"Did we get the call?" I asked.

She turned to me. "Yes," she said. She looked away and blew out a long breath of air.

I started to say something more, but then Enrico cut me off.

"Gloria? Who called?"

His voice sounded different, rich and soothing, like a preacher's voice almost. My mother looked at me for a few moments, searching for something, but for what I didn't know. She said, "Raymond called."

"Who?" Enrico asked.

"My lawyer," my mother said.

"Didn't Bub call? Has she delivered yet?"

"No. No, not yet." She paused again. "I don't want you to get your hopes up too much, Travis, but Raymond said they've agreed to settle. Or at least have made a decent offer. He's going to talk to them again on Monday."

She looked at me funny, then nodded, and I wondered for a half-second if she was telling the truth. She seemed disappointed, half-frazzled.

"You're kidding, aren't you?"

"No, honey, I promise. Monday." She took a napkin from her apron and pushed it over to me. Right below the picture of the lassoed moon were the numbers. Enough so my mother would probably never have to work again.

"Congratulations!" Boozer said. "It's about time." He immediately pulled up a clean rock glass, poured a shot of Cuervo, and pushed it in front of her. She drank it. He quickly refilled it.

"I've had enough," she said.

"I understand. I'd want to be sober too if I received a call like that."

"That's great news," Enrico said.

He took her hand and held it for a second. Just the corners of her lips turned up. She leaned over the counter and kissed me on the cheek.

"I think we should do something tonight. Celebrate. I don't want to go home right now."

Enrico insisted again that we come to his party, and my mother told him she thought it would be a good idea.

She talked to the manager to make sure we had tomorrow and Monday off so we could drive to Julie and Bub's. I started washing the glasses again, ready to be done with them, knowing I might not ever have to wash another glass in my life if I didn't want to. My mind was already off on the million things I might do with the money.

I told Enrico that I had to go to the bathroom, but instead I slipped out the back, propped the door open with a brick, and climbed the ladder to the roof. The Texas Moon was a good five miles outside of Amarillo. It was a hot, clear night, and I could see the downtown lights in the distance and a few neon signs on this side of Amarillo Boulevard, but nothing much else except a few trailer houses butting against the back parking lot. I thought, *What the hell?* I pulled about ten ones from my back pocket, threw them up in the air, watched them flutter over the parking lot like birds. I took change from my pocket and whisked quarters and nickels towards the trailer houses, listened to them clank on the sidewalk and tin roofs. I ran a couple of laps around the gravel roof, staying close, but not too close, to the edge. Then I took a five dollar bill out of my pocket, climbed up the back of the Texas Moon sign—a big, smiley-faced blue moon with a yellow lasso squeezed tight around its middle—and pinned it on the nail of the lasso knot.

"I caught you," a woman's voice shouted, and I nearly fell off the sign. "Over here, Travis." Arlene stood on the ladder, just her head visible.

"Come on up."

"I gotta get home."

"Wait." I climbed down from the sign, went to the ladder, and offered my hand.

I helped her up, and she looked around for a few minutes, commenting on how flat it was. "No water. No trees."

"Do you miss him?" I asked suddenly, then tried to take it back. "Sorry. I don't know why I asked that. It's none of my business."

"It's okay. He got me out of North Carolina. I've got a good job now. And here I am on the roof with a guy who throws money away. What more can a girl ask for?"

I asked her if she'd ever been to Palo Duro Canyon, and when she said no, I told her I'd take her out there one afternoon next week when I got back from Beaumont. "I can show you the caves," I said.

"Sounds scary."

"I'll hold your hand."

She smiled and then walked toward the Texas Moon sign. The moon and lasso blinked, casting blue and yellow rainbows on her face and the sides of her slender body. I followed her, and she turned and kissed me. My lips were dry and a little cracked from the summer wind, but they moistened quickly. For a moment I smelled smoke and thought wildly that the neon lasso had touched us and would burn holes through our shirts and jeans, brand us both, which sounded romantic, but before I pulled away I figured out the smoke was on Arlene's clothes. She wasn't burning. She just smelled the way my mother did each night when we got home.

"Good to see you two working hard." Boozer's head peeked over the ladder at the edge of the roof. "We're about to wind up down there."

"We'll be down in a minute," Arlene said.

"Why don't I get these fringe benefits?" he said, then laughed. "I'll have to renegotiate my contract." Then to Arlene: "You coming to the party?"

She quickly glanced at me. "Don't worry," Boozer said. "He's coming too."

"Yeah," she said. "I just want to run home and shower." Boozer cackled at that and then slipped back down the stairs.

We followed, and I walked Arlene to her car and promised to meet her at Enrico's. I kissed her again, but it wasn't the same, and I hoped the spell hadn't been completely broken. As she drove away, I took another quarter out of my pocket and flung it as far as I could. The silver whirled in the air, but then I lost it, never even heard it hit.

I decided to call the answering machine to hear for myself. I went to the pay phone at the back of the Texas Moon. The voice I heard was

Bub's: "The doctor says the baby is not in a very good position, so he may have to do a cesarean. But we'll wait and see. It could be a while."

Then Raymond's call: "I've got good news." He provided the details quickly about the settlement meetings on Monday, and he said what he thought the new offer would be. When he gave the figures, even though my mother had already written them down, my heart flip-flopped.

I was about to hang up and redial to listen to those figures one more time, when I heard another beep. It was Bub again.

"I've got bad news, I'm afraid," he said and paused. I thought wildly for a moment that something had happened to Julie, but then he said, "Julie's okay." Another short pause. "But the baby didn't make it."

I felt as if someone had dumped a block of cement into my stomach.

"Julie's okay, though. She lost a lot of blood, but she's resting now. She'll probably be here for a week recuperating." He paused again. "It was a girl," he said, and his voice shook so badly that I thought of glass shattering. Then he hung up.

I sat down on a stool by the back door. A couple of the waitresses walked by me on their way out, but I didn't want to be seen, so I stepped into the walk-in. I didn't turn on the light, so it was both cold and dark in there, just the smell of the fruit and beer. I held my breath and pushed on my stomach as hard as I could. I bit down on my finger. I felt that I should go break the news to my mother, but I couldn't move. I didn't know how she would take it. We'd known there were complications. We knew that she might lose the baby.

But still.

In the dark chill of that freezer, I made impossible comparisons. I wondered if losing a baby was as hard as losing a father or a brother. They'd sent us lists of prospective names. And what were we going to do about the boxes of stuff we planned to take tomorrow? I had even found in our attic the mobile that went over my crib, little blue and red wooden ducks.

I thought, *Here I am. Sweating, joking, flirting, doing tequila shots.*

Throwing away dollar bills. Pitching quarters off the roof. Kissing Arlene underneath the neon sign on top of the Texas Moon. I've made plans.

Wouldn't it have been better not to know? Wouldn't it be better never to hear that phone call or, for that matter, to see that policeman at the door, snow flecked and cold and ashamed and somehow still proud to be carrying the news, to be the one to knock on the door and stare at his boots and, later, to tell his children, "I was the one. I had to tell them. That was my job. You should have seen their faces. You don't know what it was like. Particularly on such a miserable day. So cold that frost built up on the inside of the windshield. So cold."

Like the inside of the cooler. Locked away with the beer and the fruit and the ice, I was convinced it would have been better not to know, better never to know such things. I opened my eyes, but it was just as dark. My nose ran, and gooseflesh covered my arms. I pried open the door, and the heat blurred my vision.

When I went back into the bar, most of the bouncers and other waitresses had already left. My mother sat at the counter, her head in close to Enrico's and Boozer's. There was only a thin glow from the neon beer clocks. My mother whispered something to Enrico and Boozer. I couldn't hear what it was.

"I thought you'd flushed yourself down the commode, boy," Enrico said.

They all smiled. I searched my mother's face. She smiled too, her smile—the corners of her lips barely turned up. "Are you ready?"

I planned to tell her right then, right there, but she fingered the bump on her nose, leaving me speechless.

"Let's go, kiddos," Enrico said. He threw the bar rag on the counter and grabbed my mother's hand. Boozer edged around the corner of the bar and threw his arm around my shoulders, the way Carroll used to do when he was drunk or feeling brotherly.

My mother asked me to drive. The Texas Moon sign clicked off as Boozer and Enrico wheeled out in front of us. We followed.

"My back's killing me," my mother said.

"Why don't you crawl in the backseat?" I said.

"Good idea," she said. "I can look at the stars and you can chauffeur me around."

At the next red light, she climbed over the seat and stretched out with her head behind me so that I couldn't see her face in the rearview.

"That feels so much better," she said and sighed. "To the cocktail party, James."

We drove down Amarillo Boulevard. I saw a few hookers in matching blue dresses sitting on the curb outside a Motel 6 and, a little farther up, a cop putting a wino in the back of his car and, not far from that, an ambulance with its lights flashing.

"It's a pretty night, isn't it?" my mother said. "Tell me what we should spend the money on. A car? A speedboat? A vacation to Acapulco? You could invite Arlene." She laughed, that rich laugh my father appreciated so much.

"I don't care," I said.

"Got you with that one, didn't I, Mr. Smooch-lips? Come on. Name something. Make a wish."

Ahead, Boozer, in the passenger seat, turned around and waved. I didn't wave back. I had to tell her, but there was something beautiful about her not knowing, all stretched out in the backseat, depending on me not to say a word. She was so vulnerable. But how could I stay quiet? How can anyone?

"I wish . . ." I choked up and had to clear my throat. "I wish I didn't have to tell you what I have to tell you."

"What is it, honey?"

"I called the answering machine."

"You did?" she said and lifted up in the seat. I could only see the outline of her face silhouetted in the rearview, no details, her profile only a silver-edged blade.

To catch the interstate, Enrico turned left down a dark and narrow two-lane road unfamiliar to me. I put my blinker on and stayed with him.

"There was a message after Raymond's," I said. I could no longer see even my mother's silhouette.

"I know," her voice said. "I know."

For a year my mother and I had been fumbling to protect each other. It struck me at that moment as a futile thing to be doing. How strange it was to think that you could ever protect someone else. Or to think somehow your life could stay the same—frozen, still and unharmed. What faith. What ridiculous faith.

Our lives were never the same after that night. The money came through eventually, and we quit the Texas Moon soon after. But the money came between us, made us feel both guilty and resentful, and separated us in that house in a way that the deaths of my father, brother, and Julie's baby could not do. I left home the following winter, not returning for my final semester of high school. I took my new car and drove across the country with Arlene, as far away from Texas as I could go.

Later, when Arlene was pregnant with our first child, we returned to Amarillo and visited my mother in the hospital. I had not seen her in several years, and only came then because the operation had been a serious one, and she had made it clear to Julie that she wanted to patch things up with me while she still had time. I felt sure my mother was exaggerating, as had become her custom.

We sat in her hospital room, playing cards. She looked tired, her hair messed up, an IV sprouting from her hand like a plastic flower stem, her gown draped loosely around her body. Doped up at first, she talked about Carroll and my father in the syrupy nostalgic way that had begun to sicken me over the years.

Then she fell asleep. We watched television for a while, and then, as I was massaging Arlene's shoulders, my mother woke and was remarkably lucid.

She asked Arlene if she could touch her stomach, so Arlene sat on the edge of the bed, and they talked about babies and doctors and hospitals and, jokingly, about the trouble women go through putting up with men. Then my mother grabbed Arlene's hand, and her tone changed. She talked again about my father and brother's accident, but this time her voice had no self-pity. She spoke lightly and honestly, in a way that made me grateful to be there.

"I didn't think I would make it," she said. The moonlight from the blinds made slatted images on the bed and on both their faces. "And part of me didn't want to. Travis's father had practically raised me. When I first met him, he was twenty-four and cocky, in the air force, decorated with medals. I was sixteen and amazed that such a man could be in love with me."

Arlene nodded.

"I never thought there would be a time without all of us together," she said, and I could sense in the shift of her voice, a slight lowering of her pitch, that she wanted me to pay attention. "And then afterwards I never thought there would be a day of my life when I wouldn't feel him and Carroll gone."

"I know," Arlene said.

"No, you don't," she said. "Not really." She closed her eyes for a few quiet moments. "For a long time, what I couldn't admit was that it was okay that they were gone. I didn't want to forgive myself for feeling good again."

Then she smiled, turned to me, and seemed to change the subject. "Remember what fun we all had at the Texas Moon, working together that year? You remember, don't you, Travis?"

"Of course," I said.

The smile left the corners of her mouth, and she seemed to stare past Arlene, past me, out the window. She tugged on her cover, pulling it up to her neck, jostling the iv so it looked like it would tear out. Her lips barely moved as she spoke. "You want to hear something ironic?"

"What?" I said.

"That was the happiest time of my life."

In the dark of the car, after my mother told me she had heard the call from Bub, I said, "Maybe we shouldn't go to Enrico's." I waited for her answer. I wanted to see her face but still couldn't.

"I think we should go. For a little bit at least." She stretched out in the seat again. "I'm going to shut my eyes," she said. "Can you get us there?"

"Yeah," I said.

"Good," she said. "I'm trusting you."

My eyes felt blurry. I blinked a couple of times to clear them, then opened them wide. I could hear her breathing in the backseat, soft and steady, and I heard my own breathing too. In rhythm. I thought of the little v-line of black hair on the back of Arlene's neck, how sexy it made her. I could picture Julie in the hospital resting, Bub in a chair beside her, waiting to comfort her if she should wake. I wondered where they put the little girl, if there was a special place for her.

Ahead, Enrico drifted in and out of his lane.

I gripped the steering wheel tighter. I could see clearly now the green and silver interstate signs for Paramount and Washington streets. Enrico and Boozer slowed down, but the car still moved back and forth like a slow-swinging pendulum. I eased up on the pedal, fell behind a few car lengths, but not far enough to lose them.

"Travis," my mother said quietly.

I didn't answer. There was no need to, really. There was a calm spot in our silence.

"Thank you," she said.

I didn't really understand then what she was thanking me for, but I said, "You're welcome." I concentrated on the road, and I tried hard to stay within the white dotted lines. I just wanted to get us there safely.

2004

The Sample Makers

How did they come to the same place, the same skill—
from Italy, from Israel, China and Chile?

The women who worked in the back behind the showroom,
in the overwarm, dustball rooms lit by industrial light.

Away from the glamour, back where the gush of steam irons
kept a thin gloss of sweat on neck and brows—

hooks and eyes, mousetraps and the tea water boiling,
women who marked their sewing machines

with statuettes and rosaries, Buddhas and baby pictures,
postcards of mountains and mall seaside towns?

Barely understanding each other, but understanding
basting, bobbins and straight pins,

the facing and the grosgrain and the seam allowances.
I worked there, too, every day after school,

taking the same greasy manual elevator, using the same
ribboned ladies room key. They would bring a muslin,

half a dress maybe, and place it, delicately, over my arm.
Someone would fit the bodice around my waist,

mark a new neckline, adjust a sleeve, pin the silk
so that it fit my body—me, the living mannequin

who teetered around them in high heels and panties.
And unlike the other women in my life,

they took my chin in their hands, fed me flan
and cannolis, they beamed and they winked and they wept.

What became of them? What of Marie with her cancerous breast,
stitching her daughter's wedding gown on her lunch hour,

and Lily, the saucy bottle-blond, who nipped at schnapps?
What became of the tiny rose, Lia from Ghana?

I remember their hands: thick molded knuckles,
elegant wrists, short, ridged fingernails.

I thought of them today, in Spring Joy restaurant—
beside a little shrine and an industrial refrigerator,

the flat golden bowl of oil, the floating flower petals
and beatific Buddha—when the clerk gave me my purchase.

She was quiet, you could tell, studious in her own way,
still girlish, as if waiting for someone,

wisps of hair falling into her face—
                        How do they survive here,
these women with soft, steady bodies and careful hairnets?

Oh little hive in the heat and the dust—
have you kept up the prayers, the garlands of herbs?

Big Yard

Antennas, office skyline, razor wire
coiled on a slant all around the top
of the roof wall, a mile to the pavement.
Some kids call it recess. We called it Big Yard.
Something, we imagined, like back yards—
all that open air.

Once, when Valerie Butoni had me flush on the wall—
raze of raw concrete on the back of my arms,
sirens, jackhammers, garbage trucks on Lexington—
in that moment I was memorizing soot:
square black flakes like fat urban butterflies—

and pigeons: greasy, with their emerald necks, those pigeon-
blood eyes, feet like scored wire. How could one kid
own the bench, the swings, the water fountain,
the breath in my lungs?
       In the grip of power
you might as well, if she told you to,
hurl yourself down.

The Fund-Raiser's Dance Card

The fund-raiser's name was Lee Ann Mercer and she wanted to go dancing. It was one of those late spring Friday nights where the wind was warm and wet and the air smelled like an overly chlorinated pool and everyone wanted to do something they hadn't in too long a time. The real estate agent and his wife turned off their television and went to get passed-out drunk at a bar with an outdoor patio. The too-young married couple with too many too-young children decided to hire a sitter and go see a movie that was not animated or a musical. The widower, who had practically *lived* in his bathrobe since his wife had died, put on a plaid blazer and a tie and said, "Let's *do* something," to no one in particular. And Lee Ann Mercer, who was hosting her annual fund-raising party for university alumni at her house at 107 Strawberry Lane, could hear music drifting from somewhere down the street and decided that she was going to go dancing.

Lee Ann stood holding a glass of white wine in the kitchen, next to the back door, and considered the implications of her impending departure. Her boss was in the house somewhere—chatting up all the wealthy white-haired men wearing tan bucks and linen jackets and their wives in their overly fancy yellow sundresses—and Lee Ann had the fleeting thought that he would resent her leaving her own party and thus violating the terms of her contract—not just as a hostess but as a university fund-raiser who was expected to put on and *stay put* at these kinds of functions. Plus, she was expecting someone in particular at the party: a thirty-nine-year-old alumnus from Raleigh, North Carolina, an ex-studio arts major and heir to his daddy's video poker fortune who lived by himself in a loft apartment with stacks of New York art magazines stretched well toward the ceiling and who regularly teased Lee Ann with promises of behemoth bequests to the university but thus far had not delivered. The last time Lee Ann had visited him—a month or so earlier—she had been in the middle of explaining his many gift options—named chairs, endowed annual exhibitions or installations, new goalposts—when the alumnus had kissed her, full on the mouth, and, to her surprise, she kissed him back, and wanted to do so again immediately after and now, too, even though he was a dilettante who left one too many buttons on his shirt unbuttoned and whose teeth were surprisingly crooked and jack-o'-lantern-like for a rich man. The alumnus—his name was Barry—had responded to her party invitation in writing, saying that he would come to the party and that he had a big surprise for her. Lee Ann did not want to miss his arrival. But no, Lee Ann quickly decided, she would not be missed: she would dance her way up and down the street, from house to house, and then slip back into her own house and no one would know the difference. "I haven't been dancing in *ages*," she told herself. Just then, she heard her boss's voice booming from somewhere in the house, and she quietly slipped out the back door, past her barking dogs, past the cigarette smokers. When the smokers asked where she was going, she rattled her glass and said, "Ice," then stepped out onto the street, and into the night.

On the street she stopped and listened for a moment. There *was* music playing from somewhere—Glenn Miller, Tommy Dorsey, someone with a big band from before she was born—and she did a happy little hip-shaking shuffle down the street as she mapped her route. First the Merrills', then the Yerinas', the Hammonds', the Cheevers', the Morriseys'; then, at the cul-de-sac, she would dance down the other side of the street: the Howards', the Charneys', the Lius', and finally the Parks' house, right across from her own. Lee Ann took in a deep breath. The air no longer smelled like chlorine but rather of sweet pesticide from the town's mobile bug fogger, but still the smell was chemical, and the sky was black and deep and it was the kind of night that made you feel very brave. Lee Ann had just seen a movie on the climbing of Mount Everest and so felt something of the adventurer in herself and she anticipated that she might, someday, tell stories about the night she danced her way up and down Strawberry Lane.

Lee Ann was not an impulsive woman, nor did she consider herself untrustworthy; but she wasn't above lying to herself on occasion, either. For instance, she lied to herself about her house all the time, and the lying did not trouble her much. Lee Ann lived in the house with two dogs and a husband. The house itself was fifteen years old and had white vinyl siding and black shutters and pillars that were not really pillars at all, but rather two thirty-foot strips of whitewashed pine that stretched from front entrance to roof. They were not pillars, officially, because they didn't actually support the roof. "Those pillars couldn't hold up me *or* you," the contractor had told her when building the house.

"They're for decorative purposes," Lee Ann had said.

"Exactly," the contractor had agreed. "Those things don't do *shit*."

"Understood," Lee Ann had told him. Nonetheless, she called the strips of wood *pillars*, and she also referred to her home as being *lakefront property*, even though the lake was only a damned-up river and even though the water was so low that one had to muck through fifty feet of mucousy red clay before one got to the lake itself, which the EPA said was too dangerously polluted to swim in anyway, especially if you were pregnant. Lee Ann Mercer was not pregnant, but one of her dogs, a blockheaded black lab named Labbie, *had* gotten pregnant and had given birth to the second dog, a runtish black and gray mutt that Lee Ann had not bothered to name and refused to let in the house. The dog roamed and smelled like fish. When her neighbors complained about the mutt, who barked at night, all night, Lee Ann simply lied and said it was a stray, and that she couldn't take any responsibility for it.

So Lee Ann lied about her dog, and she also lied about her husband, Teddy. Lee Ann's husband had paid for the building of the house when they had moved from Connecticut to South Carolina some fifteen years earlier, but he barely lived in it. He was the chair of the biology department at the university. Usually, when not stopping off at the house to nurse his broken heart or beg for Lee Ann's forgiveness or check his mail, he lived with one of his female graduate assistants. But for a while now, Lee Ann's husband had lived with the slutty manager of the bar he frequented and often, when drunk, talked of buying. He hadn't been home for several months. When neighbors asked about Teddy, Lee Ann merely said that he was busy at work but was otherwise fine, absolutely fine.

There was one more thing that Lee Ann lied about: her name. It was not really Lee Ann; it was Katherine. Katherine had taught fourth grade at a private elementary school in Stonington, Connecticut. Her husband's name was not Teddy but Ted. He'd taught biology at a private women's college in New London. Katherine and Ted were happy. They were! They were happiest when they walked the grounds of their highly mortgaged property and patted the Revolutionary-era stone walls and threw sticks for Labbie. The sticks were birch—no other kind of stick would do—and in her fourth grade class, Katherine taught her students how the Nipmuck Indians had made canoes out of birch bark and her students marveled at the native intelligence of the Indians. The descendants of those Indians were now supervising the slot machines a half hour away at the Foxwoods Casino, but Katherine did not mention this to her students, who were too young to appreciate how short the distance was from ingenuity to stupefaction.

But then Ted applied, interviewed for, and accepted a job at Clemson University in South Carolina. He did all of this without consulting Katherine first. "You'll get over it," Ted said when Katherine objected. Katherine simply stood there and glared at her husband. They had been married for six years, and this was the first time that her husband had said anything remotely like "You'll get over it." Katherine felt like she had been duped, conned into marrying the wrong man. "You'll get over it," she said and then spat on the ancient knotty pine floor of their bedroom, driving her husband from the room. Once he was gone, Katherine jammed her clothes into their suitcases and then spat on the suitcases, too.

Katherine became further enraged once they reached Clemson, because suddenly there were no more ancient, meandering stone walls and birch trees, and suddenly everything was air-conditioning and the Lost Cause and school fight songs and Jesus bumper stickers on jacked-up pickups with running boards, and suddenly being *Katherine* seemed unbearably *quaint*, hopelessly *obsolete*. So she tore the red bandana from around Labbie's neck and renamed herself Lee Ann.

She had gotten the name *Lee Ann* from a convenience store clerk at the Lil' Cricket. A week after she had arrived in Clemson, Katherine had gone to the Lil' Cricket to buy a loaf of wheat bread, which they did not have. She had to settle for Wonder Bread, which further enraged Katherine. She threw down the loaf on the counter and the clerk rang it up. Behind the clerk, there was a Xeroxed sign taped to the cigarette shelf that said: "I can only help one person at a time, and let me tell you, today ain't your day. (And tomorrow ain't looking too good, either)."

"Ain't that the truth," Katherine said, trying to be accommodating.

"No," the clerk said, "it *ain't*."

Katherine didn't know whether the clerk had gotten her point of reference or not, but it didn't matter. What did matter was that the clerk was a tobacco-stinking, bleached-out bulge of a woman who wore too-tight denim shorts and a skimpy denim halter top with rhinestone studs and who *didn't take any shit*. The clerk's ID tag said *Lee Ann*. Katherine immediately knew she had to jettison her God-given name.

"Lee Ann," Katherine said, "I need to throw the baby out with the bath water."

"Lady, you need a job or somethin'," the real Lee Ann said, giving

Katherine her change and her white bread and then ignoring her entirely.

So Katherine did what the Lil' Cricket clerk had suggested by word and by example: she got a job as a university fund-raiser and she changed her name to Lee Ann. Lee Ann had hopes that announcing her name change would do something to her husband, produce some sort of shock or regret, but when she told him over dinner, "I'm Lee Ann now," he merely smiled and said, "I know, I'm Teddy."

It was true: just like that, he was Teddy. Whereas before, as Ted, he'd been the kind of diligent, self-serious youngish man who ran 10K races for the cure—all cures—and ironed his chinos and made variations of the same healthy stir-fry meal three times a week, now he was Teddy: a slovenly, bearded, sport-sandaled, thriving middle-aged lothario who drank too much and bet large sums on college football games and told roaringly funny stories about his pickled brain and what stupid things that brain told him to do and overall Teddy was excellent company to everyone but his wife. Meanwhile, except for her job change, Lee Ann was much the same as Katherine, except older and much more permanently mired in regret and sorrow and loneliness. Lee Ann was the same as Katherine except there was more Lee Ann needed to forget. This was another reason she would go dancing.

The first house was the Merrills'. Wayne and Ellen Merrill were both history professors, both recovering alcoholics as well, and they were known for throwing parties where no booze was served but guests were encouraged to bring their own instruments—acoustic guitars, inevitably, and the rare squeeze box—for what the Merrills called "our famous after-dinner hootenanny." At one of these parties, Lee Ann had been cornered by Wayne Merrill who, armed with a twelve-string, had forced her to harmonize on a Glen Campbell song he insisted she knew but didn't and when the song—it was about the sorrows of drink—was over, Wayne had dropped his guitar and wept and asked Lee Ann if she knew how badly he wanted a drink right then? Lee Ann told him that she knew exactly what he was feeling and then fled the party and swore she would never go back, and remembering this, she considered skipping the Merrills' house altogether in her quest to dance. But there were crashing sounds coming from the side yard, loud music that was recorded and electric, not live and acoustic. These were not the Merrills' sounds, and Lee Ann remembered that the Merrills were away in Europe on sabbatical and that they had rented the house out to some students. Lee Ann heard voices that were, in turn, seductive and violent, and these voices drew her, her feet moving her in an improvised two-step into the side yard.

The notable thing about the Merrills' side yard that night was that it was lit up like a football stadium. There were two garage floodlights going and four cars with their headlights on arranged around the perimeter. In the center of all this light were two ping-pong tables; on either end of the two ping-pong tables were two plastic cups of beer, and behind each cup—four to a table—was a man, or to be more precise, a boy. Each of the boys was wearing a golf visor and baggy shorts with many pockets and no shirt and flipflops. They were playing a game, Lee Ann quickly understood, and the object of the game was to hit the ping-pong ball into the cup of beer. When this happened, the boy whose cup it was and his partner were obliged to chug their beer; the boy who'd sunk the ball and *his* partner were obliged, it seemed, to bump their fists or chests in celebration, whereupon they chugged their beer, too. Some of the beer spilled on the boys' chests and bellies during the chugging and even though some of the chests had hair on them and even though some of the bellies had already begun the outward bulge toward middle age, the effect of the light on the beer on the boys' torsos was like hot soapy water on Greek statuary.

Just then the song ended and a new one began and there was a great deal of whooping and suddenly Lee Ann was surrounded by the ping-pong players, who were dancing, and Lee Ann's first thought was, *revenge*. Because this, in a manner of speaking, was what Teddy had been doing to her for more than a decade now. There had been so many nights, at two in the morning, the hour when the bars closed, when Lee Ann lay in bed and imagined her husband desperately dancing through last call with his under-graduate lovers, his much younger sloppy bar managers, doing shots of tequila, admiring the happy wet sheen of liquor on a pretty-enough girl's upper lip. She imagined Teddy going to lick off that sheen and the girl not stopping him. It was the loneliest feeling imaginable, like writing thank-you notes from the bottom of a volcano. *Revenge*, Lee Ann thought again. Someone gave her a shot of something and she drank it and started dancing with the boys. It wasn't the kind of music she'd had in mind—not big band, but rather the famously tragic southern rock group with the famous three guitar attack—nor was it the kind of dancing she'd wanted to do—it was not couples dancing, but rather dancing in a circle, not so much moving your feet as stomping them. But still, it was music, and there was sex in it and in the dancing, too: there was sex in the way she took her long, blondish hair out of its complicated twists and knots; sex in the way she took off her light green sweater and tied it around her waist; sex, even, in the boys' air guitaring; sex especially when one of the boys—his visor was on backwards and upside down, his chest hairless—quit his air guitar and moved a little closer to her, as dancing partners should. Lee Ann had no fear that this was a pity dance: she was twenty years older than the boy, it was true, but she was still very pretty, she knew this, and while she had lines on her face they gave the impression of health and sun and not overage and while her clothes were mature they were not dated, nor were they designed to cover up her body's flaws, of which there were few. She and the boy circled around each other, dancing backward and then face-to-face, not touching, it was true, but to Lee Ann not touching was nearly as suggestive as the touching would have been.

"Is your name Ryan?" she shouted over the music.

"Yeah," he shouted back. He didn't ask how she knew his name—she had a theory that every other male born between Atlanta and Richmond between 1978 and 1981 was named Ryan—and in truth it didn't matter. What mattered was that Lee Ann had her Ryan and she was dancing with him and, for the first time in a long time, she felt good.

But then the song ended and the boys—her Ryan, too—went back to their ping-pong game and Lee Ann was left standing by herself, watching them. Was this what it was like for Teddy, too? Were twenty-year-old girls about adult sex in one minute and adolescent drinking games the next? Did Teddy wait around for them to change back? She was pretty sure he did, and for a moment she even felt a little sorry for him. In the shadows of the party, Lee Ann could see a line of girls, smoking cigarettes and glaring at her; they would wait for the ping-pong game to exhaust itself. Lee Ann knew this because once she had been one of them. Perhaps Katherine would have waited. But Lee Ann would not wait. She would not wait! That she would not wait seemed proof not of her desperation, but rather of her sense of perspective. There were other houses, other dance partners; there might even be a rich suitor with a suitcase full of cash waiting for Lee Ann back at her house. The point was, there was no point in dancing your way through the sweet, spring night if you did not give yourself over to its expansive mystery and promise. The ping-pong ball grazed one of the cups but did not go in and there was a great deal of arguing about the relevant Rules of the Game and in the midst of this, Lee Ann sneaked out of the party and continuing dancing down the street.

Had you seen Strawberry Lane that night from above, with the ability to see through roofs and walls and enclosed patios, you might have mistaken Lee Ann for a meandering drunk, for an attractive but troubled forty-four-year-old woman who had fallen off her medication. You would have seen her foxtrot into the Yerinas' house without knocking. The four Yerinas—mother, father, two adolescent girls—were sitting on the couch and watching a situation comedy about a rich family that had recently become a poor family. Both the Yerinas and their television counterparts seemed anesthetized and Lee danced around them to the show's theme song and exited through the back door without saying goodbye. There was no one home next door at the Hammonds', but the garage door was unlocked. There was a minivan in the garage and Lee Ann slithered over the hood, climbed to the roof, and tap-danced on it as in a musical she'd once seen before moving on to the next house, Mr. Cheever's, where Lee Ann ripped the glass of gin out of the old widower's shaky hands, set it sweating onto the end table, twirled Mr. Cheever a time or two the way Ginger never did with Fred, then placed the glass of gin back in his hands, sat Mr. Cheever on his couch as a failsafe against the drink, the twirling, and waltzed out of the house, pausing at the bathroom to jiggle the handle so as to arrest the toilet's running. If you were watching all this from above, and if you were a certain kind of deity, you would have right then descended to earth, stopped Lee Ann before she entered her next house, and demanded to know if she were feeling all right, if something truly bad had happened to her to cause such behavior. Have your parents died? Has your husband left you? Are you lost and far from your true home? Are you stupid and blind with grief? And while it was true that Lee Ann's parents were dead (for nearly a decade now), her husband no longer really a husband, her home not exactly her home, they could not adequately explain her dancing. Does the mountain climber climb because he was beaten as a child? Does the sailor sail because he pissed his bed well into elementary school? "Let's not psychologize," Lee Ann would have said to the deity, "let's dance," making the deity whoosh up and away, back to his privileged perch, before she continued on to the Morriseys'.

As before, Lee Ann did not knock but walked right in the front door. Thom Morrisey was standing by himself in the living room, a cigarette over his right ear, a drink in his right hand, hair slicked back with either sweat or gel. He was dressed in a cream-colored summer suit and his tie was loosened as if he'd just returned from a nephew's wedding or graduation. When he saw Lee Ann, he looked back over his shoulder toward the empty room and yelled, "Oh good, the fund-raiser is here."

"Will you please fix that fuse," a woman yelled from inside the house, and it was only then that Lee Ann noticed that the house was dark except for the light coming in off the street. Then, after a moment, the woman asked, "*Who's* here?"

"The fund-raiser."

"Which one?"

"The Yankee fund-raiser," Thom said, then took the cigarette out from the crook of his ear, then began patting himself for a light.

Immediately, Lee Ann's dancing felt diminished, demeaned, the way the mountain must be by the mountaineer's athlete's foot, the ocean by the sailor's urinating over the bow. Apparently, even if you danced your way up and down your street, you could not forget that you were a fund-raiser, that people expected you to ask for things they did not exactly want to give. And if you were from Connecticut, then you could not forget that you were a Yankee, even if South Carolina had become no less your home than Connecticut ever had been, even if you tried to explain that people and places are not that different, and that folks in Connecticut hated black people and loved NASCAR, too. And if you were the wife of a wayward husband, your dancing could not help you forget that the world was choked full with cheating hearts—because Thom, who was an alum and was assistant dean of admissions, was married to Bette, one of Lee Ann's few friends, and Lee Ann knew that Bette was in Charleston, visiting her Alzheimered mother, and that the woman yelling from somewhere in the house was not Thom's wife.

But still, Lee Ann could see no other choice but to dance. Besides, perhaps this was a necessary obstacle. True, she'd always disliked Thom, who could be trusted to be somehow both dull and offensive, who inevitably would tell familiar racist jokes and then, when someone objected, hold up his hands in mock defensiveness and say,

"What? What?" Perhaps this was a necessary sacrifice if she was to continue her journey up and down Strawberry Lane. Perhaps you had to dance with a sleezeball peckerwood before you could move on to better things.

"Let's dance," Lee Ann said.

Thom stopped patting himself and smirked at Lee Ann. "I always *thought* there was something going on between us." He held up his glass. "I need a refill. Be right back."

"You don't need a drink," Lee Ann said.

"Don't move," Thom said.

The minute Thom was out of sight, Lee Ann moved, tiptoed first in the direction of the kitchen, where Thom was making his drink and humming, then off toward the right, toward where the woman's voice had come from. The house was one of those deceptively large and meandering ranch houses, and so Lee Ann walked down a three-step flight of stairs, up another one, through a rec room, past two bathrooms, and into a sunroom—a small, entirely glassed-in room furnished with a love seat and an end table. By the time Lee Ann arrived at the room, it felt as though she were in a different house altogether. But it was the same house, and there was the woman sitting on the couch, knees tucked up to her chest. She was younger than Lee Ann, but not much younger; she was pretty, but not any prettier than Bette, Thom's wife. Her blonde hair had been overpermed or bleached over the years and looked tired. Her blue eyes were red, as if she'd been crying, but she wasn't crying just then. She and Lee Ann looked at each for a while, and then the woman said, "The power went out. I hate the dark." When Lee Ann didn't respond, the woman said, "I don't know what I'm doing here, do you know what I mean?"

"You're fucking my friend's husband," Lee Ann said.

"I know," the woman said. "Why am I here?"

Lee Ann held out her arms to the woman, and the woman rose and took her arms as the submissive partner might, and they danced. It was a very controlled dance, because of the tight quarters, but it seemed important to Lee Ann that they not leave the tiny sunroom: this was the space they were given and this was the space they would use. It was the first time she'd ever danced with another woman like this. It did not feel good or bad. It did not feel erotic, nor did it feel odd or repulsive. It felt like dancing with oneself and once the dance was over, Lee Ann almost asked the woman if she'd like to come with her as she finished her dance up and down Strawberry Lane. But then she heard Thom yelling from somewhere, deep or shallow, inside the house, "Where are you? *Hey!*" Lee Ann turned her head in the direction of the yelling and then turned back to the woman. She was back on the love seat, her knees tucked up to her chest again. Lee Ann would not wait for her barechested, visored, ping-ponging Ryan, but this woman would wait for Thom, that was what she was there for. So Lee Ann left her to wait.

A word on Lee Ann as a fund-raiser: she was good. She could sweet-talk an alumnus into buying a thousand-dollar commemorative plaque in a second. Her fellow fund-raisers would have been jealous of Lee Ann's success if they hadn't been so completely cynical about their work. When talking to potential donors on the phone, Lee Ann's colleagues made clownish, mocking gestures with their lips and their hands. When they actually did browbeat an alumnus or parent or corporation into making a pledge, they called the donators "suckers" and their donations "blood money." She wasn't like them, nor was she like her boss, an alumnus himself, an ex-second-string defensive lineman who liked to talk about his work in terms of *client* and *contract*.

"When you give money to the school," he told his prospective *clients* and his new employees during orientation, "you are not simply handing over money to the school. Rather, you are signing a *contract* for success with the school itself. And as we all know," and here Lee Ann's boss looked at his clients and employees knowingly, eyes wide open so as to ward off the temptation to wink, "you cannot honorably break a contract."

The potential donors were inevitably lawyers, CPAS, industrial managers, and so on the whole were very skeptical about *gifts*; but they were absolute devotees of *contracts*, and so this tactic rarely failed. But Lee Ann found it unnecessary hoo-ha. All she did was ask people for money; if they said no, she asked someone else. Lee Ann gave the overall impression of not caring whether an alumnus gave money to their alma mater or not, which people, of course, found attractive, and they gave to such a degree that Lee Ann was the school's top fund-raiser, more proficient, even, than her boss, with his *contracts* and *clients*.

Which was why Lee Ann was so baffled by Barry, the video poker heir from Raleigh. It wasn't that he'd yet to give her and the university his money, wasn't that he said No to her. Lee Ann could take No. In fact, she found No definitive and comforting. But Barry wouldn't say No, not Yes, either. He said Maybe, had said it a dozen times over the past four years, had said it so many times it produced something like a feeling of longing in Lee Ann. A longing for what, exactly, she did not know, but she did know that longing was one of the things to be afraid of in this world. Longing was the enemy. It made you want something you did not really want as badly as the longing suggested you did, and which, if you got, would not make you happy. You could *want* but you could not be *satisfied*. Lee Ann had even tried to use her boss's *clients* and *contracts* business on Barry, but he had been a studio arts major, after all, and had no idea what she was talking about. Which made her long for him, or his money, or both, even more. Perhaps this was why she had returned his kiss; perhaps this was why she was thinking of him now. Lee Ann was at the very arc of Strawberry Lane's cul-de-sac; she could have easily turned and watched her house, watched to see if Barry—he drove a Alfa Romeo, the only one, he insisted, in the entire state of South Carolina—had arrived yet. But she didn't; because this was what dancing was for. It could not make you forget the longing, but it could transform it. Lee Ann remembered watching her parents dance at her and Ted's wedding; they were good, dullish, ordinary people, but they were great dancers. When they were not dancing, Lee Ann forgot about them; but when her parents were dancing, Lee Ann wanted to be them. *This* was what dancing could do.

And this was what it did do, because when Lee Ann reached the Howards' house, the door opened without her even touching the knob. The Howard family—Terry, Alison, their son, Ian—was standing there in the doorway, as if arranged for a picture. Terry was sitting in a wheelchair, and he said, "We've been watching you dancing."

"What the hell—" Lee Ann began, and then, mysteriously, felt an overwhelming need for privacy. She hustled herself inside the house, then closed the door behind her.

"What the hell happened to you?" Lee Ann asked.

Terry didn't say anything; he just sat there in his wheelchair. His hands were in his lap; he was wearing the gloves worn only by golfers or baseball players or the wheelchair bound. But Alison said, "You've got to be kidding me."

"Sure I am," Lee Ann said, even though she wasn't, even though she had no idea what had happened to Terry. This was clearly something she should have known: because it was a small town, because Terry lived on her short cul-de-saced street, because she should have known that something bad had happened to him. Even if she were wrapped up in her own longing and her own sorrow, Lee Ann should have been at least aware enough to know what had put her neighbor in a wheelchair. After all, she saw him every day, at dusk, riding his bike up and down Clemson's hilly streets, the hilly streets without any shoulders to speak of, the hilly shoulderless streets on which the students drove too fast too drunk. But Lee Ann worked at the university; she would have known if a student had put Terry in a wheelchair, because it might have been something she might have had to mention in reassuring potential donors that the school wasn't allowing all of its students to get drunk and slaughter Clemson's citizen population wholesale. So it wasn't a student, but they weren't the only ones driving on Clemson's hilly, shoulderless streets. There were also the retirees, the legions of retirees, and it wasn't just that the streets were hilly and shoulderless but that they were without center lines, too, and so even if you weren't a retiree who shouldn't have been driving because you were going a little blind and even if your reaction time weren't a little dulled by your eighty-odd-year history of reacting, then it would be difficult to tell exactly where you were on the road—whether you were too far over or not over far enough—until your right fender clipped the rear wheel of the bicyclist in front of you, sending him over the ditch and headfirst into a pine tree, shattering the helmet that was supposed to save not just his life but also his spinal column, his fine china delicate vertebrae.

"I'm so sorry," Lee Ann said.

"Thank you," Terry said.

"It happened six weeks ago," Alison said. "So yeah, thanks."

"Alison," Terry said. "Quit it."

"At least Teddy came by," Alison said. "He brought a bottle of good gin."

And there it was, on the dining room table; Lee Ann could see it. It hadn't been opened. It was good gin, better than what Teddy himself drank. And apparently Teddy was a good, generous person, better than Lee Ann herself was. Ian, Alison and Terry's son, still hadn't said anything. He was looking away from Lee Ann, toward the wall, and she followed his eyes and saw that there were a dozen holes in the plaster, fist holes, and that they were both at wheelchair height and higher. Her eyes went back to Ian, whose own eyes were hollow and pitted and looked much like the fist holes he was still staring at. He was a teenager, she saw, a normal teenager except sadder, which is to say he was the saddest person she had ever seen.

"I'm not supposed to drink," Terry said. "But would you like some gin?"

Lee Ann didn't say anything. She didn't move. She had forgotten all about dancing; she couldn't remember how she'd gotten to the Howards' house, had forgotten even entering the door and closing it behind her. Outside the house there might have been longing and its opposite, but inside there was only shame and fear, which you might be able to dance away if only they didn't stop you from dancing in the first place.

"Anyway," Alison said, "we were watching you dancing . . ."

"It was very beautiful," Terry said. "Very impressive."

"And we were wondering—" Alison said.

They were wondering if she would dance with one of them. And she had to: her husband had brought them gin—weeks ago, probably—and she owed them at least a dance. But with whom? She wouldn't dance with Terry: she had seen people dance with the wheelchaired, at weddings, parties, and the dancing reeked so much of pity that it couldn't be called dancing, the people doing it couldn't even be called people. And she wouldn't dance with Alison—because Alison hated her, hated most everyone, including her own husband, maybe her own son, and because what they'd be doing would not be dancing but would instead be something closer to war.

"Come here, you," Lee Ann said to Ian.

He came to her, even though he would not look at her. Terry wheeled over to the stereo, pressed a button or two, and music came out of the speakers. It was one of those popular Duke Ellington songs that people who don't listen to music listen to when they want to listen to music. Lee Ann and Ian danced to it anyway. They danced as befitted their circumstances: stiffly, awkwardly, as though their legs were in polio braces, as though they were *both* teenagers and not just one of them. Lee Ann could dance better than this, of course—there was the time when Ted and she danced at their wedding on the heels of a dozen lessons devoted to that one dance, and their two-step had wowed their guests, if not themselves—and she wasn't trying to dance awkwardly, but she did, and it seemed to her the most genuine thing she had ever done. It was the most surprising moment of her life: she was capable of doing something genuine again; or maybe it was the first time she had ever done something genuine. And just as she was trying to remember if she'd ever done anything genuine before this moment, Ian moved his hand from her back up to the back of her head, which he cupped gently for the remainder of the song—the song that began with her doing something for him, ended with him doing something for her.

"We'll all be fine," Ian whispered in her ear. "Please don't cry." But she didn't know what he was talking about, she wasn't crying, she was certain of it, even though her eyes were blurry and her voice shook and cracked as she said, "Goodnight, take care, I'll see you soon," and then backed out the door.

Outside, something was on fire. Lee Ann could smell the smoke, feel the fingers of heat. Lee Ann was glad that something was on fire; it distracted her from the Howards. Something was on fire! Perhaps it was her house; perhaps it was her! It wasn't the Charneys' house or the Lius', she saw this as she danced past them, the smell and the heat getting stronger as she got nearer the Parks' house. She could actually see the flames now, their own shadowy dance with the magnolia and white pines. The Parks' house was on fire! It was a happy prospect—not because she didn't like the Parks, but because theirs was the last house before hers, and it seemed a suitably big note on which to end her dancing: one final, pagan dance around the fire before going home to her guests, her clients, her Barry, and all their past, present, and future contracts.

But the Parks' house wasn't on fire at all. Lee Ann saw this as she danced closer, saw that the fire was coming from somewhere off to the right and behind the house. She followed the flames until she came to, in the middle of the Parks' backyard, a bonfire. In the middle of the bonfire, Lee Ann could see the white-hot skeletal remains of wooden pallets, a recliner, a dresser even. There were a dozen or so people sitting around the fire on a variety of wooden chairs and Lee Ann suspected that those chairs would also be in the fire before too long. The people around the fire were completely quiet, as if ruminating on the fate of their seats.

"What is that *smell?*" someone asked. Lee Ann couldn't see his face, couldn't see anyone's face.

"Fish," someone said. "Who threw a fucking fish in the fire?"

It wasn't a fish, it was Lee Ann's nameless dog; Lee Ann could see it sprinting around the perimeter of the firelight, could smell it orbiting them.

"It's not a fish," Lee Ann said. "It's a dog."

"Who is that?"

"It's Katherine," Lee Ann said, because the fire, her dog, her dancing, the night had suddenly made her extraordinarily tired—tired of being Lee Ann, tired of owning a dog she didn't really own and didn't even know its name or gender.

"Hello, Katherine," another voice said. "It's Ted."

Lee Ann walked over to the voice. It was her husband, all right. He was wearing a Hawaiian shirt open to midchest; Lee Ann could see the swell of his belly, on which rested his hands, one of which cupped a cigarette; his beard was enormous and red in the firelight. Even his head looked huge; there was a long-billed fishing cap perched on the very peak of his skull, and it was clearly pushed down as far as it could go; there were angry waves of hair pouring from underneath it. Lee Ann couldn't remember the last time she'd seen him, but since whenever that was, it looked as though her husband had swallowed his former self.

"I'm so tired," Lee Ann said. "Can I have your seat?"

"Do I have to move first?"

"No," Lee Ann said, and plopped down on his lap. She did this so suddenly that Teddy jerked his cigarette away and dropped it to the grass; Lee Ann could see it glowing down by her feet, next to a beer can that Teddy picked up and took a pull from. There was no difference between how the beer smelled and how Teddy smelled. Lee Ann wiggled around until she was properly settled. It felt as though she was sitting on an inner tube that had not yet lost its middle.

"Well," Teddy said.

"I was just at the Howards'," Lee Ann said. "Just horrible."

"I know," he said. "I gave them a bottle of gin."

"That was nice of you."

"It was actually your gin," Teddy said. "I took it from the liquor cabinet sometime back."

"Oh," Lee Ann said.

"You don't like gin," Teddy said. "Not really."

"That's true."

Someone across the fire stood up, threw the chair on which he'd been sitting into the fire, threw a beer can in the direction of the dog, whose fish stink was still whizzing around the fire.

"What's going on here?" Lee Ann asked.

"Roger and Lucy are getting a divorce," Teddy said.

"So you're burning their furniture?"

"It seemed like a good idea at the time."

"Was it Roger's idea or Lucy's?"

"Possibly neither," Teddy said, and waved vaguely in the direction of the house, which was completely dark. Lee Ann had been there many times—for dinner parties, to watch the World Series, to celebrate this or that. But at that moment it was hard to believe that anyone had ever lived there.

"What were you doing at the Howards'?" Teddy asked.

"Dancing," Lee Ann said.

"I don't want a divorce," Teddy said suddenly.

Lee Ann nodded. "Me neither."

"Why not?"

"I've never liked you better," Lee Ann said. It was the truth. She had lied to herself for years about how Teddy had wrecked her life; she had longed for the time when she was Katherine and he Ted. But the truth was that she hadn't ever really liked Ted—he was officious, he was dull, but he was good, so it was difficult to actually justify or understand her dislike for him. But Teddy was easy to dislike, it was understandable why she would hate him, which made her, in turn, like him. Love no longer applied, if it ever had; sex was irrelevant, too (there was no stirring in her sitting on Teddy's lap, even though she could feel a stirring in him). But she liked him now, she couldn't deny it, and couldn't imagine her life without him, couldn't imagine him not coming home for months at a time even though he was never more than a few miles from home, couldn't imagine him not running around on her with girls half his age, making a happy debauched spectacle of himself all over town. If he kept on the way he was going—which he would—then Teddy would almost certainly die before she did, and this made her sad. Losing Teddy would be like losing one of the poles, North or South. The thought made her sad, and it made her even more sad to see him here, near despondent, watching the flames of someone else's marriage, when he should be out there, doing the things he did so well.

"There's a big party down at the Merrills'," Lee Ann said. "They're playing beer ping-pong."

"Beer pong?"

"Right," Lee Ann said. "Plus girls."

"Okay," he said. "I love you. But do you mind if I get up?"

She didn't; they both stood up. He kissed her lightly on the cheek, and without another word he left the bonfire. The other men got up and followed along, as did the dog, its smell trailing behind it. Lee Ann was alone again. She had heard other women—women who had never married, divorced women, widowers—say that they liked being alone. Lee Ann didn't believe this for a second. They were lying, she was certain of it, and this was another thing to guard against: not loneliness, which was inevitable, but lying about it. A car door slammed in the distance. It was a tinny slam, not the door of a truck but of a sports car. It was probably Barry. Perhaps he would give his gift to her tonight; perhaps not. Perhaps he would give her more than his gift. Perhaps whatever he gave her would make her less lonely for a little, but the loneliness would come back, it had to, there was no sense lying about it, and there was no sense in longing for a time when she wasn't lonely. And while she was at it, there was no sense in lying about the dancing, either. It did not make her less lonely, less likely to long. It was simply a way of getting from one place to another, and now she needed to get back home, to her party, where people were waiting for her.

2005

Kathleen Flenniken

Preservation

Bobo awaits my third grade class
at the forgotten end of the museum. I explain
when they finish beating their chests

that Bobo was a famous gorilla I saw at the zoo
when I was seven, that here he looks false
because he's stuffed and mounted upright, like a man.

We take in his flared nostrils and hair, the virility
of his chocolate-colored chest. Everyone, even Dylan,
falls silent for a moment, long enough to remember

you left me four weeks ago yesterday,
a rubber band snap to my inner cranium
for the thousandth time today.

Bess and Tran point to photos of Bobo as a baby,
dressed in a nightgown, being fed a bottle. Bobo "smiling"
at his birthday party. Happier days. I think irrelevantly

of the milk expiring in my refrigerator,
how attached I am to the date on the carton,
the day before the world went sour.

Even milk observes the rites of decomposition,
the holy rites that Bobo was denied.
Is that so wrong? Roy Rogers

stuffed and mounted Trigger, his companion.
Wasn't that sweet testament, if sad and strange?
Bobo, do you understand the impulse?

I gaze into your fake glass eyes but you decline
to answer. I'm talking to myself, your look implies.
We both stand awkwardly with nothing to say.

The kids are restless. They're talking about ice cream
and the bus outside. He was real, I remind them
but they're running up the hall.

The last time I saw him, he was alive.

Murder Mystery

You're fingering the gun in your pocket
like a detective thinking like a criminal and then

a breeze off the lake ruffles the page, you shift
in your chair and your muscles remind you

of yesterday's steep hike. Page 186 already.
Now you're thinking like somebody on vacation,

of the tinkle of ice cubes from the cabin,
of your daughter's sylph silhouette against a faceted lake

and then your hand is on the gun again and pulsing
with adrenaline, you imagine slipping in the window,

rifling through files, turning to face an opening door
the way yesterday—after hard hours of climbing—

you imagined being pushed over the cliff into that cloudless sky,
your fall more swanlike than any Acapulco diver.

Your mind has turned liquid, as changeable and elegant
as the swallows that appear at twilight, and now

a cold martini pressed to one sunburned cheek, kissed lips,
and now a distant rowboat like a slow shuttle of silk,

and now this idea you could step out of your life
unafraid, with no worldly need but to find who done it.

John Keeble

The Cross

Zeta and I rendezvoused on a Tuesday, midway on the eighty-mile journey between his house and mine. I parked in a turnabout, and he drove us along the back roads, winding eastward at first. His old Travelall was decorated with hanging things—beads, thongs, and feathers. On the dashboard was a garden of dried plants, driftwood, and stones. The garden trembled in the early morning light. The Travelall was filled with the odors of wild things. Zeta's body was poised and his hands rested lightly on the large, plastic wheel. Soon we would turn north toward the K—— River, a tributary of the great Columbia, and the K—— River Dam, where we planned to make an adjustment to the landscape.

As we drove we gazed at the forestland, which in the watersheds grew so deep as to blot out the sun. In other places the clear-cuts opened gloomy vistas of stumpage and barrens backed by beetle kills. Our project would have made me anxious in any circumstance, but at certain intervals I also found myself seized with rage, still shot through by images of what had been—feasibly, yet unbelievably!—a threat on my life two nights before. There had been sounds in the dark outside my house, then silence, and at dawn I found a decapitated calf and an appalling message left in the cab of my truck. It was a dangerous time. Brutality was on the rise and intimidation, the order of the day. I wanted to speak of this to my friend, but as if stunned by the utter incomprehensibility of it, I couldn't find the words to begin.

Zeta and I each wore black sneakers and navy blue stocking caps. Our camouflage slickers lay draped over Zeta's day pack, which sat on the back seat, heavy with tools. The Travelall broke out of the woodland into coulee country, a place of steep canyons, buttes, and a pervasive color of beige from the dead ground cover left over through the winter and not yet quite overcome by this spring's green. It was a dry country. We each drank a can of v-8 juice. It left the taste of tin in my mouth. Our conversation traced the wiggly edges of a subject that soon plunged into a lacuna of mind: Paul Wittgenstein, the Austrian pianist and brother of Ludwig, the positivist who had asserted that the problem of meaning dissolved when it was cast into sentences.

It was Paul Wittgenstein who had had his right arm amputated after being wounded on the Russian front during World War I. A man of means, he then commissioned works for the left hand alone from several composers, including Maurice Ravel. I told Zeta that Wittgenstein had objected to Ravel's concerto because of its difficulty, but later in his life, after Ravel's death, he managed to perform it and therefore concede its greatness. Whenever I considered the concerto, I imagined the one-armed veteran at the piano with the pinned-up flap of sleeve exposed to the audience, a mournful and heroic figure. Now, I took a deep breath and told Zeta that I thought Ravel's menace and lyricism at once memorialized Wittgenstein's dismemberment and made it immaterial.

By late morning Zeta pulled off the road into a wash. The Travelall lurched and its hanging things swung. We put on our slickers, walked up the road, and crossed toward a white sign with black letters that said, U.S. GOVERNMENT PROPERTY. DANGER. NO TRESPASSING. There was a roar in the distance, ceaseless and throaty. We slipped between strands of barbed wire with impunity. We were also the government! We made our way through sage and stunted conifers. Native flowers were coming out, too, such as grass widow and adderstongue, along with European weeds—toadflax, thistle, and spurge. The weeds were remarkable for their adventurousness, as they had quickly gorged the cuts in the earth. Zeta took the lead. Under the slicker his shoulders swung according to the lightness of his feet, picking the places to step. In his pack the tools clinked softly.

It was early May. The ground was still damp from the rain and thaw but dry enough to resist the weight of a footfall. Following the first steep incline, the trail turned. The river roared and the dam came into view. Its line of concrete was interrupted by spillways and capped by steel grates. It had a plank gangway, iron handholds, steel wheels, and chain drives by which the spillways were cranked open and shut. Behind it, slack water the color of a thundercloud backed up the canyon. The dam had a vintage character, the instruments of leverage protruding from its insides to be manipulated by hand. It had been in place for a century. Hauling the turbines over an arduous course by mule teams had been heralded as a brave crusade in its time.

Across the way to the north stood the black rock of the opposite cliff. At its top were lawns and white buildings with red roofs that housed the equipment and the crews that came and went. A glass door flashed open, and a man in a blue jumpsuit and blue baseball cap appeared. He also wore a tool belt. The stainless steel handle of his hammer glinted as we watched him go to another building just above the dam. He mounted the steps, that door flashed, and he passed within.

Zeta glanced at his watch. "Good. Now he'll ride the elevator to the bowels."

We stepped to an outcropping and paused. Not far below was a larger outcropping on which a white cross was bolted to a concrete slab. A year ago it had simply appeared. No one was certain who had put it up but only that the power company, a public utility, had at first proposed removing the dam from service because it cost more to maintain than the value of the electricity it generated. Local business people and politicians had objected, while the deep ecologists were enthusiastic over the prospect of what they called the river's "outing." A small knot of them held vigils on the maintenance grounds in preparation for the river's release. The Army

Corps of Engineers assessed the site. Archaeologists surveyed the banks. Biologists in diving gear explored the reservoir, where they discovered heavy silt cast in the shapes of dunes and a bizarre new dominion over which shiners, suckers, and huge, mutant carp held sway.

For months the controversy smoldered in the weekly newspaper of the region. It was featured in the daily, published in the city to the south. Senators and federal bureaucrats began taking positions on the question. Then five cases of dynamite disappeared from a nearby construction project. The FBI was summoned. All these things were thought to be bound together as is the way. The controversy had seemed on the verge of inviting civil disorder, but then the white cross materialized as if from nowhere.

The dissension abruptly subsided, but whether this was due to a natural ebbing of energies or to the effect of the cross was impossible to determine. People traveled to see it. The power company took the liberty of setting up picnic tables on the maintenance grounds, and on weekends groups gathered with their meals and bore witness by gazing over the canyon at the cross. An editorial in the regional paper praised the action of the anonymous party for reminding the citizens of the Lord's power to heal dissension. The dynamite was never recovered. In the months that followed, the power company quietly maneuvered for a rate increase to finance retrofitting the dam.

Forty feet below the cross lay the canyon bottom. It was high water and the dam's floodgates stood open. Great tubes of water poured through, plummeted straight down, cut through the surface of the river, then boiled up again a short distance downstream. A huge hole, bounded by a jagged curling wave, trapped entire logs. A cloud of vapor rose from the bottom and billowed around the cross. Looking down filled me with rue for what I must not do: fling myself over the edge and plunge into the river and come up and bob against the logs and be driven down again by the surge to the depths.

In my anxiety over our project—what we called "monument correction"—I had completely forgotten my particular sensitivity to heights. All my life an all-consuming terror has filled me whenever I stand at the edge of a precipice, but remembering it quite vividly at this moment, I found myself clinging to the branch of a gnarled fir that burst out of the face of the cliff. Cautiously, I raised my eyes and stepped back. Zeta cocked his head. He knew I'd been momentarily lost in a wild place. His thick hair was black. He had a mustache, beard, and dense eyebrows. His face, which was a dark rose color, seemed to shine out from behind the black patches.

"Menuhin," he said. "Wasn't he really another amputee?"

I looked at my friend, startled but knowing not to take him literally. Zeta had an admirable mind. He was capable of sweeping into the most unexpected quarters one moment and of mounting an inquiry akin to monomania in its singularity of purpose at the next. But of course he was not a lunatic! We spoke of the violinist, the prodigy Yehudi Menuhin. Although Zeta was an aficionado, music was one subject about which I knew more than he. As a child Menuhin's virtuosity had caused him to be regarded, he himself had said, as a "sacred monster." But at another time in his late twenties, he found he couldn't play a note.

Menuhin has claimed that he played utterly without self-consciousness until the breakdown. It was then the time of World War II, and he was touring Europe. He was Jewish. His people were marked, herded, enslaved, and exterminated. He had personal trouble, too, which led to a divorce. The sheaf of his prodigious California child, inside which he'd remained safe, rapt with his music, was ruptured. Suddenly he couldn't play at all. He had to go back to absolute zero, relearn the most rudimentary maneuvers, and reconstitute his spirit. Truly, it might be said in a case such as his that the coming into awareness had severed his body from his being.

"Too many messages about the true state of the world," Zeta said. "Too many melodies. Not enough rhythm."

It was a joke. Zeta's face glowed. He rocked gently to and fro, laughed softly, and touched my arm. We were hunkered against the cliff, awaiting the moment of our descent. A week ago we'd gone with our wives to a concert by the Ghanian drummer, Dadey. Dadey's performance on a set of five congas was impeccable and majestic. Above the crimson shells, his dark hands flickered among the pale skins. At times his playing was exquisitely simple, while at other times it filled the hall with a labyrinthine roar. The listeners were awestruck, knowing they were in the presence of a great heart. Dadey made a remark with which I'd been grappling ever since. "Melody is distance," he'd said.

Zeta and I stared across the canyon. Between us a root of the fir snaked out from the earth. It embraced a heap of gravel. At the outer verge of the root a groove had been worn, and there was a small opening in the gravel, as if something had been entered there not long ago and chafed back and forth. I couldn't make it out. "It's the cry," I said, referring to Dadey's remark. "It's the melody that's heard over great distances. The drums send messages to each other; everything else, the intricate rhythms, is maybe a way of making sure the transmission is clear.

Zeta smiled. "But people also dance to the rhythm."

I thought about Ghana. I thought of drummers in trees sending messages across the savanna, of how in the old days the messages might bear upon questions of life and death—game migrations, army encampments. I knew nothing about Ghana. I thought about the slaves in the plantation days, how the masters had outlawed drums in fear of the messages they sent—the dangerous secrets, conceivably the plots of insurrection and escape. I thought of the slaves in the fields, looking up in recognition at the sentences the notes contained. I knew nothing about the plantation days. I could only imperfectly imagine the fervency of such messages. It was a shakily formed and yet dynamic phantasm in my mind.

Zeta rocked forward and scrutinized the shaft. "There," he said. The service elevator passed darkly by the lowest window. "He'll go to the generating room." We looked up at the top of the opposite cliff. No one was there, nothing—only the black rock, lawns, picnic tables, and white buildings with red roofs. "Now," Zeta said as he rose and moved for the trail. "Be careful."

We continued our descent into the canyon. The trail cut back and forth through a string of switchbacks. The air grew chill, and the way was steep, the trail narrow and wet. A fall meant death. I was afraid and didn't know where to look to calm myself—up, down, or straight ahead. As we negotiated a sharp turn, I clutched at the rock wall. Before us the trail straightened in a final incline toward the second outcropping. The cross stood in plain view, bathed in luminous mist.

Zeta came to a stop. He gestured several feet ahead at a place where the trail angled downward toward the bottom. He pointed at a slot in the rock wall, leaned forward, put his hand into it, then held himself as he darted across. I reached out and slipped my fingers into the slot, which I found grooved as if designed as a handhold; later I would surmise that it must have been so. It was an ancient thing made for just such passage. I exhaled deeply then stepped. My legs shook. One foot began to slide out from under me. For an instant I froze. The foot slipped further. A terrible coldness rushed through my body. I moved, almost wildly, and Zeta reached out and grasped my wrist. I was across, safe.

Zeta knelt and quickly emptied his pack of the socket set, hacksaw, wire cutters, pry bar, cold chisel, rubber mallet, and can of penetrating oil. I knelt opposite him and inhaled deeply. Between us was the cross. Made of four-inch steel, it was six feet tall with a four-foot cross member, a *crux immissa*. It was heavy, beaded with moisture, and expertly welded. It was a Protestant, hard-edged thing to which one was obliged to reattach by imagination the impaled body of Christ. I reached out to touch it and felt overwhelmed by my history in this religion, as if I were a boy again: the night prayer meetings, the squared-off hymns, Sunday after Sunday attending sermons and scriptures, session after session filled with remonstrance against evil, and finally, most loathsome of all—though I didn't know it at the time, having been spun myself into a sheaf of childhood—the sinister requirement that believers evangelize the world, that the willing voluptuousness in every corner of the earth be brought under the pilotage of righteousness.

Zeta passed me the penetrating oil. The steel plate at the base of the cross was attached by three-quarter inch bolts. The heads were imbedded in the concrete slab. The slab had been poured into a depression in the rock itself. I doused the two bolts on my side with oil then looked around. We were perhaps two-thirds of the way down the crevasse. Straight across was the black cliff, the access tower. There was no sign of anyone. Below, the white froth boiled. We were now in thrall to a roaring envelope of sound. I looked back along the trail and straight up, wondering how the cross and its accouterments—bolts, cement, and water to activate the cement—had been carried here. I constructed imaginary scenarios that included managing a water vessel and negotiating that last stretch in the rail, bent profoundly beneath the cross. It seemed beyond possibility, but then it dawned on me that everything could have been lowered by rope, coming down perhaps from the outcropping above. I remembered the groove that had been worn into the protruding root of the fir and felt a grudging admiration for the perpetrators of the deed.

Each of the bolts had a hole drilled in it through which a loop of wire was passed and joined with a clamp. Zeta clipped off the loops on his side then passed over the wire cutters. I clipped the loops on my side, drew the wires through the holes, and tossed them over the edge. Zeta had the socket on the ratchet, and he started on the first nut. He had to put his weight into it. The nut broke loose with a crack. His body swung outward and back. He turned off the second nut. I braced myself and did the third and fourth. When we tried to rock the cross, it didn't move at all.

Zeta began chipping the concrete from around the edges of the base. It was painstaking and a good way to think through trouble

. . . to engage in repetitious labor, to allow the flood of trouble to compose itself into rivulets that found their way through the work. Hand on the chisel. Hand on the mallet. Driving the chisel through the concrete. Then passing the tools over and watching Zeta work his side.

Now, suddenly, I told him how our dog had barked wildly in the depth of the dark two nights ago, how it then fell silent, how the other noises—a footfall, the click of a latch—formed an ominous music. I'd lain awake on my back listening.

I had known, sensing the alert consciousness next to me, that my wife had been awake for some time. Finally, she spoke: "Maybe it's nothing."

"Maybe."

She rolled over to her side. The bed rocked. Upstairs, springs creaked as our youngest son shifted on his bed. "Probably," my wife murmured. Now that I was fully awake, she fell asleep.

For anyone to come to our house required a mile's drive from the county road. We slept easily most of the time. When we did not, we would sleep in turns, one sleeping and the other keeping vigil. I knew the shotgun was in the corner of the closet near the bed. I had timed myself because I worried about my inquiries into the neo-fascist organization headquartered not far from my home. They were building underground bunkers in preparation for Armageddon and to keep themselves safe for the Rapture. They stockpiled weapons and were suspected of running a counterfeit ring. They might well have the stolen dynamite. It took me twenty seconds to get from the bed to a fully armed condition and then ten seconds more to reach either the front or back door. A half minute. I finally fell asleep.

In the morning I found the dog closed up in a shed with a slab of meat. "And then I saw that one of our calves was missing from its pen," I told Zeta. "I felt like an idiot. We'd been complacent."

He looked at me. We had the cross free. When nudged, it rocked lightly. It was a question of prying it up over the bolts and letting it drop. I drove the cold chisel under the base. We moved close to the rock wall. Zeta put the tools away except for the chisel and bar. There was no sign of the watchman. "He should come out soon," Zeta said. "We want to know where he is—that's all."

It was remarkable how softly we could speak. It was as if we occupied our own pocket of quiet within the roar of the water.

"When I went to the pen, I found a heap of entrails on the ground and a carcass hanging from a corner post. Somebody had come in, baited the dog, killed and dressed out our best calf. I started back to the house," I said, "but I saw something on the windshield of the truck, pasted to the inside. And when I opened the door, I saw the hide draped across the seat and the calf head wired to the steering wheel, the eyes looking mournfully right at me, blood everywhere. I practically fell over trying to get out of the way of the thing. On the windshield was a note. It had a drawing of a gun sight, and it said, THE CROSSHAIRS ARE ON YOU. I told Zeta that the message also bore the red-and-black insignia—swastika, wings, and raptor talons—of the very organization I'd been researching. He already knew that my interest in the organization had to do with its professed fascism—mainly with the power of belief to mount a cover under which the faithful could creep like larvae, sealed from the light, carving out a scrabbled-up sanctum with their trails.

He held my arm and leaned near. "I'm sorry," he said. "No wonder you're edgy. We could have waited. You should have said something."

"I haven't been able to figure out what to say. It's so strange that it hardly seems like it happened."

"This was two nights ago? Have you called the police?"

"Yes. Two nights ago. And no, we haven't called the police." As I said that, I once again asked myself why: perhaps because then we'd have the police on our place, not that we had much of anything to hide; perhaps because, made a matter of record, we'd be drawn ever deeper into an imbroglio. "But maybe we should. I don't know. The kids have been driven to school the last two days."

"You bet," Zeta said.

"It's true that all day yesterday and last night I wondered if those people were onto what we were up to. Up until a few minutes ago, I wondered if it was a warning. Now I don't think so."

"Why?"

"Workmanship. I've been in their buildings and sat at their tables. They're rough-cut folks and close to incompetent. I've seen a bench collapse when one of them sat on it. They've got wires hanging out of their walls. Whoever made this cross and put it here is a different order of adversary."

"I'm sorry," Zeta said again. His commiseration was meant to strengthen me. He had perceived that I was more disturbed than I myself realized. "We could just leave now."

"No," I said.

"So," he said, "who put this thing here?"

I shook my head. "I don't know. Maybe they picked up a welder. The hell. Maybe it's a freelancer."

Zeta smiled. "Maybe it's the power company."

We laughed softly. Surely, that was an absurd proposition, yet it was funny because it seemed possible. But for the moment all that mattered was that this incidence of vandalism—the emplacement—be countered, its spell broken.

We fell silent. The elevator passed by the second window. Zeta slipped the tip of the pry bar under the base. The cross tottered. I moved the chisel. When the elevator passed the third window, Zeta levered the bar. Instantly the cross toppled and dropped from sight. The metal rang against the wall of the cliff . . . once, again, and a third time, calling out brilliantly and echoing with quickening clarity against the other side. Then there was nothing.

We didn't move. The elevator passed the fourth window. The door flashed open. The watchman appeared and started across the lawn toward the building where we'd first seen him. He glanced our way and went on, then glanced again and stopped. We didn't move a muscle.

"Does he see us?" I asked.

"Don't move."

The watchman didn't move, either. He was still looking. It was too far to make out his expression, but the inclination of his body suggested scrutiny.

"The question is," I said, "does he see what's not here."

"Right."

"He's taking a long time looking."

"Right."

"He's trying to figure out what's missing," I said.

"Or has figured it out, but can't remember how long it's been since he last saw it. He's thinking maybe it was yesterday, or maybe it's been a month. He doesn't know."

"Maybe he sees us."

"If we don't move, he can't be sure."

I looked from the watchman to the dam, that antique. It had been once an exercise of imagination and will, a form of prosthesis even, that drew into its engine the potential energy of topographical relief, of the "drop." It then harnessed the energy and articulated it out into the grid. It also severed the river from itself. There were now few trout here, the quick ones colored bright as birds, and no salmon at all coming up—blood red, filled with sex and death—to make the river talk to itself all along its course.

I looked back to the watchman. He removed his cap, ran a hand over his hair, replaced the cap, hitched up his tool belt, and walked on. He mounted the stairs of the other building, looked back again, then went inside. "Now," Zeta said. We got up, negotiated the slippery stretch with surprising ease, and went on around the switchbacks. When we reached the upper outcropping, we paused. There was no sign of the watchman. I put my finger into the groove that had been worn into the root and decided that it could well have been made by rope. I grasped the limb of the fir, moved to the edge, and looked down. I couldn't resist. It was all right. The cross was visible, a diffuse white shape just downriver from the foaming hole. A lone osprey cruised up the river, cut through the vapor, caught a draft at the dam, and shot high into the sky. We went on, pausing again at the top, and saw the watchman on the deck, cupping the brim of his cap with his hands and peering across the canyon. We froze.

"Now he sees us," I said.

"Maybe," Zeta said. "Or maybe what's missing just hit him. When he turns, move quickly." The watchman turned. We scrambled up the last stretch, ducked through the fence, and beat a path to the Travelall.

We took a different way out, along the wash to a logging road. Zeta told me about his grandfather, an old Obregónista, who'd come to this country after the Revolution and done field work in the southwest. He married and raised a family, then, when his wife died, returned to the homestead in Sonora that the Mexican government had granted him for his service. "Owning the land meant little to him," Zeta said. "But he told me how every night he fell asleep facing north where his children were. And he had his violin. Before I visited him last time, he wrote and asked me to bring four strings."

Zeta told me how when he'd arrived in the little town in the desert, his grandfather was in the hills. "Way out there with the rocks and snakes," Zeta said. "He was skinny as a rail. He had a ponytail and big curls of hair coming out his ears and nose.

"He played for me on the one string he had left. It was a tune with an offbeat in it. When he put on the new strings, he broke one right away by tightening it too much. He said it was a bad string." Zeta slapped his thigh and laughed. It was infectious and I laughed, too. Then Zeta went on, "So he had to put the old string back on, but it wasn't the right one. He had two strings of one kind.

"They were having a fiesta in the town, which was my reason for going at that time. Grandfather played in a mariachi band with three other old men. Guitar, guitarron, a trumpet, and Grandfather. They were very good. The people slaughtered a steer for roasting. An old woman killed it. Grandfather told me it was an honor for her, just like being able to play was an honor for him. She was a tiny thing, and the steer was big. But the young men had it roped up, and she popped it once between the eyes with a small sledge. It went right down. It was like she got suddenly big in the instant she swung the hammer. Grandfather broke another string, so he had to finish the night playing with three. It was clear he could play with one. Or if he had no strings at all, I guess he'd have scared up a piece of wire."

Zeta paused. The highway was in sight. My thoughts turned toward my wife and children, toward getting in my car and going home to the calf's head that was still in my truck, and the note and maybe to the sheriff's department, toward reckoning with the meaning of all that. At least I'd already hauled the carcass into the trees for the carrion eaters to have.

The hanging things in the Travelall swung, and the garden on the dashboard leaped crazily when Zeta bounced onto the pavement. He worked the Travelall up to cruising speed. We each drank another can of v-8 juice, but I wished we had a little tequila to go with it. "Did you send him more strings when you got back?" I asked.

"Of course," Zeta said. "It's my duty as a grandson. I send him some twice a year. He appreciates it, but really it doesn't matter to him. He's over ninety. All that matters is the music."

2006

Paul Guest

Elba

When she tells me her name I'm thinking
of Napoleon's exile there. Of his hand
in paintings, oddly tucked away,
and the vague memory that it meant
something, once. I'm thinking
then of Bugs Bunny aping Bonaparte
and how as a child I laughed
but did not know the thousands dead
in his name. I'm thinking
not at all what she would like
kneeling there in the aisle of this plane
when she asks if I was born
this way, and who in Chicago takes care
of me, a wife, a girlfriend—
she knows one or the other is in my life.
When I tell her which two
white rings of bone in my neck
are fused, wired, made one,
I can see her ardor marry grief
and I want to save her
from my life. I tell her
that some now think Napoleon died
of a hormonal disease
slowly making of him a woman,
his body white, smooth, hairless,
with breasts a physician thought beautiful,
and though she smiles
I can't tell which story she no longer
wants to know.

These Arms of Mine

Let's promise never to love like the octopus:
floating in darkness, in jellied ink,
its beak the only hardness it knows,
and though I can't imagine how
it helps matters, in the eight-armed
midst of its mating, a limb
will often fall away from the body,
by ecstasy amputated to the silt.
All morning I've failed to find
why, though no one fails to mention
that death soon follows all
this armlessness. It's fascinating but a mess.
Imagine if each time we kissed
my ear fell off. If the morning
was not so much for brushing
the fog of the night from the mouth,
but reassembly. You might go
out into the day with my bad ankle.
I'd never hear the end.
What would there be to talk about
except that we were falling
apart, and too soon, and how dull
it had all become, this entropy, this shedding,
this habit of the cephalopod
no one can explain. Maybe
it's like the threatened sea cucumber
everting its guts, to leave
less to hunger's hunger. Maybe
eight arms is one arm too many to bear
in the alien instant

of that inscrutable love.
That I would understand, that I could recognize
in the mirror of my skin,
in yours, there in the crushing depth
of the night. There we'd find
each other like exotic gods,
our hands manifold, our fingers infinite—
well, almost. Soon:
the subtraction, the severing, the silence like a wave.

Beasts

"Thank you, beautiful," I said as my five-year-old daughter, Maude, came skipping over from the swings and handed me a warm, wilted bouquet of dandelions. Dandelions, the only flowers no one cares if you pick. Maude smiled at me and then turned and ran screaming back to the playground. Ginger Rogers, the fat, sweet, six-year-old basset we'd just recently adopted from the pound, pulled on her leash and barked.

"Stop!" she called as she ran, her voice causing Kyle, her best friend, to freeze in mid-motion as he was about to sit on the one free swing. "It's my turn."

"You shouldn't call her that, Alice," Bibi, Kyle's mom, said. Bibi was my oldest friend; we'd known each other since college.

"What?" I wasn't really paying attention. I was watching to make sure Maude didn't bully Kyle, who was small for his age, a worrier, and easily bossed. Instead Maude turned suddenly gracious and led Kyle by the hand to the playground's other swingset, where two cast aluminum ponies hung side by side.

"Damn adjective," Bibi said, raking her long black hair out of her eyes with her fingernails. "Or is *beautiful* an adverb?"

"Adverbs modify verbs," I said, English teacher that I was. "Beautifully is an adverb. As in 'Maude sings beautifully.'" Maude, as a matter of fact, took after me and couldn't carry a tune in a great big bucket.

Bibi waved away the instruction. "The point is, Alice, you shouldn't call Maude beautiful." Bibi emphasized *beautiful* in a way that held it out like a dirty sock between two pinched, disapproving fingers.

I looked across the playground at Maude. As I watched, Maude's blond hair flew first forward than back as she swung her horse without mercy toward some imaginary finish line. Her eyes looked blue and big and bright even from a distance. Why shouldn't I call my daughter *beautiful?* Maude *was* beautiful.

And not because of hair or eye color. In Wisconsin, being blond was nothing special. Two-thirds of the kids in Maude's kindergarten class were blond. Kyle was so fair my husband Anders joked you could read a newspaper through him. It wasn't her neat, symmetrical little-girl chin and nose either. She was beautiful because in some way I couldn't quite prove scientifically, she glowed. She spun off energy like a hot new star.

Not a day went by that people in the street or at the grocery store didn't notice, didn't stop me and repeat that very *B* word. What a *beautiful* baby, what a *beautiful* girl. At the Mexican restaurant near our house where we often stopped for takeout, the señora called Maude "La Linda." "Beauty," Anders would say when Maude pitched a fit over some little thing, "and Beast."

"It warps girls," Bibi said, her voice shaking. She sounded like she might cry. "Take my word for it. I know." Of course Bibi knew. She was beautiful. And I, I was not. Nice looking, neat, maybe, but not beautiful. "It becomes everything to you. You end up spending all your time trying to *be* beautiful, wondering why no one has called you beautiful today, this hour, this minute. You live in fear of the day you'll get sick or old and turn so ugly no one will love you."

"Oh, honey," I said. I put my arm around her and squeezed her shoulder, but at the same time I thought *She's talking about her life, not Maude's.* Ginger licked the toe of Bibi's boot, adding her own dose of sympathy.

Bibi accepted the consolation of the hug, but said, "I know what I'm talking about, Alice. You should listen."

I frowned, shifting my focus from Bibi to Maude. My beautiful girl. It seemed so innocent. "Do you really think I'm hurting her?"

"Not if you stop," Bibi said.

I looked toward Maude. Was Bibi right? Maude was now spinning Kyle on the merry-go-round, her small sneakered feet raising dust. She was putting her back into it, clearly determined to go faster than childkind had ever gone before. Kyle was hanging on with both hands, squeaking *no no no* and then something that sounded suspiciously like *sssstttttooooopppp*. Instead Maude jumped onto the flying carousel and stood right in the middle, hands flung up to the sky, a blond whirligig, a Wisconsin dervish. Kyle let go of the safety bar and clung to her leg.

Bibi was looking not at the pale blur that was her son but at the horizon, at the tall chain-link fence that marked the boundary between playground and park—this side for children, the other for grass. She seemed, for a moment, to have forgotten we were there. She sighed.

"I'd better grab Maude," I said, giving Bibi's shoulder a last, clumsy pat, "before she breaks Kyle in two."

All the way home from the playground with Ginger and Maude I thought about what Bibi had said. Was she right about Maude? It was hard to know. I thought of Bibi, so bright and, yes, beautiful, sitting on the bench in her red tunic and purple velvet bell bottoms. I would never have admitted this to Bibi, but I picked clothes to be purposefully neutral. That way, if I wore the same sweater three days in a row, people assumed I owned three gray sweaters. Actually, I owned half a closet full.

I thought about what she'd said while I sorted the dirty clothes before dinner. One basket of whites—mostly towels and Anders's t-shirts—and one of darks—my grays and Anders's black jeans. In a college town like ours nearly everyone wore black, the house color of artists and academics. One basket of bright colors—all Maude's. Did beautiful people instinctively crave purples and oranges and reds? Maude had a weakness for chartreuse as well.

Over dinner Anders told about his trip to our neighborhood hardware store to get brass screws for an installation piece he was working on. Anders was a photographer who taught in the art department at the state university, but lately his photographs had begun to leap, rather inconveniently, off the walls. He cut and arranged them in dioramas and installed them in large impressive pieces of vaguely Victorian cabinetry. He'd even made an inlaid teak projector stand that spun in circles while showing magic lantern slides—he called them "moving pictures." I liked it. It was exciting to watch hand-colored prints of tropical fish spin dizzyingly around the room on the white walls above the furniture. It made me think about all the things I took for granted—real movies, TV, video, computers—miracles too much a part of everyday life to seem miraculous anymore.

These new pieces already took up an amazing amount of room in our small, crowded house, but still Anders kept buying sheets of mahogany, brass pulls, knobs, and screws, slowly and quietly building his private World's Fair. He hardly stopped except to take Ginger for her slow, waddling walks. "So," Anders was telling Maude, "I was standing in line when this woman comes up behind me and says, 'Aren't you Maude Dahl's father?'" And then the old guy behind the counter says, "Maude's your daughter?" Anders laughed. "Isn't that amazing?' I thought, 'My daughter is famous!'" Maude shrieked, she was so delighted. I smiled.

The old man behind the counter must have been the owner, Mr. Vandergraff. Maude had gone with her class on a field trip to the hardware store just two weeks before and had come home with instructions for how to make bird feeders out of pop bottles. Obviously, Maude had made an impression on him. Had she been wearing chartreuse that day?

The woman was probably one of Maude's many teachers, at school, at swimming, at Sunday school, tumbling, ballet. Unless she knew Maude from Anders's pictures. Locally they were his best-known works. They'd hung in the faculty show at the university, in the biannual survey of who was who among Wisconsin artists, and in a popular coffeehouse near campus where students hung out for hours drinking lattes. Over the students' bent heads hung Maude at four months, an upside down blur swung in front of Anders's lens, the amazing flying baby. Maude at two, with a jumbo pitted olive on the end of each stubby finger like some mutant half-toddler, half-tree frog. Anders shaped his face into an extravagantly artificial frown. "Famous on five continents, but I'm nobody in this town but Mad Maudie's dad."

"Oh, Daddy," Maude rolled her eyes. She had taken to pretending offense when he called her Maudie, his baby name for her. The "mad" she didn't mind. But wasn't "mad" as bad as beautiful? I wondered, all adjectives suddenly suspect.

"When you win the Nobel Prize," Anders said, his faux frown losing out to his usual slight, mocking smile, "just remember to thank your old dad."

"Thanks, Old Dad," Maude said, kissing him on the top of his graying, old-dad head. That done, she turned to her mother. "Is there a field trip tomorrow?" she asked. I nodded. I'd signed a permission slip for Maude and her fellow kindergartners to be taken to the State Historical Society to see a new exhibit on Native Americans of Wisconsin. I had, as usual, ducked Maude's teacher's suggestion it was my turn to chaperon. I taught freshman English at the local community college and had forty student essays waiting for me in my bulging book bag. "I want to wear my straw hat, Mom," Maude said.

"Are you sure, Maude?" I said. On family trips Maude tended to start out with a sunhat and then lose interest. Usually I wound up carrying or wearing it. And none of Maude's teachers looked like the straw-bonnet type. Maude, though, looked absolutely stunning in it. When she'd worn it to the farmer's market that past weekend, half the people who passed us hurrying in their search for the perfect pumpkin or heirloom apples or aged cheddar could be heard to remark in passing, "Did you see that beautiful little girl in that lovely/amazing/damn big straw hat?" I was sure Maude had heard them as well.

Maude nodded. "And," she added, "if they're clean, I'll wear my chartreuse socks."

That night after Maude had been steered clear of the treacherous reefs that surrounded five-year-old bedtime and was safely asleep with Ginger at her feet, I lay in bed, trying to summon up some energy for my stack of papers. When I was engaged in my teaching, full of the kind of energy I had rarely been able to summon that fall, I gave my students what I thought of as slightly mad but challenging assignments. Compare someone you love to a wonder of the world. This time I had only told them to compare or contrast two people, places, or things. So I knew without looking I was doomed to comparisons of dogs to cats, Big Macs to Whoppers, Frisbee golf to Hacky Sack, Wisconsin to Iowa, or, at best, Illinois.

I gave up on my students' attempts to find meaning in the subtle variations of daily life and began leafing through one of the many back issues of the *New Yorker* I hadn't gotten around to reading. I glanced at the listings for photography shows. Anders was too busy building his vision of the Past/Future for gallery openings in Manhattan to interest him. I had grown up as an army brat, moving every four years. Anders had been born in Wisconsin in the same small town where his great-grandparents were buried. He'd left Wisconsin reluctantly to go to grad school in New York, serving time as if in the foreign legion until he could at last return home, return to a place where the people had the innate sense to call all cold fizzy drinks *pop*. His plan, he told me on our first date, was to be like Frank Lloyd Wright, a fellow Wisconsin native who also hated cities and who had made the world beat a path to his low, well-designed door.

When we met, Anders had been a new assistant professor. He was experimenting with color film, giddy with the extravagance of having unlimited access to the department's color processor and printer. He blew up everything he shot to poster-size. He would stay up all night printing what he'd shot, then drag it still wet into class the next morning for his students to see.

After we started dating Anders begged me to model. If I would, we could spend all our nights together. So I had agreed to pose. But first we'd gone shopping. Even then my wardrobe had been better suited to black-and-white photography, so we'd gone to a vintage clothing store near campus and bought a big red satin shirt the color of Technicolor lipstick. Then we went to an all-night drugstore and bought lipstick to match. The first night he took pictures of me leaping off a chair, a blurry, midair kiss of a woman. Then on other nights, juggling—and dropping—green apples. Then, in an artistic breakthrough, throwing lime Jell-O into the air.

Some of the shots looked like Kodak ads—all color, no content. But some, when I had tired of the games and the endless delays for moving the spots, metering the lights, and reloading the camera, when my mouth was a weary smear, my eyes were narrowed, my neck bent with fatigue into a slightly odd and painful angle, then voila! there was tension and a hint of a story that would forever remain tantalizing and unknowable. There was art.

After the photo sessions we would make love on his futon, and then he would leave me to a few lumpy hours of sleep while he went to his darkroom on campus to develop that night's film, make color prints from the negatives he'd taken the night before.

By the end of the semester it was clear that I was going to move in with Anders and his futon. So when Anders asked me to pick up the four-foot party sub he had ordered for his end-of-class party, I agreed. I'd walked through the door carrying this most ridiculous of foods, and the assembled photography students looked up and cried as one, "It's her," as genuinely star-struck as if they had spotted Madonna. "It's the Jell-O Woman." For a moment, I was famous. But where was there to go after fruit-flavored gelatin? I was relieved when Maude came along to model for Anders.

But how long had it been since Anders had taken a picture of Maude? I tried to remember. Not a roll of holiday snapshots, but an honest-to-God photo as art? I couldn't remember. Last summer?

Earlier this fall? At any rate, it had been before Anders bought a table saw and began building his mahogany boxes.

Anders came to bed, crawling over me to get to his side, picking up a magazine along the way. Anders actually read the long *New Yorker* profiles of people you never knew existed until you saw the columns of tiny type about them. I propped myself up on one elbow. "Why don't you take pictures of Maude anymore?"

"What?" Anders was flipping through his issue, squinting at the cartoons. "Oh." He blinked, as if he hadn't really realized he had stopped. "No reason. Just that that last time it didn't work out. She posed too much."

"What do you mean?"

He shrugged. "She didn't know what to do with her hands or with her mouth. She kept smiling like she thought she should smile in a picture." He turned back to his magazine. "You can't be yourself if you're worried all the time about being beautiful."

That's it, I thought, as we settled down to sleep. I was going to go cold-turkey on all words—adjective and adverb—that referred to the illusion we call our bodies, bodies that were bound in the course of things to grow sick or old. No more *beautifuls* or *lovelies*. Not even a stray little *don't-you-look-nice*.

Thursday was Bibi's and my annual night out to celebrate our birthdays, which fell a mere ten days apart. Our tradition was to go to a bar we'd never been to before, get good and drunk, exchange small gifts, and sometimes break into fits of inappropriate song or dance. Once we got bounced from a bar for doing an imitation of the Rockettes, high kicking and singing *New York, New York*, in my case shrill and off-key. Then, our birthdays duly celebrated, we'd take taxis home where families and hangovers awaited us. In other words, for one night we acted like we were still in college. Anders and Bibi's husband Lloyd had seen the ritual enough times that they kept the aspirin handy. This year we'd chosen the town's first martini bar. We found a table, then we each pulled out our presents and set them in front of us. Mine for Bibi was in a small gold gift box that had obviously been wrapped at the store; Bibi's present for me was in a red handmade paper bag pulled shut with rough twine.

Bibi and I had known each other as undergraduates, floormates in a large, rowdy coed dorm. But we hadn't started this tradition, hadn't become best friends, until we were in grad school. Bibi was in her first semester of art and I was working on my master's in English, already teaching freshman composition, though I hadn't known then that I had stumbled into my future. At that first birthday-party dinner Bibi had handed me a scroll tied up with gold ribbon. I unrolled it, expecting to see words—maybe a hand-set poem or a Zen koan done in calligraphy. Instead, the paper was blank. I turned it over, looking carefully at both sides. It was odd paper, as blue and fuzzy as dryer lint. I looked up at Bibi, trying not to look too puzzled. "I made it," Bibi said, "in my papermaking workshop. You whiz snips of old blue jeans in a blender with water and Elmer's glue, then spread it out to dry on an old window screen."

It is lint, I thought. "It's amazing," I said, knowing it had probably taken Bibi hours to make.

"I'll show you how to frame it." Bibi smiled lovingly at the first piece of paper she had ever made. She, too, had found her life's work.

I still had Bibi's first gift and her second, a blank book. I, on the other hand, doubted Bibi still had the first gift I had given her, a literary guide to Wisconsin. Bibi had flipped through it, peering at the foldout map, at the black-and-white photos of authors and their houses. I didn't know then that Bibi was badly dyslexic, could hardly read and so had good reason to prefer her books blank. It was me, crazy English major, who liked them dense with type.

The second year I made a better choice; I gave Bibi a pair of earrings. Big purple glass grapes, a bunch for each ear. That set the pattern. Every year was a paper anniversary for Bibi. I, on the other hand, worked my way up from glass to silver. Last year I'd even sprung for an odd bobbing pair of fourteen-carat-gold plumb weights. This year, though, I'd broken with tradition. Instead of earrings I had gotten Bibi a pin. A single smooth nugget of amber the size of a baby's heart bound with a band of silver, with a sharp dagger of a pin set in the back. It looked like something a Goth might have used to close his rough woolen cloak. I couldn't wait to see Bibi pin it to her bulky lime-green-and-orange sweater.

Before we opened presents we always had at least one drink. Bibi got her martini with vodka and a pickled baby Vidalia onion. I, ever the more conservative, went for gin and an olive. But after the first glass of pure alcohol I loosened up. Bibi talked me into ordering something off the specials board for my second. When it arrived it was a lovely, sad blue. What liquor turns a martini aquamarine? After one sip I felt like crying. Then I was crying, not from sadness, really, but a sudden acute sense of time slipping past me. I could hear it rushing like water. I remembered our first birthday bash—our skin had been peach perfect. I remembered Maude in my arms for the first time, a red-faced blue-eyed little radish. Where were any of us headed? Suddenly the rush of time made me dizzy. I wanted to stop the relativity train and get everyone I loved off before we all came to some terrible end.

"Are you okay?" Bibi put her hand on my arm, her concern touching and genuine though she knew from experience I was a maudlin drunk.

I nodded, wiped my eyes with my cocktail napkin.

"Hey," Bibi said, picking up her present, "may I?"

I nodded. "Tear away."

Bibi tore into her birthday gift, shredding the wrapping. She had a casual attitude toward machine-made paper. She held the amber up to the light and let out a long happy "Ooooooh."

"Be careful," I said, reaching out to touch the brooch's silver pin. In my martinied state I misjudged this distance and pricked myself. As if in a fairy tale, a single drop of red blood appeared on the white tip of my finger.

"Close your eyes," Bibi said, unknotting the string on the present. I did, and heard a soft *whoosh* like moths fluttering past me. Bibi put something over my head, placed it gently around my neck. Could you knit scarves out of paper? I opened my eyes. This year Bibi had given me jewelry. A necklace of folded paper strung on silver cord. A lei. *Aloha*, I thought, my mind ever the dictionary, *a word that means both hello and good-bye*. I reached slowly up to touch it, almost afraid the paper might startle and fly away.

"It's *beautiful*," I said.

Bibi gave a wry laugh. "Oh, I almost forgot," she said, positioning the amber over her left breast, then stabbing the silver pin into her sweater. "Can you watch Kyle for me on Saturday?"

I noticed my finger was still bleeding. It had left a red smear on my cocktail napkin and probably, though I couldn't see it, on the paper necklace as well. "Sure, what time? Maude has swimming lessons at 8:30, but we can be home by 9:15 if I tell her Kyle's coming. Otherwise she takes forever in the shower."

"No rush," Bibi said. She was signaling the waitress for our tab. "I'll drop Kyle off around 10:00. I have to go in for another biopsy—this time on my right breast. Lloyd's going to drive me. I should be home by 2:30 at the latest."

I started to say something, I wasn't sure what, but Bibi put a finger across my lips.

"Later," she said. "No matter what they find, they won't do anything. Not then."

Saturday, Maude was up before the alarm went off, digging through her drawer for her bathing suit and goggles. We had taken the summer off from swimming lessons, and now she was eager to start again at the Y. She had forgotten last spring's tears over her inability to float on her back. I made a pot of coffee and toasted a bagel. Friday morning after my night out I had been wretched, as sick as I had ever been in my life. "Think of it as nature's way of keeping you sober," Anders had said, shaking his head. This morning I still felt a little shaky. *This is what age does to you*, I thought. Throw a little party and it took a week for your liver, cranky old housekeeper, to clean up the place. Maude, a healthy five, ate a heaping bowl of Cheerios.

Maude swam with great splashing enthusiasm, cheerfully venturing in over her head. It made me nervous to watch her, but her teacher was full of praise. He moved her up from Minnow to Fish. "The spirit's there," he said, when the class was over and the kids ran shivering for the showers. "Her body will catch up."

In the locker room Maude's class struggled into their clothes as the next class wriggled into their suits. Lockers banged and girls shrieked. A baby, sibling of some young amphibian, cried at the top of her lungs. I felt yesterday's hangover in the base of my skull, clearly planning a comeback. I was pretty sure I had some Tylenol in my purse and I desperately wanted to wash them down with Diet Coke, that perfect shot of caffeine and NutraSweet. Maude, sensing where her mother was headed, begged a quarter off me for the gum machine. I hesitated. Anders disapproved of gum. It stuck to your shoes and wasn't even food, but, then again, he wasn't there. I opened my change purse and dug out a quarter for Maude. That and a few pennies were all the change I had, but I knew from Maude's past swimming lessons that the Coke machine took dollar bills.

What was Bibi doing and thinking right then? I wondered as I dug through my wallet for a bill that wasn't too wrinkled. They wouldn't let you have breakfast, even before a minor surgical procedure. She must be starving. Bibi always ate a good breakfast. Maybe she was brushing her teeth, over and over. That was okay as long as you spat and didn't swallow. She wasn't worried, she'd told me the night before. This was her third biopsy in as many years. Her mother had been the same way, Bibi said. Biopsies every year and never anything but harmless fibroids. And now, with mammograms, every shadow made the docs jump. They'd be negligent not to follow up.

I fed a bill into the Coke machine. It sucked it in halfway, then spat it out. Damn. I smoothed it, running the bill back and forth across the sharp corner of the candy machine. I had had only one lump, one biopsy. It happened just before I met Anders. The scariest thing had been the changing room at the university hospital, a locker room full of women coming in for biopsies, women getting the news from ones already finished, still others on their way to a dose of chemo or radiation. No privacy. In the corners women wept. Bibi said it wasn't like that now. Each woman had her own little curtained cubical with a La-Z-Boy recliner to lounge in while the nurse started her pre-op IV.

The Coke machine emphatically and finally rejected my dollar bill. I turned my back on the idea of liquid refreshment. Maude was sitting on the couch by the door, looking glum. Wasn't the gum machine working either? "What's the matter, Sweetie?" I said.

"I swallowed it."

"The gum?"

"The quarter."

I didn't know what to say. I had heard plenty of jokes over the years about kids swallowing things, about parents keeping watch over toilet bowls to get back diamond engagement rings. Surely, surely swallowing change was not that serious. Maude looked okay. We could afford the quarter. Maybe we should just go home and see what Anders thought.

"It hurts, Mom," Maude said, pointing at a place just below her heart. Now, suddenly there were tears in her eyes. "It hurts right here."

We went to the emergency room. There the triage nurse was openly concerned. "You didn't call 911?" she asked me.

I shook my head. The nurse frowned, then turned to Maude. "Tell me what happened, dear. How did you swallow the quarter?"

Maude looked embarrassed. At five she knew she was old enough to know better. "I don't know," she said. "I didn't have pockets so I put it in my mouth, then I was just standing there looking at the gumballs and I forgot and swallowed it."

It made sense, I found myself thinking, drawn in by Maude's slant logic. I had noticed how few clothes that were made for girls Maude's age had pockets. Boys' pants always had pockets. What were little girls supposed to do, carry purses?

"Did you cough or choke?" the nurse asked. She was writing all this down.

"No," Maude said. "I tried to spit the quarter out but it was too late."

"Are you having trouble breathing?"

"No," Maude said, "but it hurts." And she looked like she was going to cry again. I put my arm around her.

"It'll be okay, Sweetie," I said. The nurse, I noticed, looked less sure.

"The peds doc will probably want an x-ray," she said. She put us in a cubicle to wait for the pediatrician on call. A cubicle similar, I imagined, to the one where they would put Bibi. *Bibi.* Had I told Anders that Bibi was going to drop off Kyle? I had forgotten my watch, but surely it was ten already. There was a phone on the wall beyond where Maude lay on the narrow examination table with a paper sheet pulled up around her neck, but it was a blinking maze of buttons. I ran my hand over Maude's damp hair. "Does it still hurt?"

"A little," Maude said.

"Rest, Sweetie," I said to my daughter. "I need to call Daddy." I stuck my head out of the curtain. "Excuse me," I said to a nurse—not our nurse—behind the desk. "How do I get an outside line on this phone?

The nurse made a sour face, as if all the indigent moms in town came in here to make phone calls. "Press nine," she said, "then your number."

"He's here," Anders said about Kyle. "He's petting Ginger and watching me stain plywood. Where are you?" I told him. "What does the doctor say?"

"We haven't seen one yet, but Maude seems better." Actually, Maude now had the paper sheet pulled over her head. "I'll call when I know something. We may be awhile." I hung up the phone and peeked under the paper covers at my daughter. "Are you okay, Maude?"

Maude was crying again. "Why did you have to tell him? He'll think I'm stupid."

I sighed. We were in the adjective swamp again. And *stupid* didn't seem an improvement on *beautiful*. "I had to tell him," I explained. "He was worried. Besides, just because you do something stupid doesn't mean you are. Your father knows that. Everyone does stupid things sometimes." I patted Maude's paper-covered knee. "I certainly have."

"Knock, knock," a woman called, then flung back the curtain. "I'm Barbara. The doctor sent me to take you to x-ray." The woman spoke directly to Maude, not looking at me. *You let your daughter swallow a quarter*, I thought, *and they all know what kind of mother you are*. The x-ray technician held out her hand, and Maude hopped down off the table and took it. "Where does it hurt?" she asked Maude.

"Right here," Maude said, pointing.

"Her esophagus," I heard myself say.

The technician looked at me as if she were surprised to find me there. "Are you a medical professional?" she asked.

"No," I said. Just a person with a passing knowledge of body parts, I wanted to say, but didn't. "I'm an English teacher."

"Oh," the technician smiled. "In that case, I'd better watch my grammar." She started to lead Maude down the hall. I began to follow. The technician waved me back. "We'll only be a minute," she said. "And Maude's a big girl, aren't you?"

Maude nodded emphatically and abandoned me, the mother who had given her the ill-fated quarter, without a backward glance.

Actually, they weren't gone long. Maude reappeared with two heart-shaped stickers on her purple turtleneck. The first read *I Got An X-ray Today!* and the second *I Was Brave!* "She was super," the technician said, holding up the black-and-gray picture of Maude's insides. She snapped it under the clip on the light box. "I'll go get the doctor," she said, and left.

"They make you hold your breath," Maude said, hopping back up on the table. She was taken by her stickers. "Just like in swimming class." I wanted to sneak over and flip the switch on the light box to illuminate Maude's irradiated bones, but before I could move, the doctor was there.

"Dr. Jorgenson," he said, holding out his hand. I shook it. He looked about the same age as my students, and his palm was almost as soft as Maude's. "So," he said, "let's see where the foreign object in question, the . . ." he glanced at the notes the nurse had taken, "quarter has gotten too." He flipped on the light. And there was the missing quarter, floating like a bright, full moon in the night that was Maude's chest.

The doctor pulled at his smooth, young chin. "How long ago did she swallow this?"

I peeked at the doctor's watch. It was nearly ten-thirty. "A little over an hour."

"Hmm, it's sitting right where the esophagus opens into her stomach. A tight squeeze for a quarter," he said. "Let me go talk to the pediatric gastroenterologist on call. We may have to go get it."

"Operate?"

Maude was excited. "Will I have a scar like Madeline?" she asked. The doctor looked puzzled.

"It's a children's book. The heroine has her appendix out."

"Oh," Dr. Jorgenson said. "No, no scar. We have this long rubber tube, an endoscope. We slip it down your throat and grab the quarter. Bring it up, good as new."

"Yech," Maude said. Thinking, I imagined, about where that quarter had been, but the doctor thought Maude meant the idea of the endoscopy.

"You'll be asleep," he said. "You won't even know when it happens." Maude nodded. "Be right back," he said to me.

Maude sat swinging her legs. I wondered if now was a good time to check in with Anders—I didn't like the "asleep" part—but Dr. Jorgenson was back before I had a chance. "Dr. Gert says Maude should rest here for a while to give her own muscles some time to squeeze that quarter through. We'll take another x-ray in thirty minutes, okay?"

I didn't like the idea of more radiation either, but it sounded better than anesthesia. "Okay," I said to Dr. Jorgenson. He patted Maude's foot.

"Relax," he said.

After he was gone, Maude asked, "What did you do that was stupid, Mom?"

I almost said, "You mean besides start this conversation with my five-year-old daughter?" But it was too late to back out now. I thought of the time I had eaten a large dose of hash in sloppy joe mix. For a week I'd thought my roommates were planning to kill me. Then of the time I slept with my Theory of Composition professor even though I knew he thought my teaching was hopeless. But those didn't seem quite the right examples for Maude. "Well," I said, "last year I backed out of the garage too fast without really looking and knocked the side-view mirror, *bam*, right off the car."

"Really?" Maude asked.

I nodded, not adding that I had told the insurance company someone had hit me in the grocery-store parking lot. Or that I sometimes dreamed a big guy in an Allstate jacket was chasing me, calling me a liar and a lousy driver. "What else?" Maude asked.

"I jumped off the garage roof and broke my collarbone." Maude nodded. She knew that story. "I swung a baseball bat without looking and hit a kid who was standing behind me in the nose." Maude lay down again.

"It's really hurting now, Momma," she said, touching the same spot under her ribs. *If only*, I thought, *I'd given Maude a dime*. Maude turned over on the examining table, clutching her wrinkled paper towel of a sheet.

"Shhh," I said, stroking her hair. If Maude got any worse I was going to fling back that curtain and go find Dr. Jorgenson. I put my face next to Maude's on the little paper pillow. "Then there was the time . . ." I had gotten as far on my list of stupid-things-I-did-as-a-child to the time I'd given the family dachshund a crayon to eat when Barbara, the x-ray technician, reappeared.

This time Dr. Jorgenson brought Maude back himself. He snapped the x-ray into place on the light box and flipped it on. I couldn't see through him—he was no x-ray—but I didn't have to. Dr. Jorgenson took one look then whooped and made a fist, pulling victory down from the air. "Way to go, Idaho," he said to Maude. Then he stepped back and I could see the full moon of the quarter was much lower and off to one side, no longer centered over the orderly ladder that was Maude's spine. "Into the stomach and on its way home," Dr. Jorgenson said.

Maude poked at her ribs. "It doesn't hurt anymore," she said, as though that surprised her.

"You know, kid," Dr. Jorgenson said, still admiring the x-ray. He tapped Maude's faint curving ribs. "You've got a *bea-ut-i-ful* set of bones here." He stretched out the word I had banned from our lives into four comic syllables. "You must drink a lot of milk."

"Ice cream," Maude said seriously. "The secret is ice cream."

"Really?" Dr. Jorgenson said. He stuck his hand into the pocket of his lab coat, drew out a prescription pad and some children's Motrin samples. He shook his head and tried the other pocket. "Then you'd be a good candidate for one of these." With a flourish Dr. Jorgenson handed Maude a slip of paper. It read, "Rx: one ice cream cone to be taken internally. Fill this prescription at the University Hospital Cafeteria. ASAP."

"Please, Momma?" Maude said. Part of me wasn't sure girls who swallowed quarters for a main course deserved dessert, but I was so grateful to have Maude unsedated, unintubated, that I nodded in approval.

"Sure," I said. "But remember, Kyle's waiting to play, so we can't take all day." Would Anders have heard from Lloyd about Bibi yet?

We found the hospital cafeteria in the basement—weren't they always in the basement? It smelled unpleasantly like dishwater and overcooked broccoli, but the lunch rush, if there was one, hadn't started yet, and the large woman in the hairnet working the food line was happy to scoop Maude out a very large Cookie Dough cone. I grabbed a stack of napkins and followed Maude to a table near a row of dusty plastic plants. "Work on it a little," I told Maude, watching my daughter digging the chocolate chips out of the ice cream with her tongue. "Then we'll risk taking it in the car."

I spotted a pay phone on the far wall. "Stay right here, Sweetie. I'm going to tell Dad you're okay." I got change for my wrinkled dollar from the cashier. The quarters looked huge in my hand. Would I ever look at one the same way again? A woman with a stroller beat me to the pay phone, and I stopped short, trying to signal that I wanted to make a call but not wanting to seem like I was listening in.

Luckily it was a short conversation. "No. No. Okay," the woman said. "All right, then, pick us up out front." I smiled at the woman and looked into the carriage to smile at her baby as well. As a mother I felt obligated to do that kind of thing. But the child in the carriage was much older than a baby, would have been a toddler if he had been able to walk. Twin oxygen tubes ran into his nostrils from a tank at his side. A blank rubbery expression filled his round face. I forced myself to smile anyway. The mother nodded at me as she pushed her son past.

I felt dizzy, but I made myself pick up the receiver of the pay phone. Then I leaned forward, resting my forehead on the cool metal of the coin return. After a moment I straightened. Maude was still sitting at the table, working hard on her cone. This was the first time Maude had ever been to an emergency room. She had never had more than a cold. Anders had had nothing worse than the flu. We had been living, were living, on the lucky side of the planet. *Lucky*, another word you couldn't trust. We were lucky. The other people in this room—some trailing ivs from tall t-shaped stands, others just sitting wearily over Styrofoam cups of coffee waiting for news that was not likely to be good—they, clearly, were not.

But if beauty could desert you, then so could luck. Was Bibi, across the highway in ambulatory care, still one of the lucky ones? I thought of the boy in the baby carriage, then of blond, sweet, perpetually worried Kyle. I knew Bibi would say she had been lucky so far. Maybe that was the best any of us could say.

I dialed my own number. "Hello?" Anders said.

"We're coming home," I told him.

At the house Kyle ran to greet Maude with Ginger at his heels. No kid's idea of a good time is spending Saturday with someone else's parent. I told Anders the good news. "It might take as long as two weeks," I said, repeating what Dr. Jorgenson had told me. "But unless Maude starts throwing up or running a fever, the quarter can be considered safely on its way."

"Two weeks?" Anders said. "After that long it should come out two dimes and a nickel."

I nodded, then belatedly realized he was making a joke, and tried to smile. I hadn't done anything all morning except sit around and wait but I felt exhausted. "Did you hear from Lloyd?" I asked. "Do they know anything yet?"

"Yes," Anders said, "and yes." He looked over his shoulder. Kyle was sitting on the living-room couch. Maude was standing in front of him, tracing the path of the quarter with her finger. Anders lowered his voice. "It's malignant. Lloyd said they want to do a lumpectomy, probably tomorrow."

God, I thought, *lumpectomy*. What an ugly word. I knew, though, that there were uglier ones.

"Then," Anders was saying, "Bibi will have to choose between chemo or radiation. Apparently it's her choice. I told Lloyd I'd help him do some research on the Web tonight."

I shook my head. Printouts about odds would never help Bibi decide what to do. Bibi was Bibi. I imagined her flipping a big gleaming quarter—heads I choose death rays, tails poison cocktails.

Anders looked at his watch. "Lloyd said he'd be by for Kyle as soon as he got Bibi settled at the house."

Kyle was looking at us, looking even whiter than usual. He knows, I thought, somehow he knows. For a chronic worrier it must make a kind of perfect sense. He'd been preparing for bad news all his life, and now it had arrived.

"Dad, Dad," Maude was pulling on Anders's arm. "I need you to put on some music."

"What?" Anders said, for once not on his daughter's five-year-old wavelength.

"Kyle's playing audience and I'm going to dance."

"What kind of music?"

Maude shrugged. "Dance music." Anders put on the Supremes. Then, at Maude's insistence, he sat on the couch next to Kyle. "Stop, in the name of love." Maude was wiggling around, mouthing the words.

"No, no," I said, "like this." I spun into the routine I'd learned from Bibi in our dorm days, one she and I had done in a sports bar on the memorable occasion of our first birthday night bash.

"Stop!" I held my hand out like a school crossing guard. "In the name of love," I crossed my heart. Maude threw herself into it, wagging her finger along with me. "Before you break my heart." Ginger lifted her head and howled. I heard footsteps on the front porch.

"Come on in, Lloyd," Anders called over the wall of sound.

"Nice moves." It was Bibi, standing next to Lloyd and looking as if on this Saturday nothing had happened to her that hadn't happened a thousand times before, as if under her sweater were no fresh stitches and beneath them, no tumor, hard and hungry and growing.

"Auntie Bibi," Maude said, catching her hand, pulling her into the middle of the room. "You dance, too. We're a girl group. We're . . ." Maude paused, frowning with the effort of making up a name, "We're *The Beautiful Girls*."

Bibi didn't flinch when Maude said *beautiful*. Instead she smiled, began making the hand motions I remembered so well from the early years of our Beautiful Girl lives. As one, the three of us pivoted and turned and mouthed Diana Ross's words as if nothing in this world could ever be less than lovely. As if there were no tragedy or loss, no unlucky quarters in stomachs, no blank-faced children who couldn't breathe or walk, no ugly cancerous lumps. As if the world were all beauty and no beasts. Kyle and Anders on the couch gaped in amazement. Lloyd, still standing, the long folds of his face damp from tears, sang along. Their girls were breaking their hearts. "Stop," we girls sang. "Stop." But, for now, there was no stopping us.

2007

Mari L'Esperance

Pantoum of the Blind Cambodian Women

Years later my mind returns to them
Their sightlessness a physical mystery
Blindness a deliverance from memory
Eyes darkened in mute refusal

Their sightlessness a physical mystery
As if it were all that was left to them
Eyes darkened in mute refusal
It is this that has kept them alive

As if it were all that was left to them
The women have turned inside themselves
It is this that has kept them alive
Through the burning, falling world

The women have turned inside themselves
There is no returning, the boats departed
Through the burning, falling world
Their vision turned inward to the bearable

There is no returning, the boats departed
Forced to watch their daughters bayoneted
Their vision turned inward to the bearable
This is the story of their turning away

Forced to watch their daughters bayoneted
Blindness a deliverance from memory
This is the story of their turning away
Years later my mind returns to them.

Finding My Mother

Near dusk I find her in a newly mown field, lying still
and face down in the coarse stubble. Her arms

are splayed out on either side of her body, palms open
and turned upward like two lilies, the slender fingers

gently curling, as if holding onto something. Her legs
are drawn up underneath her, as if she fell asleep there

on her knees, perhaps while praying, perhaps intoxicated
by the sweet liquid odor of sheared grass.

Her small ankles, white and unscarred, are crossed
one on top of the other, as if arranged so in ritual fashion.

Her feet are bare. I cannot see her face, turned
toward the ground as it is,

but her long black hair is lovelier than I remember it,
spilling across her back and down onto the felled stalks

like a pour of glossy tar. Her flesh is smooth
and cool, slightly resistant to my touch.

I begin to look around me for something with which
to carry her back—*carry her back*, I hear myself say,

as if the words spoken aloud, even in a dream,
will somehow make it possible.

I am alone in a field, at dusk, the light leaving
the way it has to, leaking away the way it has to

behind a ridge of swiftly blackening hills. I lie down
on the ground beside my mother under falling darkness

and draw my coat over our bodies. We sleep there like that.

Katherine Vaz

Lisbon Story

I opened the door to my father's apartment in the Campo de Ourique district of Lisbon—he'd sent me to sell it quickly before he died—and even before my eyes adjusted to the dark, I could feel that a stranger was lying in the bed. I froze in the hallway. He seemed thin and long but heaped, a tangle of cords more than a body. I jostled my suitcase, but he didn't stir. I inhaled the scent of what might be the corpse of a drug addict who'd wandered here from the Cais do Sodré station and persuaded the excruciatingly bribable *porteira* downstairs to let him expire in some warmth.

As always in Lisbon, my heart throbbed semaphores to call Tónio. That's all it ever takes for him to gather that I'm in town, but I'd also taken the precaution of sending a letter asking him to try some advance work toward the sale. He's an orbiter, an arranger, a whisperer in kings' ears, though what he actually does for a living, like many of the refugees from Angola, is construction work. He'd written back that he'd tracked down a possible buyer . . . though (*Ai, querida, you know the story here*) there were a few complications, which he'd save for my arrival.

I touched my way into the small, narrow kitchen, where I snapped on the light. The tiled picture of a caravel was tilted; a knife black with jam was tipping the bark canoe of a cheese rind on the cutting board. While I was grimacing at a cleaned-out tin of sausages, a young man wrapped in a sheet appeared in the doorway.

I shrieked—one of those girlish but full rending affairs.

Inside the *V* where he clutched the bed sheet, his chest revealed enough of his ribs to suggest the inner planks of a one-man fishing boat. His eyes were clouded but bright, beaming a child's buoyancy toward sickness.

My brain switched to Portuguese; I stammered that he could call me Catarina, and I sketched the outline of why this place was getting hurried to market . . . and was he perhaps a friend of António Magalhães? Was he the buyer for my father's apartment?

His name was Mateus Soares, and he spoke somewhat the English from watching many movie programs on the television set. He pointed a finger at me and said, "Bang, bang, especially your westerns." Toninho was a friend, yes, but as for owning a genuine roof over his head, no, ha ha and again ha ha, he barely had money for a dinner of pork fat.

"Well, now," I said. "How about if you go into the other room, and we can talk? You can explain where you belong, how's that sound?"

His answer was for his legs to buckle. He stayed kneeling, gripping the doorframe. He was wearing my ex-husband's sweatpants. Water began to gush from his skull.

When I'd tucked him back in the gray wet bed, I whispered, "*Tens* SIDA, *Mateus?*" The room smelled of spilled intestines.

He nodded. His eyes flickered, as if fireflies had stepped in the quicksand of his irises and were pulsating ferociously before they went under.

What had possessed me long ago to paint the bedroom the shade of a toy pig? Now that it had faded to a hybrid rose, the furnishings—rickety iron bed, splintery armoire, beige hooked rug, and spindly dresser—suggested probing insects resting indefinitely inside a flower.

"Let's see what you've hidden in this mess to feast on," I said.

I'd come to esteem Lisbon as a refuge after college and still loved to escape here. The narrow, tiled staircases edged with plants, the shirts with extended empty arms flapping in the breeze along the lines, balconies where no one appears: Lisbon rises before me as real as a dream printed out of my brain. I kept lots of provisions on hand so that I'd enter, after a lengthy absence, into a well-stocked home, but almost everything had been eaten. The cupboards, canary-yellow and apple-red, cheery plastics I'd installed in the postrevolutionary seventies, offered a lone tin of tomato soup that I brought to lukewarm. The freezer was empty except for a heel of bread.

I sat on the edge of the bed to feed Mateus. I was wearing a black skirt, white blouse, and lilac pumps—only British tourists wore sensible shoes—that kicked at his splay on the floor of magazines on American basketball. The pages exposed unearthly jumps and skeins of muscle. The dryness of his hand scraping mine alarmed me: a husk of a dead starfish. He grabbed the spoon and, smiling, splashed at the red pool in the dish in mock complaint and said, "You serve me the food of jails."

"My father was in a jail in this country, and trust me, he never got anything this good," I said.

"Your father is a criminal?" Thrilled, eager, he flopped toward me.

"No. No, you might say he's the opposite of a criminal." I eased backward.

"I don't understand, pretty little girl." *Menina bonitinha.*

"Don't call me that. I'm forty-five years old. *Jesus.*"

We stared at the room's sole attempt at decoration, Dad's framed poster of Wales, my mother's birthplace. He'd been born in northern Portugal and met my mother after his release from prison. She'd been on holiday in Lisbon and found it touching that he acted unstrung while riding in the funicular. They'd bought this place to live in as newlyweds awaiting their immigration papers to California, and they'd kept the property but never returned. He'd asked me to leave the map on display, so that Mama's ghost could visit if she liked.

Came a small voice from the bed: "I meant you are pleasing with the long dark hair and green eyes and your smallness."

"Don't say that either."

"My mother, she owns the green eyes." His voice spooled out the scratchy tape of his story. She was Lisboan and his father was

Mozambican, and they lived by the Museum of Costumes and did not approve of him. He was only thirty-three. His boyfriend had thrown him out when he got ill.

I murmured about his bad luck. I was sorry.

He quoted a Portuguese line about destiny: If shit were worth money, the poor wouldn't have assholes.

Mateus could easily be one of Tónio's lovers; he was forever breaking up with one man or another, though he'd sobbed terribly over a guitarist from Cabo Verde. Beyond the rattling pane, Lisbon was coming to, the trucks grinding and trolley wires singing that pitch best heard by animals, while the Christmas lights—in tints from eggshell to vanilla, strung as bells and holly—buzzed in their sockets over the streets.

I repeated that my father was dying of stomach cancer in California, and letting go of this perch was his last unfinished business. He wanted to survive long enough to sell his spot here and divide the profit among his three grandchildren, my brother David's three.

"I cannot buy nothing," said Mateus.

Right. Quite so. I'd help him get into a hospice that dealt with AIDS patients—wasn't it good to be in a country with socialized medicine?—because I had another sick man to put at peace.

"Ai, no," he said, turning over to face away from me. "My desire now is to die in a nice house. I am not going to no hospital."

Americans solve their problems by fleeing. From the hallway I left a message on Tónio's phone machine to meet me at once at the Santa Apolónia station. I trusted my voice to find him immediately and have him plain materialize. I abandoned my luggage and, without saying good-bye, raced the four flights down and stood on Rua Carlos da Maia to stare at the ground-floor windows and shut curtains of Deolinda Simões, the porteira, the gorgon at the gate. My father never failed to mail her checks to watch his property, though we were sure she rented it out on her own and pocketed the cash and, up until now, managed to spirit her renters into some fissure if my brother or I planned to visit.

I bolted over the dragon's-tooth mosaic sidewalks, past the Chinese restaurant run by immigrants from Macau, and hurried to the taxi queue on the Rua Ferreira Borges. My cabdriver inquired if I was about to become ill, did I need help? I was hoping I looked merely deep in prayer. My hands were sealed over my eyes as we climbed the Calçada da Estrela, where the cobalt and turquoise tiles gleamed on the shops stocked with King's cakes, glacéed citron, baskets spilling pineapples from Madeira, and port bottles with chalky stenciling to show their age. The cable on the Prazeres streetcar ahead of us fell from the overhead wires, and my driver, grizzled as scraped toast, slammed on the brakes but hummed a sweet, broken tune. When the streetcar jolted forward, its cable like a femur bouncing on the wire, we tore east along the waterfront and I almost catapulted through the windshield from the force of his stop at Santa Apolónia.

On a plate-glass window looking into the station's waiting room, my reflection was smeared, as if I'd thrown my face to splatter on a mirror. Ostensibly my father wished to spare me the trauma of prolonged deathbed scenes; he intended to go to his Maker in a pine-scoured room with trained caretakers. He'd been fond of his forty years as a nurse at Children's Hospital and regretted that he couldn't die with their teddy-bear wallpaper as a backdrop to David and me. But the other reason for packing me off to Lisbon was that the year before his cancer was diagnosed I'd imploded into jigsaw pieces after my husband, James, blurted that I "represented confinement." I was, with unforgivable timing, my father's last nursing project; childless and solitary since my divorce, I was going to send him worrying into the other world.

I scanned the crowds, anxious for them to present me with Tónio. The Tejo across the road lapped against the hulls of boats, an incoherent lullaby. Toninho! There you are! Tónio Magalhães! Grinning at me from the opposite side of the Marginal. Wearing broth-colored khakis and a blue-striped shirt, a vastly different getup from the one he'd been sporting when we'd first met twenty years ago. I'd been walking down the Avenida da Liberdade when an African in a bell-bottomed, chartreuse tie-dyed pantsuit pinched the back of my calf and said, "You are the first white girl in this city I have made smile." He later denied that he ever wore such an outfit.

He tapped with a what-goes-on-in-that-mind-of-yours brisk-ness at his temple to convey, *You said the* south *side of the highway, minha sempre-perdida Catarina!* He looked gaunt, but then he was lamppost-tall, and perhaps his habit of manifesting out of nowhere suggested the notion of the spectral.

I barely missed getting hit by a car as—horns blaring—I dashed through the traffic into his arms. "My God," he said, "you almost got yourself killed and then I'd have to die, too!" My hand on the giant rosary-bead decades of his spine. His scent was of Mustela oil, like a pressing of hazelnuts and lab-invented musk, and we were of a perfect mismatch of height for him to settle his head on top of mine. Though we often sleep side by side, we'd never tangled in the ruinous desperation of love that leaves no one standing.

"Cat, I am so sick, oh my Lord, about your father."

The sun scorched off my corneas, broke the membrane sealing in the water, as if it were only simple, physical laws that had me crying.

Ai, Catarina. Não chores como chuva. He cradled my head against his chest. My father used that expression: Don't cry like rain. When the sorrow bursts out of you as a visible storm.

"Honey pie," he said. *Unny-pah.* He'd picked the word up from the fifties sitcoms hailed down into his war-pounded Luanda. He tossed it at me often enough, but it never failed to crack me up.

"You need to tell me everything, Senhor T," I said.

"Honey pie, I must sit down. *You* want to sit down, too, believe me, Catarina."

We found a green bench with a view of the dock. Discarded napkins from a stand selling lemon squash and coconut tarts scuttled like albino crabs around our ankles. He was mottled with sweat as he took my hand in his and said, "Your father is not the only one to possess that apartment, I am sorry."

"He's owned that place for sixty years. I sent you a copy of the deed."

"Honey pie, I discovered that after the revolution some *grande queijo* in the Communist Party said, 'okay, I am making a new deed, I own it, not some American who doesn't live here anymore, it's mine.'"

"If someone else stole it, why hasn't he ever tried to move in?"

"Because he died a few weeks after making the false deed. I found it when I was nosing around the Associação Lisbonense de Proprietários, and when I tried to track him down I met his widow. She was in the dark about it. When I showed her your father's deed and said the place was for sale and I hoped she wouldn't try anything ridiculous, she said that she hated all Communists, including her dead husband, and she wants to buy an apartment for her grand-daughter. She'll pay your asking price. António Magalhães forever at your service, Cat-Cat."

"So why do you look as if you've swallowed a bucket of nails?"

Ah. Just one slight problem. Mateus.

"I was once insane about him, honey pie. We were never lov-ers. Even dying, the bastard knows I worshipped him and will do as he asks. I paid your porteira to let him stay. The one little catch is that the widow who wants to buy is superstitious; she refuses to make a transaction while a dead man is in residence. She thinks it is more with the grace to let my friend be there to his end before the sale begins, so that he does not feel rushed, with the roof being transferred from him, if that is his final wish with God."

"*His* wish? Mateus—I'm sorry for him, I am—but he can go to a hospital, and this woman can lose her voodoo hang-up and sign a check, and then I can go home to my father. Whose last wish includes cleaning up his affairs here. By me. For *his* grandchildren. This is *absurd*."

"Yes, of course it is. But you're here to sell it, querida, yes? You asked me to wave my magic wand and help. I thought you'd be glad for a buyer this fast. Fast . . . with a small delay so that Mateus—"

"Mateus can go stay with you. Since you're so in lo-ove with him."

"He wishes to approach his death in a pleasant home. You are aware, honey pie, that my flat is a shit-hole. I am the wizard with arrangements for everyone but myself, as you have pointed out a few times. Also, and perhaps I am handing you the gun to shoot at me with, but his parents have said they will take him in, but they do not like him. His mother will read to him from the Bible with the parts underlined about the sodomy, and that is to go to the other world with a nightmare in the ear and in the eye and right up the ass. No good."

"You had *no right* to move your *friend* in. There's no *time* to fuck around."

"Your father can go to his rest, and may God bless him very much, knowing a finish to his business in Lisbon is near, while another dying man—"

He caught my arm as I seized my purse to leave. He'd used the words "father" and "dying" in the same sentence.

"Cat, I'm so sorry, don't cry," he said, tightening his grip on me. "Please. Don't run away. We're fighting like tired married people. We get so much almost right."

Seagulls wheeled and cawed and plunged into the river. I collapsed back onto the bench and said, "T, tell me this isn't some assisted suicide thing."

"Okay, he did ask me that. But baby, you know me, I told him I could not kill anyone. He agrees to stay until he is so bad he won't know where he is, and then I'll take him to the hospital. Don't you see, honey pie? It is a chance for me to tend the passage of someone in a good way. Plus the sale is for sure, God willing. Maybe God prefers that your father not watch his place in Lisbon go away in his lifetime."

"You're making me crazy, T."

He put his arm around me and said, "I forget your father is American and you people think that things get finished. I wanted to buy time and make everybody happy. But okay, it is my job now to take care of you. I'll tell Mateus to go to his parents."

The roof of the daylight sky rippled early to let the sharp stars streak down as tinsel pooling around our feet. We were wading forward, with the world shrunk to an arcade with its top and walls draped with people and buildings and newsstands and here and there a fresco curve of sky. Sometimes a few flowers. Chatter and, from somewhere, a moan going toward diminuendo. We passed a contingent of young women wearing belts that wrapped around and stuck out the back loop of their trousers. Some American imports had once flooded in, and everyone figured this must be the style; who could have waists so large? A model was being photographed against a white stucco wall and I stepped into the road for a closer look: her skin and hair were damp and she seemed naked under a tease of a lime-colored raincoat. I did not detect the Prazeres streetcar bearing down on me until Tónio threw me onto the sidewalk and from there I saw the aghast face of the conductor gliding toward the cemetery at the end of the line, his hand still blasting the horn. Cemitério dos Prazeres, the Cemetery of Pleasures. Did that mean that earthly pleasure was strong enough to continue past death? Or that death brought heavenly pleasure? "That streetcar almost killed you," said Tónio. "Jesus and Madonna, Cat."

Tónio's arm stayed fixed around me as we barged into a piano melody filling my father's apartment. Rachmaninoff. Blaring.

Mateus was sitting in bed with the sheet tented over his knees and, in the way that presence speaks to presence, he sensed that Tónio had given him up. His wailing caused Tónio to cross the room, where Mateus clung to him like a frightened child, and drove me into the living room, where I picked up the plastic cassette holder. It belonged to Mateus; maybe he'd bought it from the transients who hawked music outside the train station. It certainly did not belong to my father or to me.

Tónio was chanting, *No, it's not her fault. Pá, it's time to be a son again for your parents, you must tell them good-bye.*

The living room was as motley as the rest of the place; it retained its original wallpaper with violet sprigs, an *oratório* to Saint Anthony, and a cabinet my parents had filled to bursting with tableaux of miniatures, Russian dolls, toy soldiers, farm beasts, and enameled and ceramic figurines. I'd added a rug busy as a tapestry and an incongruous oak dining set. A nearly blind great-aunt had passed her gentle widowhood here, and I needed only to stroke the furniture to absorb the heat left behind by the wandering pads of her fingertips. I parked myself on the sofa, which was upholstered in a print of stylized compass roses that wear and blur had changed into blastulae.

Look, brother, I spoke out of turn, Catarina's here so end of story, okay, pá? . . . go home where they love you, of course they do, shh, pá . . .

The piano music was helping drown out their voices, but it was also making me as queasy as it always used to make my father. He'd spent a lifetime trying to hide this from me, but once, at the Guerreros' Christmas party, when I was ten, I watched him brace himself against a wall while someone thumped carols on the Steinway. I asked my mother why he'd gone home ahead of us, complaining of nausea.

It took another week before my mother broke her promise to my father never to tell me that when he'd been young in a village up north, he'd been required to play the piano loudly enough to cover the screams of the men being tortured in the makeshift jail during the fascist regime. Mother was big-boned, fair but jet-haired, a pragmatist; she'd been a vet's assistant in Wales and then in California, and dispensing the truth about animals had tempered her quiet tone into the straightforward.

My father's original career had been as a journalist. The trouble broke when he wrote a newspaper article scolding the government for not providing better medicine for the poor. On the same page as his editorial, some other newsman—or a shaving of metal fallen onto the printing press—had altered the line "Rare men run this country" to "Rat men run this country." *Ratos* instead of *Raros*. (I learned on my own that *rata* was also slang for cunt.)

The editor was exiled to Galicia, no one confessed to the alteration, and my father was arrested at the house he shared with his elderly parents and brothers. The soldiers explained that his job now was to entertain them with his musical talent.

He was a decent player, nothing special. The piano was a moldering upright in a corner of a drafty edifice serving as a jail, and the screams from someone invisible in the depths pierced him. The notes he hit muffled the sounds before they swept down into the valley.

He quit playing.

They said, Keep going or we'll chop off a finger.

He did not attempt Debussy; too airy. Liszt would be better. Liszt ranges over the keyboard, gets showy, never settles down.

The screams escalated. A man emptying himself out.

My father dropped his hands into his lap, and a boy in a uniform several sizes too large raised a knife and, at a slant, sliced the fat pad off my dad's wedding-ring finger. The miniscule chopped part would heal, but it would remain a flat, dead spot.

My father managed scales until his blood streaked the keys. The shrieks turned into primitive gasping, hitting a crescendo. Once again my father wrapped his notes around the noise. Then he took his hands off the keys yellowed as bad teeth and said, Cut off my head. Do it fast. I quit.

The unseen man was delivering staccato, roof-lifting, gut-contorting calls. Then the sound stopped cold. My father gaped through the window at the beige fields and waited for the torture of the man in the back room to continue, but there was only a quiet of epic, multiplying shape.

My mother said that it was utterly impossible to gauge whether the man in the back room had been killed, or dragged off, or—this was the guess she imbedded in herself as true in order to convince my father it was true—someone had been deliberately hollering to frighten him as his punishment before he got shipped out to a year of solitary confinement.

Mateus was lightening up on his infernal crying, subsiding into gulping and choking. I snapped off the music and pitched myself at the telephone.

I started out wanting merely to report to my father that we'd found a buyer, but he snatched up his receiver before the end of the first ring as though he'd been waiting at the ready, and before I could speak I heard, "Catarina, there are problems, naturally. Tell me." I didn't get far past explaining about Communist leaders and the superstitions of their widows and delays when I blurted about a man in the house. Sick. No, dying. AIDS. Displaced. African, sort of. Would my father please calm him down, since he had a lifetime of speaking to patients in their beds, persuade him that it was time to leave? He had parents willing to take him in, though he was estranged from them.

My father would be sitting in the velour chair worn down to its shining warp. Even at eighty-five he looked remarkably like James Joyce: trim, nearsighted, cerebral, and given to bowties. The carpeting was a cornflower tint, and geodes caught sunrays on a mantel that had been barnacled with them since my childhood. His feet would be on the footstool I'd done in needlepoint the summer my mother died of breast cancer; I'd stitched a pride of lions with manes of orange tendrils.

"Put him on." He sighed with enough force for his words to billow out of the phone as a mist that dampened my ear. I pictured the fog that continually wraps pieces of San Francisco as if they're ornaments to be swathed and shipped.

I signaled for Tónio to pick up the line in the bedroom while I unplugged the phone in the living room and found the jack in the hallway. When I sat on the bedroom floor to listen in, Mateus and my father, who'd lived in California over half a century but remained instinctively Lusitanian, were fording that tributary-rich stream of politeness that must precede diving into business. Mateus, now dry-eyed, assumed the pose of a teenager set for a lengthy gossip, head propped on pillows. . . . *if it might be acceptable to speak cordially with thee, esteemed owner . . . and before I might trouble you regarding my home, in which you are presently lodged, I should inquire as to your profession . . .*

"I used to be a fry-cook at Café Nicola," said Mateus. "It is an art of timing, pá."

"You are possibly aware, my friend, that the Japanese word *tempura* comes from the Portuguese word for *time*, and from the Portuguese teaching them about the right timing and degree of heat for frying." My father had a habit of figuring that exchanging colorful facts sufficed as intimacy with strangers.

"Imperialists, pá."

Tónio was on a chair by the bed; he bent in two, his elbows on his knees, and his head plummeted into his hands.

"Excuse me?"

"Missionary imperialists in Asia. In Africa. You white people should stay home, pá."

Senhor T's head sunk lower, as if something very interesting had materialized on the floor.

"Young man, that's a funny thing to say. Since right now, as I understand it, you're in my home."

"Dad?" I said. "Listen. I'll figure this out. I'm sorry I called."

"You're dead, I'm dead, it doesn't matter who goes first, pá."

"You keep calling me Father. As your father, more or less, I'm wondering if you might remove the rudeness from your tone."

"Father? You're not my father," said Mateus. "My father is a God-fearing son of a bitch who despises me. He is dead to me."

"Dad, he's not saying 'pai,' he's saying 'pá.'"

"Pá. He's saying 'pá.' What does that mean?"

"Pal, man, guy. It's every other word here now."

"How delightful. My beautiful language mutilated. I'm not your 'pal.' You are in the place I plan to give to my grandchildren."

"Your imperialist grandchildren can go to the devil, pá."

Tónio stood and pressed a hand on Mateus's forehead, aiming to push the fury back inside him or at least pin it in one spot.

"*Credo.*" The word means "I believe," but when stretched to contain ten *E*s, it means *I do not believe this!* My father was aiming for thirty *E*s.

I set the phone on the floor, where sound buzzed around the edges of the receiver. Mateus lapsed into a fast slang I couldn't follow. Tónio snapped on the small television on the dresser and returned to stroking Mateus's head until the venom seemed to retract. When I retrieved the phone my father was sputtering.

"Catarina, what's that racket?"

"There's something called the Ducky Song that comes on the TV to send the children to bed. I guess it soothes him."

My father considered television a sinister drug. He hadn't been allowed to silence it in the large ward at Children's Hospital, so he'd arranged a card table to show how to fold origami. One victorious night, all the patients gave up television to shape giraffes, pelicans, and many-sided stars.

Mateus slammed down his phone to attend to the ducks.

"I'm still here, Dad."

"They need ducks to tell them to go to bed. Don't children there ask their fathers for a night blessing anymore?"

"It's a catchy tune," I told him. "The cartoon ducks play xylophones. The problem is the music gets stuck in your head." I'd started despising his night blessing when I was fourteen. He'd make the sign of the cross over me and ask God in Portuguese to make me a big saint. When he'd borne enough of my complaining, he remarked that perhaps I'd become too mature for this kind of good night.

The cord was long enough for me to hide in the hallway. "Dad, Tónio is here, too. He's trying to talk Mateus into going home. Then we can proceed. With the sale. It's all so ridiculous, but I don't think I can handle calling in the white coats to have him forcibly removed."

"No, no, don't do that to someone who's sick. No."

"I could find out who else is out there, on the market. I could find someone this afternoon. Or it could take months, Dad. Longer."

"I like that the buyer will be a woman putting her husband's theft to right. Erasing a sin is good, even if it isn't yours. Even if the harm never came into view. Listen. I'm proud of you."

"Good night, Dad. Daddy? I'll be home soon."

Tónio had finished delivering Mateus to his rest and was unrolling a sleeping bag for me in the living room. I climbed into it. He collapsed next to me on a nest of blankets.

"I'm such a coward, honey pie."

"You're not a coward. How are you a coward?"

He said that Mateus wanted to pretend he lived in his own grown-up home before he left the earth. Perhaps he should have helped him die with that vision intact.

"Tónio, I've read those Hemlock Society things. You have to put a plastic bag over the person's head to make sure he's dead."

"This is about giving a man his last wish."

"I know," I said, sharply. "That's why I'm here, remember?"

In the cabinet filled with miniatures, ceramic bluebirds in a disheveled, merry row were playing ceramic instruments. I'd never noticed that in the dark the dots of violets on the wallpaper, and the amber drips from the sweating of the glue and aging of the print, formed a halo of quarter and whole notes around the outside of the cabinet. Tónio burrowed down so his head fit against my breast. I said, "I don't mean to bark at you, T. What did you love about him?"

"He was a genius of a cook. His timing, it's a gift. He snuck into the Nicola to cook a fish for himself and steal it. But he said he fell in love with standing there waiting for the fish to get done. I liked that. But the real reason I fell for him is his singing voice. He can go over high C. Can you believe it? A voice that deep. Where does it come from? It's like he doesn't produce it himself, he offers a place for a sound above high C to hide. But I could not bear waiting for him to be done with one person and then another, it was too much like watching myself, and I became the one he'd come crying to when something ended." He fidgeted on the floor, his elbow barely missing my face. "Honey pie, I cannot sleep with that looking at us." He got up and closed the little doors of the oratório to Saint Anthony, my grandfather's wedding gift to my father and mother, on a lace runner on a side table. In the hollow in the chest of the wooden saint, under a thin glass pane, was a sliver of finger bone that was supposed to be from someone who'd touched the saint during his lifetime.

When he flung himself back down onto his bedding, he hooked a leg over me, and I said, "If he's shut in his coffin, Senhor T, you're stuck protecting me from the ghosts with their daggers and the screaming scary stuff."

He said I shouldn't imagine otherwise. Hadn't he always kept me safe and sound?

I stroked his blanketed leg. "Yes," I said, and that was enough for him to drop into an instant slumber. He'd forgotten that in my family "safe" and "sound" had never quite fit together. My ear rested as a stethoscope where T's heart pressed up to send a pulse through the side of my face. This must have eased me into some kind of rest, because when whimpering filled the air I sprang to attention in my sleeping bag, unsure where I was. Tónio stretched, half awake, and groaned, "I put him to bed, it's your turn."

With his head stuck below his pillow, Mateus looked like an ostrich, gawky. I removed the pillow. His hair looked singed, and I stroked the tufts of it and uttered that timeless night litany: *Do you need water? A story? Where does it hurt?* until I fathomed what he wanted: my hearing his calling out. My stroking his hair.

I'd slept in this room with Tónio our first night together, never undressing. It was more of a clutching, my astonished inspection of how thin he was, and his embrace of me at first was so ferocious I seemed to be underwater and breathing through a straw that pierced the surface. There was a package of condoms near expiration left over from a love affair with a fellow I broke into fragments over, but when I mentioned them, Tónio said, *I don't like you like that but, please, if you do not mind holding me.* The war in Angola had left him an orphan adrift, one of the earth's totally fucked. I quit my usual anxious wondering what was supposed to happen next, until I had a sense of being pressed whole to the inside of him, and I left that print of myself there for him to carry around, and his physical weight sank inside my ribs, where it expanded so he'd stay trapped in the barred cage of my chest. But I was aware that my arms were mine and his were his, and my legs belonged to me and his—his were so long the muscles seemed a topography rolling away. The light from the streetlamp outside exploited a weak horizon in the blinds so that it seemed to have hurled a knife in to cut the throat of Wales, but out of the slit spilled a brilliance. The plastic over the framed map had refracted this dazzling strip onto us, laying a cool cloth of light over both our foreheads.

I kissed Mateus's fevered temple. He had drifted away.

When I lay down next to Tónio he lifted a lock of my hair to fit behind my ear and said, "I wish I could desire you, you need so much."

"Go to sleep," I said. "Stay with me, Tónio. I love you to pieces."

But as he slumbered my own sleep was so fitful you'd have imagined I was choreographing abandoned sex with someone a movie studio still needed to superimpose on the film. I got up and peered through the window every hour. Night in Lisbon speckles itself blue, tosses sapphires onto black cloth. The sapphires dissolve by daybreak, but the sky keeps the saturation of the gems of the night in the same way that clear water, amassed, holds blue.

I came to with a start to find Tónio missing. The phone rang, and my father's panic trilled over the wire. "Catarina? I keep falling. This is going to be the first day I can't go see your mother." It was nighttime in California, predawn.

"Dad? Is David there? Call David to come take care of you."

My father—even when he was ill—visited my mother daily in her cerulean vase in the Columbarium, a minute's stroll from the scene of their married life on Arguello Boulevard. She awaited him in the niche they'd tiled with *azulejos* as their final home. One evening, after he'd again put on his suit and tie to go calling on her, I'd said, "Daddy, isn't it time to move on?" He'd tried to check the disappointment in me that made him tilt his head, as if he couldn't possibly have heard me correctly. "I was faithful to your mother," he'd said. "Why shouldn't I stay like that, especially since she's in a weakened state?"

"I'm coming home, Dad. Enough already."

"No. Something good and without death will arrive so the sale can happen. I can't guess what but I have faith. I'm a week away from the hospital. You can visit me there. I couldn't stomach my daughter hovering, bracing herself about taking me to the bathroom."

"Call David."

"I couldn't bear him hovering either. Is our patient surviving over there? Allow me to chat with my fellow countryman. I have a joke for him."

"A joke."

"Yes."

Tónio came in, carrying groceries. He set bottles of Luso water and Sumol pineapple seltzer on the kitchen counter and lingered in the doorway, watching me. He'd brought in the scent of the ocean. Fish.

He assisted me in performing the same fandango with the telephone lines so that I could listen as my father said to Mateus, "Young man? Good morning. Is it morning? In Lisbon? When I was a boy in Portugal, my father inflicted a joke on me to start every day."

This was news. The sepia photos of my *Vovô* with his scrub-brush mustache and crazed leopard's squint didn't suggest a laugh riot.

"What happens when five Portuguese people argue politics?"

Tónio was leaning against the armoire. In its oval mirror I could see the whorl at the back of his cropped hair, as if it's where the entirety of his body refuses to vanish despite being down his own drain.

Mateus said, "Wait, wait, wait. It's on the tip of my tongue."

The pregnant pause across the seas between Lisbon and San Francisco was interrupted by my father's ineptitude with comic timing. "They form seven political parties."

Mateus laughed. "That's it. Good one, pá. Are you buttering me up before you scream at me to leave?"

"I don't have the strength for the scream in me," said my father. "I was hoping you'd offer your personal assurance that the *ginjinha* shop is still open in the center of town. I've been wondering. My wife and I went there after we got married, to toast each other."

"You must not have had many friends, pá. It's the size of a closet."

"It was mostly the two of us, back then. Has it been torn down?"

I could have told him it was thriving, a pint-sized dispensary serving nothing but cherry liqueur on the Largo do São Domingos.

"It's always the same, pá," said Mateus. "Who knows how the owner survives."

My father said that the ache in him was awful. When he was much younger he'd drink some ginjinha whenever his system was upset. He filled Mateus's ear and mine with the war story of Monção: when the town was surrounded a woman scraped together the last of the flour to make two buns to throw at the enemy. The invaders withdrew, unnerved at the town's defiant wish to speed up hunger rather than surrender. He said he felt like that, under siege and pretending he wasn't starving.

"I'm starving. I can only swallow applesauce," he said. "Catarina, could I trouble you to stroll out for some ginjinha? It'll quiet me if you're drinking it. Buy some for our patient there, too."

"Why, thank you," said Mateus. He said he'd been craving something without knowing what. Cherries in firewater. Yes, good.

"Call me back and describe it," said my father. "Please."

"I think I can manage that," I said. "Good-bye, Daddy."

Tónio picked up a towel lying on the floor, blue with nearly scrubbed-away roses, and wiped Mateus's face. He lifted the towel and stared at its underside, as if expecting his friend to leave a veronica imprinted on the cloth. Then he studied Mateus, as if by chance he'd find, instead, the faintest outline of the dissolving roses on his face.

"Pá," said Mateus, and he gripped Toninho's arm, "I'm not sure why I always seem to get my way, but I've got nothing to show for it."

Toninho's face split open to spill out his radiance. "You fucking idiot," he said softly. "Nothing to show for it? You've got people here dancing for you, dancing around you, dancing—"

Mateus grinned. "okay, okay."

"Dancing off on an errand of mercy," I said from the doorway, trying to raise my tone into light animation. "Say thank you."

"Hurry back," he called out at me. I had to take him as boyish; ill or not, he didn't come across as a man in his thirties and surely never had. "Thank you for hurrying," he said. It was the first time we were both smiling at precisely the same moment.

Tónio said he would cook an early lunch for the lord and master. I walked past the Pingo Doce—the Sweet Drop—grocery store, where pigs' heads hung on hooks, to be stewed for sausage for the holidays. My father had refused to take us to the *matanças* in the valley, because he said the squeal of the pigs when the knife came down was unearthly and no one who heard it could ever get rid of it.

Angels, droll and flirty, were stenciled around the entranceway of the ginjinha shop. Shallow shelves housed the liqueur, the bottles glowing crimson, like the blood of Saint Gennaro readying to bubble alive. The cherries swelling in a vat on the counter looked like the eyeballs of cows or a hen's painful laying of eggs. The owner and I commenced an argument about why he could sell me liqueur but not glasses to carry it. I offered to pay lavishly. His glower suggested his disapproval of foreigners who thought they could march in and make demands. He wasn't in the business of selling glassware; obviously I had mistaken his humble but dignified establishment for a kitchen-supply emporium. A fellow customer said, "She's the

American girl who was on the television last year about her book. She's one of us, in a way." I'd taped a segment for my novel about a Portuguese nun. Television is one of the magic words of the universe. The owner frowned but gave me what I asked for.

I carried two glasses like chalices brimming garnet, toasting the streets. Here's to the gargoyles on cornices; here's to you, funiculars and iron Juliet balconies, and to you, azulejos—tiles of griffins, bears, and explorers in the hues of sky and ocean, cloud and whitecap.

The men were in the kitchen when I arrived, with the deep fryer on the stove. The fumes of the oil heating mixed with the boozy cherry aroma I brought in. Tónio was extracting *carapaus*, their eyes like cross-sections of marbles, from their waxy paper and dipping them in beaten egg and rolling them in cornmeal while Mateus was slumped on a chair, waiting for the oil to hit the proper temperature.

"Cheers," I said, handing a glass to Mateus, who downed it fast, and to Tónio, who snaked an arm through mine. From the center of the caduceus we made, he and I took turns drinking. T's Adam's apple pushed out and I brushed it with my fingertips and felt it jump as it got painted with alcohol.

"Stand back," said Mateus.

He got up from the chair and studied the cauldron of oil, took one of the fish by its tail, and plunged it mouth first into its bath below a rolling boil. Waiting with the scoop made of metal netting, he looked like a marionette with the strings cut, a dry creature glued to sticks. But happy somehow. In the pose of his element. He looked away from the cauldron, as if to show that he was not in a hurry.

He extracted the first carapau and Tónio said, "Perfect."

Mateus was elated. "Perfect to the end, pá."

The carapau looked as if it had tumbled in sand on the beach, and then it had flipped fore and aft in the sunlight until it was done. I said, "Unbelievable. Goodness." He nodded. A tremor almost dropped him to his knees, and I eased him into the chair near the stove. He needed to rest before doing the same for the other two fish.

I set the table in the living room with placemats from the Maritime Museum—prints of sea monsters on indigo—and found some pale orange tapers. Oscillating from the clotheslines of the buildings across the courtyard were vibrant linens, as if someone had savaged sky-sized bouquets, the petals stuck and writhing. Mateus said he was getting wobbly and would eat on the sofa. Tónio sliced up a pineapple.

We didn't speak as we admired the fish and the fruit and the teardrops of fire quivering in place on top of the candles.

That pause of beholding it all was our grace.

The air was drinking the vapors of brine from the fish. It had been drinking up some salting of the air for so many years here. This place could have been mine. But I'd told my father back when final promises needed to be made to give it to David's children. I had many friends I could stay with in Lisbon.

Soon that widow and her granddaughter might be doing nothing more than strolling through this room, suddenly at a loss. They'd tear the engorged salted air and there'd be a storm of weeping and it might frighten them, their inability to say where it came from.

"Amen," said Toninho. "Get out the shovels and begin to dig."

We rattled our knives and banged our plates and lowered our heads and got to work.

Mateus said, "I believe someone is in need of calling the father, yes? Tell him the drink put a lamp in me." His hand rested on his gut.

I dialed California and said, "Dad? The cordial tastes like the inside of a cherry tree. Mateus says thanks. We're having a feast. Tónio cut up some pineapple. Mateus fried three carapaus."

"You can't find those here."

"I know." With Tónio pulling his earlobe in that universal signal of *This is so fine*, I tucked the phone where I could speak and listen and took up my fish knife again; I take pride in my Lusitanian skill at filleting a fish so that head and spine stay intact, and the skin, skimmed off whole, stays a flap that can be folded back to re-cover the fleshless place.

"Tell him the pineapple looks especially well presented," said Tónio.

"Dad? Our pineapple is that good miniature kind, deep yellow."

"How about the coffee?" he asked. "When I first left with your mother we searched for coffee like we had there."

"They import the coffee here from Brazil," I said.

"Africa," said Tónio.

"I miss the food," said my father.

"You're forgetting the people, Dad," I said.

"No, I haven't, not for a single minute. They're as gentle as God makes them."

Mateus leaned over and erupted in choking. His plate spilled off his lap and clattered onto the rug; his gnawed fish came to rest in a pear tree. His whooping noise settled into a gagging and he used up his strength to get to a sitting position, and Tónio leapt from his chair and pounded him on the back, but he couldn't fill his lungs. His eyes bulged at me. He raked his nails on a round ochre pillow.

"Dad, hold on, Mateus must have swallowed a fish bone."

With the phone pinned between my shoulder and ear, I got on one side of him and Toninho stayed on the other. Mateus's skinny arms were flailing; a curtain of scarlet rose below his skin.

"Catarina," said my father, composed. "I taught you the Heimlich. Put the phone down and try that."

Mateus was weightless enough for me to get behind him and brace my fists below his ribs while Tónio held him steady, and I banged upward. Nothing. I tried a few more times, my fists bashing so hard I was afraid of cracking something.

I grabbed the phone and yelled, "Dad? Dad? It's not working!"

"Be calm," he said. His words, as he spoke, had spaces between them. "Go into the kitchen and put on rubber gloves. Tónio's there?"

"Yes. Yes, yes."

"Put on your gloves, and have Tónio pry the patient's teeth apart and hold them open. Press his tongue down with a spoon. The bone's probably in his throat. Go on now."

I dashed into the kitchen and struggled as the gloves stuck, and when my fingers were in them Tónio yelled, "Christ!" because Mateus was going into spasms. The two men were wrapped up in a writhing way, with T's eyes lit as he looked at this convulsing kindling. I seized the phone and my dad said, "It's the last cat in the litter waiting to be born. Pull it out to save the mother. Go on."

I told T to pry open Mateus's teeth and keep them apart. Plying a fork because we hadn't put out spoons, I pressed the muscle of his tongue down with the tines. A pin-sized white object was down in his throat. I made a pass at pulling it out, but I only made him gag.

I snatched up the phone and shrieked, "Dad? Dad?"

And I went sheer blank for a second, the way we do when we wish ourselves far from where we are. Tónio came to my rescue by yanking the gloves off my hands hard enough for the phone with my father inside it to fall and hit my foot, a good rap that doubled me in two, so that, head lowered, I heard my father, as if he were shouting up from the earth, "*Know* you're going to save him! Now *do* it!"

Tónio heard him as well. I tilted back Mateus's head. Toninho was already wielding the fork while reaching past the wet rim of the dying man's mouth. Saliva pooled into the cavity. My forehead was against Toninho's and a last exhalation jet out of T's nostrils. I quit breathing, too. The phone spun around on the floor, as if it were a little boat with my father in it in a tiny whirlpool.

Tónio reached in for that infinitesimal swelling, the claw of an almost-newborn cat reaching the hook of itself upward, and the plastic of the glove gave him traction, and he pulled, and the bone slid out, along with the sloshing return of the feast, the contents of Mateus's gut. He tipped forward and vomited onto the shoreline where the oak planks of the floor met the medieval rug with its fruit trees and birds, and Tónio dropped the fish bone and rested his head on Mateus's back.

The bone was shorter than the length of my ring finger, only the width of a wire.

Tónio held a palm to Mateus's forehead and muttered, "I'm here, pá. I'm right here. It's over now."

We stretched Mateus flat on the sofa, and I groped around shaking to retrieve my father and said, "Dad, are you still there? We've got to clean him up but he's fine. I mean he's breathing." The stench of stomach juices was of the slaughterhouse, a blast of a carnal odor I knew from my relatives who were ranchers in the San Joaquin Valley. The spores will always be lodged on the nerve endings in my nose.

Tónio got paper towels and a bucket and mop, and while he began sponging the rug my father said, "Shall I give the patient my good night blessing? It's early yet, but he should rest."

"My father wants to know if you'd like his good night blessing," I said to Mateus, whose eyes were shut. "Would you like that? Did your parents give you one when you were small?"

His head shook and I couldn't tell if he meant yes or no. I went through the exercise of transplanting one phone and propping the other at Mateus's ear. Tónio was running a faucet, rinsing the mop. Mateus curled on his side so he could listen without the exertion of holding the phone. A glycerin finish was brimming back onto his dull skin. *In the name of the Father . . .*

I couldn't focus for a second. The room smelled like a person disemboweled, poured inside out, and I was sure I'd faint. I revived at . . . *Ghost. May God bless you and make you a biiiiig saint . . .*

Had it been thirty years since I'd last heard that warbling play with *muito grande* until—*I* after *I* after *I*—it stretched accordion-wide?

Good night, sleep well, young man.

Mateus tried to speak but he was too undone. I told my father something to the effect that he was beyond words. Before I hung up the phone I said, "Thank you, Dad. Good night. Good night."

Mateus passed out while I was helping Toninho reswab the floors, filling the place with the pungent smell of a hospital. Already the remainder of our fried fish was looking like tarnishing bronze; the pineapple was exuding its insides. We hadn't eaten much, but we were no longer hungry. I blew out the candles and Tónio and I worked without speaking in the kitchen, washing plates, drying them. Of course Mateus would have the instincts of someone who shows up to offer help once the work is done, and the very second I was putting away the last plate we heard him call out hoarsely, "Cat, the phone, if you please!" He was languishing regally against the cushions. "I must thank your father, now that I have a voice."

"Big of you," said Tónio, bringing him the phone and setting me up with my connection, "since it's his bill in both directions, pá."

Mateus hauled my father out of his own nap; he was groggy.

"Senhor!" Mateus croaked. "You sound sleepy! Allow me to sing the Ducky Song to put you to rest."

"Heavens, won't that be soothing," said my father. "On one condition. You will tell me why you cannot speak to your parents."

"Ai, well," said Mateus, shifting around. "They have their religion, they push it down my throat, I choke on it, that's the story."

"Have you read Tolstoy? I've just reread *Anna Karenina*."

"Who? No," said Mateus.

"I am at the part, near the end, where the fathers are speaking of the difficulty of creating children, saying that the struggle to train them is so endless that no one can think of bringing them up by his strength alone, and that is where religion comes in."

"Fathers drive their children away."

"Yes," said my father. "They send them off, it's true. They are frightened at how they want them near."

"If I go home," said Mateus, "I suppose my reward will be great in heaven, for putting up with their need to think they're good to me?"

"How should I know if there's a heaven?" said my father. "The reward will be on earth for you. That is the certainty. This is a chance for you to change your history. Sometimes grown-ups do what they should, not what they want."

"I don't see how this is any of your—"

"Let me put it to you another way."

I pressed the receiver closer to my ear.

"If you do not give the gift of yourself to your parents, if you miss this chance to be an adult, you will perish in my rooms as a homeless soul. I can't return to my country in this lifetime, so it will be up to my soul to go back where it belongs. But if you die there a wanderer, you will haunt my place."

Tónio arranged himself to sit behind me on the floor, his legs in a grasshopper-bend around my sides. His arm pinned me to the front of him.

Mateus said, "I'll think about it. Will that be sufficient?"

"Good," said my father. "Torment me now, patient dad that I am, with the Ducky Song."

Mateus didn't hit high *C* or his magical spot above it. The tune didn't require that, even if his throat could have managed it.

All the little ducks have finished playing
Finished playing . . .
It is the hour for them to go to sleep . . .
Go to sleep . . . Turn out the light. Turn out the light.

But his singing vaulted during the phrase *a-CAB-am de brincar* and ricocheted into me, and the echo made by the impact chimed outward.

Tónio took the phone and said, "Senhor Alberto? I wish we had met. Cat and I, we are good friends. She is stubborn, as you know, but smart, and she will be able to take care of herself. I can promise you that, Senhor Alberto. Our patient here is fine, and thanks to your instructing me I am fine also, very fine."

When I managed a good-bye to my father, he said, in parting, "No more fighting. Buy carnations for the dying young man. I can't fight anyone's need for peace."

I replied faintly that the corner market would be open.

The evening was glistening. Tónio and I set out; disinfectant coursed like liquid moon through the cracks in the sidewalk. I'd have thought that my father's years as a nurse would have put him off carnations—that pungent odor of the water they decay in!

We greeted Esteves, the owner of the Canto Belo, and brought him a dripping armful of carnations from the bucket set in front, under the awning, by the bins of dates and walnuts. From a spool of pearl-gray ribbon he tied a bow around my carnations, and he rasped the blade of a scissors on the ribbon to curl it.

"Ah!" said Esteves. He had a gold molar and an immaculate apron and a pocked complexion, like the top of an overboiled custard, that spoke of a deathly shy adolescence. On display were girls' jewelry boxes, with the ballerinas intact but the musical gears extracted to exhibit the ground spices.

Esteves's shop wafted a perfume of cloves, mace, and allspice as I took Toninho's arm and stepped with my bouquet into the street, where we stood together, arrested.

Women were leaning over windowsills, looking altogether like open flaps in an Advent calendar.

A billboard was advertising the Lalique exhibit at the Gulbenkian Museum. The pictures of milk-colored cameos throbbed like pure light.

A hobbled man with a lion's head cane undertook the extreme exertion required to lift his homburg and wish us a good evening. Out of his smoke-damaged throat issued, "I see that a flower is carrying flowers. You are a bride."

My father's plea for peace unlatched the lockbox in me where his old stories lay. In 1974 Lisboans listened for a song on the radio as a signal to go into the streets when the dictatorship was teetering. A woman who had not sold her flowers that day began sticking carnations into the gun barrels of soldiers. Everyone followed suit, helping to speed to an end, with the force of flowers, a reign of oppression.

My father wasn't having me bring Mateus carnations because they were hospital flowers; they were signaling my father's surrender. Mateus could stay as long as he liked. He'd get to decide. It was a last pleasure for my father to converse on the level of deep history, native son to lateral native son, and a last pleasure for me, perhaps, that he trusted me to interpret his language. A beat or two late, but I'd gotten it. My father had not been present for the Carnation Revolution; he'd only watched the newsreels on the Luso channel at home—one of the rare occasions when he'd allowed himself to succumb to television.

If he protested when I showed up, I'd quote back to him his line about parents being too frightened to say they wanted their children near. That was how I would read the carnation story back to him: peace had arrived when people declared, All of us will face what we must face, even if we perish together.

As Toninho fit my key into the building's front door, I glanced between the parted drapes of the porteira and saw her in a torso-sheathing apron decorated with daisies. Rock-bodied, shelf-breasted, in her cat's-eye glasses, she was feeding a baby in a high chair. A woman slightly under my age was sitting pretzel-limbed on a stool: leg spiraling around her other leg, arms that would complete a perfect straitjacketed pose if she weren't puffing a cigarette. The unwed daughter. The two women caught me spying. I'd once come across Deolinda pawing through my trash to bolster her contempt for prodigal Americans, but her daughter pitched a friendly wink at us through the glass.

When I set the carnations in a vase on Mateus's nightstand, he plucked out one and handed it back. He could comprehend how my father was talking to him. I said, "I'll leave in the morning. You'll need your rest."

"Tell your father they are my favorite plant," he said. "Good night, green-eyed lady. I'm going to die with your kindness on me."

I reserved, at a staggering cost, a seat on a morning plane. Tónio promised to stay with Mateus until there'd be no putting off the hospital. And he'd finish the sale of the apartment without me. I called my father to say I'd be racing home.

"That would be a good idea," he said. "I'd like that, Catarina."

"It's almost Christmas, Dad. I'm going to take care of you whether you like it or not." The cord of the phone swayed and quavered. Sometimes creation itself speaks out of a deep silence, to say: *This is the true story*: Tell us how your love will deliver us all to a heaven you have made. For everyone, including God the Father Himself, needs a father, a mother, a sister and brother, and that is why He invented you.

Toninho snored that night next to me while I stayed flat on my back. The hours dissolved without my knowing it. I woke in the dark, when it's hard to guess the time. Tónio stirred gently as well. He sat up and scrubbed at his face with his hands as I went to the window and lifted the blinds. I suspected it was five in the morning, an hour I worship; the sky pounds the black pearl of the night until it is in pieces and for a brief time, right then, the white of day is the grout holding it together, a perfect tiled mosaic to greet us, the hour that's the artwork most like making love, opposites fixed all the way up to heaven.

But then the beauty of it dissolves.

Tónio joined me in regarding the sky. I clutched his hand as we stared straight ahead. "Honey pie, that nun you wrote about," he said. "I'm afraid she's you. I'm afraid you're turning into one of those pretty women who's sad, and you'll fold yourself up and up and I won't be able to find you anymore." He asked me if I was aware of the quote by Claude Lévi-Strauss, *I am the place in which something has occurred.*

I said I was glad to learn it.

"Well, okay, Cat," he said, kissing my left palm. He got doubly gleeful whenever he landed on a bookish fact I didn't know. "I think I am the place in which *someone* has occurred. That is you."

I stretched my arms toward his neck to hold him and said he was my country, too.

I also noticed the mute alarm clock.

Time to leave.

When my flight was called Tónio reached into his breast pocket to give me a comb as a gift. It had hammered gold oak leaves finely tooled with veins, arranged on the tortoiseshell spine so that, if I were standing outside, or at a window, the sunlight would snag on the edges of the leaves and drip its blood, and the back of my head would throw out spokes of autumn red. I dashed myself onto the shoal of his neck as he started to wail. He understood it was likely to be an indefinite while before I returned in the flesh, that I was the type made comatose by events. He'd grasped long before me that grief begins as a crawling and wailing thing, and then it grows older. The second and endless half of grief is quiet, because the best part of you gets spirited away and, rage extracted, undone—why most people begin to figure from the calm of you that you're just about happy.

One month to the day before Mateus followed suit, my father died. Tónio reported that the date of my father's death coincided with Mateus asking to be taken to his parents. He stayed in his boyhood room and endured his mother's scoldings and his father's silence. He never made it to a hospital; he died at home, and Tónio was with him. I wish my father had known this before he passed away. Toninho thereafter concluded the apartment's sale to the widow of the Communist leader for her granddaughter. My niece and two nephews each have a modest sum that college will eat up.

But the granddaughter suffered a compound fracture of the leg soon after moving in and took it as an omen that she should be healed by moving to the sea. She negotiated with her grandmother to sell the place for a profit to her divorced cousin, who happened to be the head chef at a three-star restaurant not far from the Castelo de São Jorge. Tónio was irked at a summons to show the apartment, but soon thereafter he moved in with the chef, Bartolomeu, who had custody of his ten-year-old son.

The house is crowded, querida, but I am glad. The porteira had quit radiating disapproval, since Bartolomeu brought her cash but also trays of food, including a menagerie of creampuff animals under a spun-sugar cage.

Cat . . . our home is really yours . . . Come when you can! But also I carry you around wherever I go, you are so very light.—Your Senhor T.

I managed a final outing with my father, to the Japanese Tea Garden. It was one of those strange last days when he seemed on the mend. We ordered jasmine tea and fortune cookies and rested with the scent of the old redwood bridge still strong near the bamboo. He'd taught me how to paint bamboo on paper, with black ink, in segments made with single, firm gestures aiming to convey a lifetime of knowledge. *Don't worry your lines. Just draw them, dear.*

My fortune read, "You will meet a tall, dark stranger."

"I can't deal with this," I said. "This couldn't be for me." I handed him the slip of paper.

"Oh, yes." His grin was a marvel that drew in his whole face. "The busy gentleman with the scythe."

I grabbed the fortune from my dad's hand and put it in my teacup and dowsed it with the last of the lavender-tinged water.

Without moving his head, his vision went from the oleander and dragon statues and carried itself past where we were, into the far manzanita and vents in the desert, the screech of the steam spraying from the center of the earth.

"Dad?" It was the first time in all our lives that I was bringing up the subject with him. "They were probably trying to frighten you by yelling in the back room. For writing about better medicine. That's what Mama said. But they didn't frighten you, not so much, did they?"

He finished his jasmine tea and studied the dregs of the leaves. "No, I'm afraid that's not the case," he said. "Look, promise me you won't let anyone hurt you. Because I love you like mad."

"Don't worry about me. I love you, too."

"There's no mistaking that scream. It's too raw. It can't be faked. That high note. If you try intellectually to scream like that, you can't. It's like the difference between what's real and genuine, and what you pretend might be real."

The pot of tea was finished, but I made the gesture of pouring.

"There's a sound all creatures make when they've been inflicted with a mortal wound. It goes into your head like an arrow and stays."

His stare left the far plains and came back, to be with me for a little while more.

I paid for my father to be transported to a private room at Children's Hospital. At first I thought it was my gift to him, but then I saw it was his gift to me, for him to be a child as I held the covered plastic glass of water with its straw for him to drink. I sat by his bedside, folding cranes. Stringing a thousand of them for a wedding is meant to call upon joy. It gave me something to do so I could bear the agony of his drugged breathing, his gazing at me until we both had to look away.

"Allow me, Catarina," he said, and I handed him a square of golden paper and his hands stopped shaking as he shaped the beak of a crane with a perfectly mitered point. I'd been folding in a hurry, but he moved slowly so the edges were exactly met. He was beaming as he handed his work of art over to me.

He had stayed here overnight many times in his career. When an orphan named Eddie Martinez was dying, my father was with him in the final week, sleepless on a cot next to him, alert to the little boy's cries; on other occasions he'd nap in the hallway and spring up when pain made the children bellow from a distant room.

But he would not cry out himself. He would not alarm the dozing of the night nurse.

"Papa," I said, smoothing his spare white hair out of his eyes. He looked straight into mine. "*Deus o abençoe e o faça um santo muiiiiito grande. Boa noite, durma bem,*" I said.

God bless you and make you a biiiiig saint. Good night, sleep well.

That was when I felt his spirit detaching from the loosening paste of his skin, to burrow inside and wrap his soul to carry him away. I knew he'd wait until I was gone to attend to the business of dying. David had come and gone, quickly, but that was how my father preferred it. He'd said earlier he would always be with me, it wouldn't matter where he was traveling now.

As I leaned down to kiss my father's forehead, he kissed my chin. That was how the night blessing played itself out. You asked for a kiss to take with you, especially since you or he might not wake; who knew what fate would bring? And then I said what the parent might utter in a still further closing to the child, the equivalent of how we wish someone sweet dreams, the thing he'd left off saying to me when I was fourteen: *Sonhos cor-de-rosa*.

Pink dreams. Go to the land where you dream in color.

I'd found him a set of pajamas covered with whales and dolphins, something sporty for a large teenager. I stood framed in the doorway to give him a last picture, and he turned his head to watch me leave. It is never too late to save someone, to grant him peace. It is never too late to save yourself by saving someone. I smiled and so did he, and then all that was left for me was to leave him and imagine his journey; it was beginning. The marine animals around his remains were floating at the ready to coast him that night across the sea, to wash up on the shore of his long-lost earthly home, and from there to lift as fallen rain does in an exaltation of quiet back to the wide blue sky.

2008

Kara Candito

Self-Portrait with an Ice Pick

Imagine the impact—wrecking ball, welcome
   injury or collision, like some secret screamed
      in a late night taxi. And while it was happening,

bile rising and the blind urge of its happening—
   the ice pick striking the white wall of the freezer,
      the neon sign glowing through the window

like a red undertow, a sliver of the street corner
   where Essex looked like Sex Street and a low
      winter sun vignetted the room, the wedding band

left on the nightstand because betrayal was a tender
   industry then; *siempre* its one urgent slogan.
      There was the mind's syncopation—fractured,

freezer-burnt, mesmerized by the shards of ice
   that ricocheted across the floor; cuts covering
      the knuckles and a hole finally carved out,

big enough for the bottle of vodka where
   Van Gogh's wheat fields trembled. What the body
      wanted was its penance; scar, reminder that I

could love anyone, gnash my teeth on their
   shoulder, then forget them in the subway car,
      the stale air and grime of it, metal bar still

warm from a stranger's hand and the shock, almost
    erotic, of being jostled by so many limbs.
        Follow it back to that bar where the drinks

had lovely Storyville names—Chloe, Justine,
    Simone; names like a girl on a swing with her hair
        blown back; espresso, nutmeg, chambord,

grenadine; flower petals ground down to powder;
    names I stumbled through that year when
        my one job in the world was to smile in a way

that meant, *Say something interesting and I might stay*
    for five minutes. I remember Alex, the Bellini-eyed
        waiter lighting a match, flicking his wrist

like a gambler drawing fate closer. I remember walking
    home past empty fruit crates and the truncated
        frames of bikes still locked to street signs. Helicopters

circling the East River, like a repeated phrase. There was
    no aubade, just sunlight breaking the bones behind
        my eyes. What the body wanted was a blank room;

its own pain, untranslated, self-contained. If I can see
    myself there, it's my eye in the windowpane, hazel
        speck reflected back against a daze of sirens.

Carnivale, 1934

Burlesque Dancer

Tell me about the Badlands,
     where we hid in the dry riverbed
and whispered *deluge* until our breath filled
     the cracked cups. How it was dark
when we dug up the baby and wrapped him
     like a little papoose again.

It wasn't like headlights, the seams
     they left on the side of the road.
It was more like the dotted lines I drew down
     my sister's calves where stockings
belonged. How it was hot in the tent
     and we put peacock feathers

in our hair and danced until we forgot
     the men's hands in the matinee.
How we swore we'd drive out to Los Angeles
     where the fog unzips its white dress,
and I'd learn to dance like Shirley Temple.
     Smile and slap my dimples.

Look at the girl splayed out on the dusty stage.
     Look at the stars, at Orion unbuckling
himself. That means we're in Cheyenne,
     that means we'll never see the coast.
Tell me the things you say to yourself
     when there are stray dogs
                    at the edge
                       of every town.

Vincent

You all know the story of Vincent, the man with the scraggly red hair and wild eyes, wearing the wrinkled linen suit, with the battered straw hat sitting askew upon his head, Vincent who at first seems destined to be a respectable, if slightly eccentric, art dealer, like his burgher uncle. But at nineteen, Vincent is stranger than he was at eighteen, at twenty stranger still. Vincent reads the Bible, the same Bible that his father, Pastor Theodorus van Gogh, read to the assembled congregation on Sunday, in his quavering voice that didn't quite reach to the back of the small unheated church, to the bored Dutch peasants for whom the Sunday visit in their dark clothes to the dark church was but one more thing to be endured in a life filled with things to be endured.

But when Vincent reads the Bible he hears the voice of God who calls him to the wilderness to face him, the mad holiness of scorned John the Baptist; when Vincent sees the blackthorn hedges around the snow-covered fields, their twisted bare black branches become characters upon the white paper of snow, reminding him of the pages of the gospel.

Vincent goes to preach in the coalfields of the Borinage, where to mortify his flesh he will sleep without a blanket on the coldest nights of the year, while the wind sails freely through the cracks in the rude hut. It is there that the children will chase him in the street, throwing rocks and calling, "He's mad! He's mad!" In the underground mines of the Borinage he will see the pit ponies, born in the darkness of the mines, dying without ever having seen the sun.

This is where the Hollywood version of his life begins, immediately after the opening credits, which give the great museums of the world, the Louvre and the Museum of Modern Art, top billing, above Kirk Douglas and Vincente Minelli even: without their help and that of private collectors across the world, this movie could not have been...

There's another film, now, a Robert Altman. This one opens not in Vincent's boyhood home nor in the coalfields of the Borinage but at Sotheby's. The climactic scene of Vincent's afterlife: the sale of *Sunflowers*: suited men in white gloves wheel out the painting: "£5.5 million . . . £8 million, 500 thousand . . . £10 million . . ." The auctioneer's voice fades but is still in the background beneath a scene of filthy, tortured Vincent, pipe clenched in his teeth, lying on a filthy bed in a filthy hovel, rowing with his brother Theo. As Theo storms out, the auctioneer's voice rises: £21 million. . . £22 million, 500 thousand." The gavel pounds. Judgment passed. (I suppose those of us who aren't philistines are meant to read this as irony.)

Vincent turns away from this evangelical path, writing to Theo: "I think that everything which is really good and beautiful — of inner moral, spiritual and sublime beauty in men and their works — comes from God, and that all which is bad and wrong in men and their works is not of God, and God does not approve of it. . . . To give you an example: someone loves Rembrandt, but seriously — that man will know there is a God, he will surely believe it."

Only this time around it's not 1885 but 1985. Theo doesn't live in Paris but in a co-op on West 53rd Street in New York. He's still an art dealer. He's just pulled off a real coup: selling an installation called *Empty Space*: one steps into a gallery, the walls are white-washed, the artist's name appears in block letters on the wall — and there is nothing else. Theo, dressed in a slouchy teal silk shirt and wrinkled black linen pants, urges prospective buyers to simply allow themselves to experience *Empty Space*: the whiteness of the walls, the sounds of the city as they filter in through the silence. He may quote Rilke on the two subjects that the artist has, childhood and death, and how this installation starkly confronts us with our blank beginning, the abyss toward which we rush.

Theo's gone to see a therapist. She's helped him work through the thicket of guilt and envy, the legacies of that dysfunctional family, his neurotic need to support his manipulative, artist brother, the one named Vincent, the one who writes, "It is very urgent for me to have: 6 large tubes of chrome yellow, 1 citron, 6 large tubes malachite green, 10 zinc white," followed by another letter that asks, "Do you know what I have left today out of the money you sent this very day? Well, I have 6 francs. . . . So I really beg you to send me a louis, and that by return mail, please." The therapist shakes her head as Theo tells her that this Vincent was born a year to the day after the first son, also named Vincent, arrived in the world stillborn. Theo works it all through and writes to his brother:

> Dear Vincent, I know that what I am going to say in this letter may well prove hard for you to hear. I have given this matter a great deal of thought. I realize that I have supported you financially as a way of not dealing with my own feelings of guilt and envy, that I have needed to feel superior to you. I have decided that I can no longer send you money as I have in the past.

So Vincent will never write those hundreds of letters to his brother filled with good elder-brother advice (*"Ora et labora,* let us do our daily work, whatever the hand finds to do, with all our strength and let us believe that God will give good gifts. . . . Courage, boy"); passages where his love of color melds with his feeling for the places he has traveled through, his love for his brother ("Before sunrise I had already heard the lark. When we were near the last station before London, the sun rose. The bank of gray clouds had disappeared and there was the sun, as simple and as grand as ever I saw it, a real Easter sun. The grass sparkled with dew and night frost. But I still prefer that gray hour when we parted"); biblical quotations ("God hath made us sorrowful yet always rejoicing"); and, later, his cool assessments of his mental state ("As far as I can judge, I am not properly speaking a madman") and the brotherhood of the asylum ("Though here there are some patients very seriously ill, the fear and horror of madness that I used to have has already lessened a great deal. And though here you continually hear terrible cries and howls like beasts in a menagerie, in spite of that people get to know each other very well and help each other when their attacks come on"). No, this time around Vincent does not fill up reams of paper with his firm, penciled script.

This time around, when Vincent gets this letter from Theo he crumples it up and throws it into the corner of his hotel room, a room cluttered with canvases and paints. *Trust in the Lord*, he tells himself. *He will provide.* He paints fifteen hours a day, devotes the few remaining hours to sleeping, eating instant oatmeal made with tap water as hot as he can get it out of the stingy faucets of the Metropolitan Hotel. (Vincent is the only resident who takes to heart the injunction intoned by the manager and repeated on signs Scotch-taped to the walls throughout the establishment: ABSOLUTELY NO COOKING IN THE ROOMS, while the hallways are thick with the smells of curries and boiled cabbages and hamburger grease.)

But then, when the landlord changes the lock on Vincent's room, demanding the three weeks' back rent, adding, "And don't think I'm going to store that junk of yours for long!" Vincent sets out to find a job. He scavenges newspapers from trashcans and looks through the classifieds; he walks from McDonald's to Wendy's to Burger King, dutifully filling out applications. PAST EMPLOYMENT HISTORY: art dealer, minister. REASON FOR LEAVING: heard the call of God, loss of faith. Poor, mad Vincent! For two weeks he tramps the streets in the linen suit that shrunk and was thus passed down to him from Theo, so short that it shows a gap of pasty flesh between the top of his sock and the cuff of his pants, a porkpie hat set atop his wild flame of hair.

Finally he goes to Social Security to apply for benefits. He takes a number (32), like in a deli. Sitting next to him in an identical molded plastic orange chair is a boy with a bright red seizure helmet; across from them a retiree. Hours pass. Finally a voice mumbles his number.

"Name?" says the worker by way of greeting, following that with "Address?" Vincent gives the address of Our Place, a Bowery social service agency that collects his mail for him. "Date of birth?"

"Have you ever been diagnosed as having a psychiatric impairment?"

"No. But the children chase me in the street and throw stones at me and call 'He's mad! He's mad!'"

The intake worker: a man with a shaggy bowl cut like the Beatles had in 1964, a man who wears a too-large pair of glasses that slide down his nose, a "C" student.

"The regulations of Social Security," he says, with his eyes fixed on a point on the distant wall, "provide for benefits to those who can be shown, by objective tests and measurements," pushing his glasses with his forefinger back up the bridge of his nose, "to have an impairment, whether mental, emotional or physical, which prevents them from engaging in employment."

"Oh," says Vincent, "I can work. I paint fifteen hours a day. It's just that everyone thinks I'm mad."

"Objective tests and measurements," the intake worker repeats, backing thirty seconds into his speech. The wheels of Social Security grind slowly, and they grind exceedingly small. Vincent must wait, and wait and wait. The landlord burns his canvases, throws away his paints. Poor, mad hungry Vincent walks the streets of New York. My art is what I see, Vincent tells himself. My art is an ever-changing canvas I paint in my head.

Finally a notice arrives at Our Place. "An appointment has been scheduled for you."

Vincent enters the psychiatrist's office. The shrink is mid-forties, a smooth dome pate, not very successful, and so has ended up taking these cases. Mostly he weeds out the fakers, the ones whose notions of craziness have been formed by TV, and tell him of arms reaching out of the walls, monsters trailing up the stairs, vivid hallucinations;

he winnows them apart from the more steady parade of those quag-mired in misery.

"Mr. Van Go."

"Van Gogh," Vincent corrects him.

"Van Goff."

"Just call me Vincent."

"Mr. Vincent. Have a seat."

Irritable, the shrink notes; that and the fact that this Mr. Vincent has chosen the seat closest to him.

This is not a standard psychiatric first encounter. There is no silence as an opening gambit, no "What brings you here today?" no patient wait for the patient to begin. Instead the doctor, yellow legal pad on his lap, writes briskly: name; address; with whom do you live? Do you work? No? Have you ever worked? Parents living? Sisters and brothers? Names; ages; what do they do? Glancing at his watch, he sees it's time to move on to: Ever hear voices? Have mood swings?

Vincent does not dissemble. He tells the bored shrink everything. Yes, he hears the voice of God. It speaks to him sometimes in the night; it speaks to him through the flowers and trees, the blades of grass pushing their way up through the Manhattan sidewalks. He tells the shrink that he read Thomas à Kempis's *Imitation of Christ* and tried to live the life of a true Christian, taking seriously the biblical injunction "Take all you have and give it to the poor," doling out his bedclothes, his food, his clothing.

Poor self-esteem, the shrink notes.

Vincent's chair will hardly contain him. He waves his arms so wildly that the doctor moves objects back on his desk: the vase holding the dried flower arrangement, his black lamp. Several times the shrink murmurs, "Calm yourself, Mr. Vincent," and "We need to move on, Mr. Vincent."

At the end of the session Vincent is dismissed. "That's all?" he asks. He had spoken to this man with such rare honesty, it seemed their souls had touched: the doctor had murmured, "Yes, tell me more" as Vincent told him about the face of God glowing through the sunflower.

That night as he drives home on the Long Island Expressway, the doctor dictates a letter to the Social Security Administration. In bumper-to-bumper traffic, the drivers around him bopping about in their bucket seats to the songs blasting out of their car radios or with blank, unfocused stares, the doctor speaks into the voice-activated mike: "On September 21, 1985, Mr. Vincent—Estelle, get the information, Social Security number and everything from the notes, which I'm attaching . . ." Vincent has dropped himself neatly into the category of schizo-affective disorder: the religious mania and the sheer joy, the inappropriate ecstasy, that the color yellow evokes in him.

The next morning Estelle types the letter; by that afternoon it has been signed, folded, placed in an envelope, stamped, and mailed.

Yet Vincent hears nothing from the Social Security Administration.

What do we imagine happened to that letter? That it traveled promptly through the mails to Washington DC, and there was delivered to a mausoleum-like building of granite? That within that building a woman sits alone at a battered wooden desk, a battered wooden desk with a few devices upon it: an elaborate rack holding rubber stamps, a stamp pad, a letter opener, and a stapler? That in the top drawer of this desk sit identical purple-inked stamp pads, shrink-wrapped in clear plastic; that the bottom two drawers are filled full with neat stacks of boxes of five thousand staples each? That behind her is a mountain range of letters—letters from doctors, petitions from rejected applicants, requests for clarification from muddled recipients?

She swivels slowly in her wooden chair and extracts a single letter from one mountain. Her eyes travel slowly over the address. At first one thinks of the gaze with which a letter from a lover is studied: the eyes caress the handwriting; one stares at the stamp: if it's a commemorative, you imagine that she went to the post office, chose carefully, the one you would appreciate most. If it's a standard American flag you figure that in her hurry to get it off to you, she rummaged in a desk drawer, grabbed the first thing that came to hand.

But this woman isn't alive with desire. With a slack jaw, a dull gaze, she makes sure that the envelope is properly addressed: if the zip code is wrong, she leans slowly forward, slowly turns the metal rack of rubber stamps in front of her until she finds the one that says, "Incorrect Zip Code/Return to Sender." If the address is off by so much as a single digit, it too is sent back. If all is in order, with practiced slowness she lifts the letter opener, inserts it into the ungummed corner, slowly, slowly tears the envelope open, lifts the letter out, unfolds it, smoothes out the creases; lifts the largest of her rubber stamps, her very favorite, with its elaborate rubber loops of numbers, its cogs and arrows, presses the stamp firmly against the purple ink pad, then finally against the letter, rocking it ever so slowly back and forth: "Rec'd SSA, 10:00 a.m., September 24, 1985." Every hour a buzzer rings, and she pushes the time arrow ahead an hour. At 10:00 and again at 2:00, a skinny young man wheels in great baskets of mail to add to the mountain behind her.

Vincent, poor Vincent, wanders the streets of the city. He has not eaten for days. The first day or so without food, hunger makes you peevish, self-pitying. You notice how much of the world is given over to eating: two or three storefronts out of every block are restaurants: diners sit in windows, waiting patiently at their white-topped tables with a basket of French bread set in front of them from which they occasionally tear a piece, munching slowly, thoughtlessly (what you wouldn't do, Vincent, for a taste of that bread!); they eat pastrami sandwiches and pizzas, glistening with fat, dripping mustard or globs of tomato sauce onto black beards, blouses; mom- and-pop stores display their cans of fava beans and *frijoles negros*, their potato chips (Cajun, sour cream and onion, bleu cheese), Fritos, Cheetos, candy racks holding Baby Ruths, Oh Henry's!, Fifth Avenues, Butterfingers, Lifesavers; women emerge from grocery stores, pushing carts loaded with children and paper or plastic sacks heavy with frozen corn, spinach, peas, broccoli; fresh oranges, apples, cucumbers, celery; tins of tuna, cans of condensed milk; steaks, tofu; boneless, skinless chicken breasts. Thin women with good cheekbones emerge from take-out emporiums with white containers; signs blink EAT, EAT, EAT. The world seems to be organized around a single principle: the shoving of food into a great maw, outside of which you stand, gaunt, pale, with a stomach that twists and cramps with unsated desire.

In the midst of your frantic yearning, you know—the knowledge a dim reality—that in a day or two this hunger will cease to bedevil you; it will be replaced by a feeling of pure, transcendent calm. The pangs of hunger will burn themselves out, burn away all longing. In another twenty-four hours you will walk through the canyons of New York, beaming benevolently at all the rushing yups, the dawdling homeless, the hue and cry. You will have slept the previous night under a blanket of light from the moon, will have awakened this morning in Central Park, the birds weaving a canopy of song over your head, trilling, "Vincent, Vincent, Vincent." You will be happy.

Impossible, however, to live for too long in that holy state without food. On your wax and feather wings of hunger you know you are soaring too close to the sun: your happiness becomes frantic, high-pitched, a few steps away from madness. So you scavenge garbage cans for returnable bottles, panhandle, look for the odd penny or dime lying on the street. You go to a McDonald's and buy a small milk, a single hamburger, which, like a drug, is both salvation and damnation, a holy paradox. You are saved from the ecstatic state that can only end in death but delivered again into that cycle of need and want, the reawakening of the flesh.

And the reawakening of despair. When you are not eating the food you imagine is the stuff of dreams: home-baked bread dripping with sweet creamery butter, salads of romaine lettuce dressed with extra virgin olive oil and tarragon vinegar, salmon so delicate it dissolves in your mouth; a cheddar that your grandfather unwrapped from a cheesecloth and granted you a sliver of one Christmas Eve. And then there is the reality of the cloying milk and the hamburger that tastes of metal and decay. And the reaction of an empty stomach to food, which forces you to rush down an alley, pull down your pants, and allow the shit to hiss and roil out of you.

Meanwhile, she sits, the mountain of letters growing ever taller behind her, and with studied lassitude opens an envelope, pulls out the letter, stamps it with her "Rec'd" stamp, staples the envelope onto the back of the letter, rolls the letter and inserts it into a pneumatic tube, which carries it down. Down to a vast underground nest of bureaucrats, who, like the pit ponies of the Borinage, have never seen the light of day. They are born, mate, reproduce, and die in this fluorescent-lit hell. Only through dim recounting do they have any knowledge of the world above: that day gives way to starry night, that the Social Security numbers they give out and process are attached to living human beings. They do not know that the struggles for the twelve- and then the ten-, the eight-hour day have been won. Pale as white worms, they labor fourteen hours a day, wearing old-fashioned green eyeshades and creosote cuffs. They sleep next to their desks on folding cots, covered with Civil War–era army surplus scratchy wool blankets. They mate quickly, furtively in cubicles and broom closets, give shameful birth in stalls of the women's room. The new forms (SSA-L8170-U3; SSA-561-U2) appear mysteriously in the supply room; they take comfort in the notations in the upper-right-hand corners—"Form approved OMB"; religiously follow the directives, "Exhaust existing supplies of SSA-L8710-U2" or "Destroy prior editions," which they do in rituals held around the paper shredder. These are directives from their God, OMB whose face they cannot imagine, whose name they are forbidden to speak.

Vincent falls in love with a prostitute. Even in the Robert Altman version, where we see Sien crouching over the chamber pot to piss, even in that raw and gritty film, she's not ugly. But I've seen Vincent's drawings of Sien. She was. Her breasts weren't symmetrical and they lay in flat folds against her chest. Her face was drawn. I know Sien. I pass her every day in Detroit's Cass Corridor, she sits in the booth next to me at Coney King, in Parker's buying a single beer and a half liter of Pepsi. On a rich woman her fine features, the skin tight against jutting cheekbones, would look beautiful or at least dramatic, but on her poverty, exhaustion, bitterness leave her looking haggard, too thin, as she lurches forward on spiked heels.

Poor Vincent: you shocked your uncle Cor by telling him that you loved ugly women, that you would rather be with someone whose pain and past were written on her face. But even Altman won't allow an ugly woman to appear on film.

Vincent, starving Vincent, refuses to allow Sien to give him any of the money she gets from ADC. So he goes down to General Assistance. Literally: the GA offices are in the basement of the City/County Welfare Building, the building with the marble facade and the white marble figures with perfectly muscled bodies that embody justice, civic duty, freedom, down into the linoleum-paved hallways, half lit by flickering fluorescent lights. Nearly two hundred of them, men (a few women), most, but not all, of whom have bathed within the past week, wait. Some scratch, some rock slowly in their seats, some keep up a steady flow of curses. Vincent waits and waits and waits; at the end of the day he is given a number and told to come back again; the next day he waits, and the day after that is given $160 a month, found eligible for food stamps, given a Transit Pass.

He sells his food stamps for 65¢ on the dollar, stands at a freeway entrance holding a sign that reads, "Will Work for Food," although who would dream of asking this man to do odd jobs at her home, what restaurant owner would offer him work busing tables? But cars do stop, offering folded dollars, spare change. With the money he scrounges, Vincent buys a canvas, paints.

Vincent is going to paint light.

But before he can paint light he must paint darkness. He must paint the picture of the five homeless people in the abandoned building, four men and one woman, a flashlight dangling from a rope tied to a lighting fixture above them casts deep shadows on their faces, as they share a meal of two orders of large fries and Chicken McNuggets, the puny light turning the white paper gray. He must paint the picture of the Haitian refugees working in the dusk, not turning on their lights, doing illegal homework in their one-room apartment. He must paint the still life of the three pairs of shoes that he pulled from trashcans and dumpsters; he must paint the skull against black holding a burning cigarette in its teeth.

While Vincent yearns toward the light, in Washington DC a Programmer descends into the dark bowels of the Social Security Administration. Wiry-haired, wiry, with an astonishingly large Adam's apple that jounces up and down as he speaks, speaks the language which they, the underground beings, recognize as English, although its meaning is incomprehensible to them: "swizzling between multiple files," "I've hacked lisp machines," "the code that you snarf from the net," "the domain of munging text." He is here to devise a vast Network that will link this mother-office to the offices on the surface, to take this system where clerks still scratch with quill pens and rolled documents are pulled from pneumatic tubes and bring it—not just online but into the greatest mainframe humanity has ever known.

At first the Programmer sends up three times a day for double espresso, which arrives in ecologically correct paper cups with not quite so ecologically correct plastic covers. He downs one at 10:00 a.m., one at noon, and the third at 3:00 in the afternoon. Each morning he descends in the elevator and each evening ascends.

He is happy, if such a mundane word can be applied to a man who mastered differential equations at the age of seven, who can recite the entire dialogue of every episode of *The Prisoner*. He daydreams of installing a terminal in every maternity ward and birth center. Infants assigned Social Security numbers at birth, entered along with their weight, height, sex, and Apgar scores! Terminals in every morgue and funeral parlor, to close the files of the dead!

He imagines himself as Colonel Kilgore in *Apocalypse Now* (he has seen it thirty-seven times, twelve at the movies and twenty-five times on video). He inwardly crows, "I love the smell of napalm in the morning!" as he strides through the sub-sub-subbasement, past the GS 2s and 3s whom he leaves trembling in his wake, although they see in his unnaturally long stride, the way he pumps his arms in front of him, the off-gait of the maniac, declaiming to his assistant, "The question of whether C or Lisp or Emacs Lisp or ML or Shell or any of the little languages is the appropriate method to attack a problem is a religious one . . . I want tools that work together, not one program that generates VSAM fixed-length eighty-byte record files and can't play with another, can read only other format files. I want to be able to glue those programs easily and trivially reap the benefits of coarse-grain parallelism."

At first he dutifully clocks in, 9:00 to 5:00: no work-obsessed Yuppie he; he knows where his real life lies: in front of the television he jerry-rigged himself with the remote control feature that enables him with a simple motion of his thumb to make the screen go fuzzy, the browns red, the blues magenta, turning back episodes of *Dobie Gillis* and *The Avengers* into expressionist art. His real life lies with his elaborate computer game in which he casts as villains anyone who has ever wronged him: his third-grade teacher, Mrs. Kaplan; his older brother who lives in the Bay Area and disputes arcane points of Trotskyist doctrine with his coreligionists; the gang of kids who took one look at him on a Cambridge street five years ago and beat him senseless: all stand in the way of the elusive, nameless Maiden, a woman he once saw in a white dress, backlit by a porch light, coming down the steps of a California bungalow, whom he has loved devotedly ever since.

But one evening the Programmer looks up at the clock, realizes that time has flown by: it is 7:30: he has missed the *Dr. Who* rerun on Channel 42. He slams his fists on the computer keyboard, shouts, "Fuck! Fuck! Fuck-Fuck-Fuck-Fuck," but then goes back to work.

Before long he has almost become one of them. No longer do the espressos arrive from above at three-hour intervals: instead his assistant finds that his duties have devolved to being merely a cappuccino runner. He ascends to the above and fetches double lattes, caffè macchiatos, triple mochas for the Programmer, coming back trembling at what he has seen: the brilliant pulsing yellow globe of the sun, the flickering green leaves, the stark white marble and granite buildings of the Capitol, the wild buckets of flowers set out for sale next to the Metro station. He returns dizzy, almost nauseous with the riot of color, afraid to speak of it to those who live underground, pale as blank slugs in their murky world of slate, smudged brown, mole.

At 3:00 one morning the exhausted Programmer, who has an 8:00 a.m. meeting, decides it isn't worth going home to sleep, and so sets up a cot next to his terminal. As he pulls the scratchy wool blanket, redolent with a century's worth of odors, up to his chin, he little imagines how few times he will again see the sun. The next evening he will leave after 9:00 and fall asleep in front of the vid running episode number 15 of *The Brady Bunch* (he displays his porn proudly and keeps his *Brady Bunch* tape under his socks in a bureau drawer). Then for four more weeks he will not even surface again.

Meanwhile he has had installed a La Pavoni, the queen of espresso machines, at which his assistant now toils, making him endless cups of brackish espresso. He has almost ceased to eat.

The clerks with whom he must interface stare at him slack jawed, refuse to comprehend his frenetic speech. And endless glitches appear in the circuitry. They think they've found the root of the problem when they discover that the circuit boards are being deliberately mis-soldered, electrical connections skewed by the workers of Multinational Memory's On Wok Long Factory No. 3: unionization efforts there having been stymied by repressive legislation and random firings, the workers have formed the Rosa Luxembourg–King Lud anarcho-syndicalist collective with the slogan "The Barricades are in the Circuit Boards." But even when the circuit boards are repaired and Legal has filed a multibillion-dollar lawsuit against Multinational Memory that promises, in its scope and complexity, to take years if not decades to wend its way through the court system—

But we have almost forgotten poor Vincent! Where is he? The last time we saw him he was standing at a freeway entrance holding his sign. We return to that same freeway entrance, but he is not there: we search the city, checking out each of those unshaven, unwashed men holding signs, the men huddled around burning barrels, hanging on street corners outside shelters and service providers and liquor stores. He's nowhere. Has he died in some back alley? Left Manhattan on foot, walking across the Brooklyn Bridge, trudging through Flatbush and Prospect Park, heading out to find the Long Island that Whitman wrote about?

But no, Vincent has not left the city, not gone into the countryside to paint light: he's sleeping some nights in a Bowery flophouse, sometimes sleeping days and walking the streets all the dangerous night long. Weekly he treks to Our Place, where the volunteer behind the desk flips through the *V*s and says. "Nothing. Sorry." Vincent turns and walks away, then turns back. "Perhaps it was—under *G*?" he ventures.

She sighs, rifles the letters filed under *G* and says, with satisfaction, "No."

Every week Vincent returns to Our Place. Once there is something for him, but when the letter is handed to him Vincent is dismayed to see that it is merely from his brother Theo: a card of a Seurat print, "Think of you so often and hope that you are well."

But then, at last, one day it is there: when Vincent goes into Our Place and stutters to the woman at the front of the line: "Van Gogh, it's two words, v-a-n and then g-o-g-h, and so sometimes I get filed under *V* and other times under *G* . . . ," he is handed an official letter. It would take the talents of one of the great romantic poets to describe the throbbing of Vincent's heart inside his pale chest, the rush of delighted color flooding his cheeks. With trembling, trembling hands he tears open the envelope. Without salutation the letter begins: "We are increasing your benefit amount" and then goes on to say, "We cannot pay you any benefit at this time." Vincent reads these words over and over again. He can make no sense of them. He meditates on this bureaucratic koan.

Vincent does not know that the first part of the Network has at last gone online and begun to generate these letters. Ten years previously a consulting firm (which actually consisted of a woman with a master's degree in educational psych and a part-time secretary) landed a multimillion-dollar contract to draft these epistles, mandated by an act designed to simplify the baroque language of the Bureaucracy, as convoluted as medieval Latin, into a Basic English understandable by over 95 percent of the U.S. population. So now instead of Byzantine incomprehensibility we have a clean Zen paradox: "We are increasing your benefit amount . . . we cannot pay you any benefit at this time."

And that letter from the good doctor that officially certifies Vincent as mad? Where has that gone? Thank God we are the Godlike narrator of this piece, that we have the power to peer into the great mountain of letters and immediately find Vincent's, that we do not have to paw through the tens of thousands of pieces beneath which it is buried: pleas from former miners with brown lung, desperate letters from mothers of chronically ill children, Xeroxed medical records still awaiting their official purple "Rec'd" stamps. There it is, about three feet down, waiting, waiting still.

But the Programmer is hard at work. Geeked on espresso, his fingers roil over the keyboard as his plans for the Network become ever greater: now it will be linked into banking system computers, spying on recipients to ensure that they are not collecting unreported interest on their checking accounts, depositing unpedigreed sums of cash into the computers of every college and university; it will be modemed into links between doctors' offices and medical labs, insurance companies, it will pick up credit card transactions, driving records, so that when an applicant shows up at an office of the Bureaucracy, the tapping in of her Social Security number will produce a complete educational, medical, social, and psychological profile.

Alas, the poor Programmer! Unbeknownst to him, a tumor is growing in his brain, fed by the electromagnetic fields that pulse from his computer; his story, like the story of Vincent, is tragic. He will not live to see the Network go online.

"Caffè macchiato," he calls out to his assistant. "Make it a triple." He, who once checked his e-mail every waking hour, has become so obsessed with the Network that sheaves of messages pile up: from hackers in Australia and Azerbaijan, from his college roommate who is trying to get him to come to a celebration of Nikolai Tesla's 129th birthday. The message that follows: "All work and no play make Jack a dull boy," scrolls endlessly down the screen.

Vincent, who has not been able to scrounge any more money for canvas or paint, a street-corner crazy, perches himself on a broken-down chair he has found in an alley and, palette-less, canvas-less, begins to paint in the air. He paints the *Cafe Terrace at Night*, the yellow light spilling out of the bar, the night-blue sky above, alive with the dotted streetlights that glow like fireflies. Holding an imaginary brush in his hand, he leans forward to his imaginary canvas, swiftly painting the black, yellow, orange, and blue streaks that make the sidewalk. How thickly he would lay on the texture of the zinc white that costs $8.58 a tube.

Poor, mad Vincent: he sits in the public library and stares, stares at the man sitting opposite him, imagining how he would paint him: exaggerating the fairness of the hair with oranges, chromes, even pale citron yellows. Behind the head he would paint infinity, a plain background of the richest, intensest blue that he could contrive: a mysterious effect, so the face would be like a star in the depths of an azure sky. The face has something more to say to him: he stares and stares, until the man slams the book he is reading shut, gets up, and moves to another table.

Poor, mad Vincent: his imaginary paint never speaks back to him the way real paint does. It never refuses to do his bidding, surprises him. Vincent, in real life, pardon the expression, you dipped your fingers into the paint and made the curving petals of the sunflowers with your thumb. Later on, Vincent, when you were going mad, you drank turpentine, tasted Prussian blue paint, profane Communion.

Leaning in a doorway, his shopping cart filled with aluminum cans, Japanese prints torn from art books in the library, sharing his bottle of Midnight Express with a companion he has just met, a Black man who tells Vincent that whites are the devil, marked by those eerie blue eyes of theirs. "Hiroshima," the man ticks off, "slavery," taking a swig, "concentration camps . . ." Vincent, who believes so easily, believes. He remembers that Christ said, "If a man hate not his life, he cannot be my disciple," and, full of self-hatred, stares at his pasty white flesh with its mottled blues and yellows and pinks. He stares at his companion: missing half his teeth, his face covered with odd bumps, his fingernails thick and yellowed, more like the hooves of cattle than the smooth, shaped nails of that other race, the rich. Together the two men dream aloud of the sun-drenched skies of Martinique, Java, Africa. There they will know the truth: that the only real infidels are those who don't believe in the sun.

There's a high yellow note Vincent has to attain to do his best work: to get there he has to be pretty keyed up, on endless coffee, loaves of Wonder Bread, and cheap, cheap wine. But on it he will paint the colors beneath the stark flesh-colors called black and white: the orange and yellow and green hues of his own skin, the same tones that underlie his companion's skin, to bring together for a moment in color what history has rent apart.

You all know how this story ends: Vincent dies. In the Hollywood version, he is at his easel painting *Crows over the Wheat Field*, a shrink's dream of a painting made by someone with bipolar disorder: the yellow fields of joyous wheat, malevolent skies brooding above, and the crows—the only living thing in the painting, the crows—carrying darkness down into the light. Kirk Douglas's face expresses agony, torment, and he pulls out the revolver. The camera cuts discreetly away to a farmer passing in a wooden wagon and we hear the shot.

But this time it isn't in Hollywood and it isn't in Auvers. At the very moment when Vincent fires the shot, at that exact moment, the white woman behind the wooden desk at last reaches the letter from Vincent's doctor and stamps it: "Rec'd., July 27, 1990, 11:00 a.m."

2009

Dust

Our last night together, in the small hours, she took me by the
    hand into the bathroom, ran the water
and soaped me down. Her hands moved over my skin, separately,
    though in concert, like two people
who know each other well but are not lovers, slow-dancing
    together in the bar's farthest corner for the last song

of the evening, that time of night everyone alone dreads. But we
    were not at that moment in a bar—
we were in a Vancouver hotel bathroom, on a warm, late July
    evening, which I admit sounds wonderful
though if I had the night to do over, I might have avoided
    bathing in the small white tiled bathroom

so similar to a Winnipeg hospital room last December, where
    outside the north wind blows the snow
in whatever shapes snow dreams it might be, where from his
    hospital bed my grandfather asks what's new
in the world, looking to the window as if questioning not me but
    the snow swirling past, a man trying

to understand how the cancer comes on, almost imperceptibly, as
    in, *One day it's just there in my chest,*
as in, *How does it happen, Shane, can you tell me?* And because I
    have no answer for that question,
I respond with another, *What about getting you a shower, Grandpa?*
    And then he turns to me,

and I am slipping his moccasins over the cracked skin of his feet,
    topographical maps bearing the marks
of places he's been: baby shoes in Boston, brown feet on the Red
    River's sandy banks, soft leather
brogues on the cold streets of Sault Ste. Marie. Then I shift his
    legs, spindly after weeks

in bed, and the green cotton gown rides up, revealing the place
    where the clear tube leaves him,
snakes down into the plastic sack, browning with the waste of his
    body. He's so light that with one arm
I lift him, and he pauses, arms hanging over my shoulders, and
    looks around the room with what I imagine

is wonder at the sudden uprightness of the world. And then we
    are walking slowly, in step
with each other, down the hospital corridor, one of his arms over
    my shoulder, the other on the cart
that holds the oxygen canister, and with one hand I steady the
    cart, in the other the bag of piss

swings, and I think of those times during my childhood, grocery
    shopping with my mother,
when she let me push the cart, my hand beside hers on the metal
    bar, how I would concentrate
so hard, that this might be one thing important, one thing to
    help, as I am helping now, moving down

the hallway with my grandfather, and as we pass the open
    doorways I notice he does not look in
exactly, but pauses almost imperceptibly before the large flat
    diamonds of light on the floor,
the harsh light of a prairie winter coming through the windows
    in patients' rooms, and if it is true

that what is captured in the mind remains the same, then perhaps
    what he hesitates over on the polished
gray floors are the prairie winters of his youth. Without asking, I
    have no way of knowing this,
and because I know that for him just moving is tiring enough I
    am silent, my mind returning

to the light of his past as I have held it since tenth grade history
    class, not flat and steady but flickering
black and white in those films from the thirties—the prairie a
    broad dusty tabletop full of ramshackle
cars, jerking across the screen, faces furrowed like the empty
    field, tire marks left in the chaos

of dust. In truth, I watched little else of those films, preferred
    instead to whisper with my friends,
but there was one time when the screen held us all, a close-up of
    a boy our age wearing
flat cap and britches, scowling into the camera—mad as hell to
    be lining up for bread when just last year

his dad's acres spanned whole continents of wheat in his mind.
    But if my grandfather's youth
was that boy I'll never know, for even at this late stage in his life
    it is old-time prairie pride
that prevents him from halting for more than a quick breath at
    the first diamonds of light his skin

has felt in weeks. Pride for the old woman who spends her days
    yelling at the nurses for more
food. Pride for the man who complains loudly the doctors are
    poisoning him. Pride for the woman who calls
out to a family who never comes. If it's for anyone I think it's for
    these people my grandfather's pause

is as slight as a whispered secret, the kind a lover breathes late at
    night in a bath, for some reason
you can never know, when her hands take hold of the soft
    sponge, the bar of soap, and in the bald light
of the bathroom's too-small tub, she rises up from the water, runs
    the sponge along the length

of your arms, leaning into you, so that her breasts swing out
    close to your lips and you think
of taking a nipple in your mouth, but giving way instead to some
    sense of decorum, decide against it,
and for this, then, or some other reason, she smiles, just as my
    grandfather smiles now when

I help him stand in the white tiled shower room, after I've
    removed the green gown, and he leans
into me, and the water splashes down, soaking my hair, his hair,
    my shirt and his naked body.
And when I pick up the soap and begin, my hands moving slowly
    over the places he points to,

I try to imagine the way he might do it, I do not ask how it feels
    when I rub the dark bruises made
by daily needles in the crooks of his arms, do not ask because this
    is simply a job to be done,
the way those prairie people in the flickering movies of our
    minds did the things they had to, silently,

to stay alive. And my hands, graceful in their ignorance, move
    over his body, not knowing
this is a rehearsal for something they will witness later, in a
    Vancouver hotel room, when the hands
of another person will dance over my body, because this was
    right now, and right now the knowledge

my hands carry of how this dance will disappear and return in my
    life is hidden well enough
to keep us both, the old man and me, still moving in my mind,
    two dancers in the smallest hours,
in the farthest corner of a dimly lit bar, our slow turning in one
    spot a kind of contemplation,

of wheat fields, water, snow, skin and dust.

Ted Gilley

Physical Wisdom

In the spring of the year that we moved from Chicago to Loma Feliz, California, I began to be afraid to sleep indoors.

I was sixteen, living with my parents in the house my father had rented after walking away from a well-paying job with a Chicago psychiatric firm—his words—to take a civilian position at Camp Pendleton, counseling marines who'd had second thoughts about serving their country. I understood, as we packed the rental truck with the things we hadn't sold, that my father had taken a step down in the world. But this knowledge didn't jibe at all with his cheerfulness as he stood high in the back of the opened-up truck, looking both clumsy and powerful stripped to a T-shirt and cutoffs, flexing his white, heavy arms and slapping his hands together impatiently as I struggled toward him with yet another load.

August was nearly done. A layered, warm-and-chilly wind blew in from Lake Michigan, flipping what was left of my father's hair across the smooth crescent of his bald spot. I was to start school, in California, in a week.

They're modern parents. Talk, talk, talk. They'd asked me what I *felt* about moving—and what could I say? Wasn't it already decided? My father laid a map out on the kitchen table and reached way across America to the dot that was Loma Feliz, a town so small its name had been edged offshore where it drifted, an orphan in the blue Pacific. I scanned the intervening space—the vast, empty squares of the western states—while my father described our new home: a "vintage" ranch fifteen minutes' walk from the ocean. Avocado trees in the backyard. A large, bougainvillea-covered shed that my mother, at that time a painter of sensual reinterpretations of biblical themes—her Mary Magdalen was less than entirely penitent—planned to set up as a studio.

"Robert, are you awake?" My father nodded absently, straining his attention westward, intent on getting us to a motel before night fell. Anchored between us, my mother squeezed my hand to let me know she was happy. I looked out at the dimming, surreal desert landscape and felt sure I would never see a tree again—a real tree. I remembered avocados from the supermarket in Chicago: the size, heft, and weight (I guessed) of hand grenades.

My father drove north to Camp Pendleton every weekday morning at seven. Mom needed more time to get started. She routinely dumped the breakfast dishes into the sink and made a second pot of coffee, poured a cup for me, then sat quietly at the kitchen table, wrapped in the camouflage of an exotic, flowered robe, smoking the cigarettes my father couldn't abide and gathering herself for her day's work.

I walked to school through the village in the cold morning sunlight—not cold by Chicago standards, but damp. By afternoon, when I walked home, the sky would be bright, glaringly blue, and the day hot. On the hottest days, it was really only when you got close enough to the ocean to hear the breakers' echoing aftershocks that the air cooled. Coming home one day I stumbled; I thought I'd caught my shoe in a crack in the sidewalk. But suddenly I seemed to be drunk, or what I thought drunk was: I lurched and nearly fell. Then I lost my balance and fell down. My books tumbled out of my arms, one of them opening neatly on the grass.

The earth was moving. I sat on the ground and felt the world trembling; beneath my hands I felt its hairy body shaking with tremendous mirth. A radio was playing in a nearby house and the music, a waltz, floated strangely on the air as the earth shook. I heard a woman calling a man's name. Telephone wires twitched as if tethered to invisible, restless dogs. The sky's inverted bowl of unshakeable blue burned over me. Birds raced in all directions.

Then it was over.

When I ran down our street a few minutes later, my mother was waiting for me in the front yard. She was dressed in her paint-crusted coveralls and still held a brush in her hand.

"Hey! Are you okay?" Her eyes were wide. She was happy, all right. She clapped her free hand dramatically to her heart and looked up and down the street. She would have liked to share her excitement with the natives, but we seemed to be the only people out of doors.

"*Carl*. Our first earthquake! Well—strong tremor? But that counts. We're really Californians now. Okay?" She put her hand on my head, stroking my hair. "Carl?"

"Yeah," I said. "It was neat."

But that was a lie. It hadn't felt neat at all. I couldn't catch my breath, and I kept sensing flashy, furtive movements at the edge of my vision and turning my head to catch them. I had slipped into a universe that wouldn't stop moving.

Panic had hit me in the stillness after the tremor. I had run the few remaining blocks home, and now I felt that I wanted to keep running: only swift movement would pacify the tremendous power that was pressing against my skin from inside. Running would conceal the shaking I felt certain was visible to my mother.

"Carl," she said, her voice low. "Honey. It's okay." Her hand slid lightly over the back of my head. She gingerly rubbed the place between my shoulder blades where an evil current flashed sparks down my spine, plucking at the muscles of my arms and legs.

"I'm sorry," I said.

My mother spoke softly. "*No*." Keeping her hand on my back, she moved to my side and we stood together facing the house, listening (I thought) to the noise of my breathing. When it quieted, she said, "Let's go in. I'll fix you something."

We had reached the front door when I remembered my books.

"Okay," she said. "Hm. Okay. You go and get them. Or—" a flourish of the brush—"I could come with you?"

"No, Mom, I'll go. I'll be right back. Thanks."

"All right, Carl." She smiled at me—and the earth began to shake again.

Seconds later it was over. I extricated myself from my mother's arms and together we walked back to where my books lay. I gathered them up and we walked home. I did not speak, but my mother, who loved California suddenly, all at once, and just like that, remarked brightly on the varieties of its flowers and trees—the flush of life surrounding us. But all I could see, in spite of her enthusiasm, was a deceptive veil of vegetation concealing an angry and treacherous earth.

I entered my bedroom that night with suspicion but everything was as I had left it in the morning. There were no signs of violence: the walls stood smoothly upright, the windows were intact. I had assigned reading, but once in bed I found I couldn't concentrate on the material.

My father had come in upset from work. A young marine in his care had jumped from a third-floor barracks window, breaking a leg and fracturing his skull. When the boy recovered, my father said with a tight and angry smile, he stood a good chance of being court-martialed for trying to kill himself. During dinner, my mother mentioned the tremor—which the news people were calling an earthquake—but my father only said distractedly, "Oh? We'll have to expect those, I suppose." I didn't say anything—didn't tell my father that I felt I had been pushed from a high place and was still falling—and we passed the rest of the evening in a gloomy silence.

When I switched off the bedroom light, my fear returned refreshed from where it had been working out. I began to sweat. As my eyes adjusted to the darkness, I made out the familiar outlines of the windows, the long, ghostly panels of the closet door shimmering into shape, the front edges of my desk brushed with a single stroke of light from the street. But it was all unfamiliar, too; it could've been any room. Like the motel rooms we stayed in on the trip west, its uniqueness had been stolen. Feeling on those nights an eerie kinship with a silent, migratory procession that had no beginning and no end, I had told myself, *It's just a motel room*, and then I had slept.

But I didn't sleep now. When I considered switching on the light for comfort, I felt ashamed and angry. The room seemed to sense this weakness and its hatefulness hardened into glee. I lay rigid, staring at the ceiling without blinking until its plastered creaminess deepened into a wavering illusion of troubled water. But when I rubbed my eyes and looked again, it was once again a solid surface, and more sharply focused. Just as I turned my head, something up there caught my eye.

I took the flashlight from the drawer of the night stand and followed its beam across the ceiling until it fixed on what I had spied: a long, meandering crack that cut right across the plaster.

Taking my pillow and blanket—and, after a moment's thought, the flashlight—I crawled under the bed. I set my mind on waking up at my father's first stirrings, and then I slept.

My new friends Henry and Paul were talking about the quake in school the next morning. Henry, whose locker was next to mine, slammed it shut and leaned against the metal door.

"Hey, Carl, did you feel it yesterday?"

"I did."

"So?—what did you think?"

I shrugged and twirled the locker's dial.

"Man, that was *nothing*," he said.

"It was less than nothing, dickweed," Paul said. "A *negative* quake." He looked at me. "You don't have quakes back east, do you?"

"Chicago is pretty stable," I said.

Henry drummed on his locker. "The big one! It's the big one! We're all gonna die!"

"Women and children first!" someone shouted, and everyone laughed. I twirled the dial.

"Yeah," Paul said. "Far out, man. When the big one comes, this place'll be history."

"So will *we*," Henry said. "Tidal waves, you name it. Look at this guy. Been here three months and can't get his locker open." He looked around. "Hey, *Carolyn*," he called, "by any chance do you know Carl's combination?"

Carolyn Wilson looked over from her open locker, smiled, and shook her head. She didn't have to speak, and we all knew it.

"This damn lock is broken," I said to Paul.

"You're pathetic, man," Henry said. "Hey, *Carolyn*, help this guy out." She was walking by. She was slowing down.

She actually stopped. We all froze.

"What seems to be the trouble, gentlemen?"

Cool and beautiful. Shoulder-length hair the colors of washed-out rock maple leaves in October. Freckles in a constellation across the nose. Smart, I had heard. *And you*, I thought, *you spent the night under the bed.*

"Beats me," Henry said. "Chicago here seems to be locked out of his locker. It's puzzling."

"Broken," I croaked.

"I see, said the blind man." She grinned at me.

The bell rang. Doors opened and the hallway was immediately, loudly jammed. She moved off, still smiling, and I jumped at this lingering contact.

"So what'll I do?" I called out.

"Suffer," she called back.

My father lowered his fork and looked at me across the table.

"Sleep out? What in the world for?"

I shrugged. "Why not? It's California, Dad. It's not like I'll get frostbite."

My mother didn't say anything. She ladled some more

California-style vegetarian stew onto Dad's plate. Then she caught my eye: we held our look for a moment—my gaze bland, hers appraising—before she turned to Dad.

"What can it hurt, Robert? Sounds healthy to me." She looked down. "This needs something. Cheese?"

"I love cheese," my father said. "I'd kill for cheese. Carl, check the fridge."

I fetched the cheese and grater and a bowl and brought them to the table, grated the cheese, and passed the bowl to my father. "So, can I?"

"What? Oh, sure." He heaped cheese onto his stew. "Better wrap up, though. Nights are surprisingly chilly out here . . . Oh, this definitely helps. Delicious."

"I think next time I'll use more pepper," my mother said.

"Carl, get the pepper," my father said.

My mother glanced up. "You're full of orders tonight."

"Can't help it," my father said. "Semper fi."

Mom sighed, got up, and brought coffee to the table. She poured cups for herself and my father.

"How about me, too, Mom?"

"None for you tonight, Carl." Again, that appraising look. "It might keep you awake."

I unrolled my sleeping bag and lay down on it, letting my gaze drift upward through the branches of the avocado trees and blowing clouds to the stars. I thought about Carolyn Wilson and felt foolish, happy, and relatively safe.

The back door opened and closed, and I heard the click of my mother's lighter. In a moment she came into view. She opened her hand and a stocking cap fell onto my stomach.

"Your father insists that you wear this."

"Okay." I put the cap on. I hadn't worn it since Chicago and already it seemed like an odd hand-me-down, a token from another life.

We'd spent our last day there visiting with my grandparents, and after we'd said good-bye my mother ran back and held her father and cried while I stood in the middle of the yard, waiting, and my father sat in the truck with the motor running.

"Great," I said. "Thanks."

"You're welcome." She took a drag from her cigarette. "Carl, what are you *wearing*?"

"My sweat suit."

"It's not enough. Really, you'll freeze. Come in and put something else on."

"Mom. I'm not even in the bag yet. When I get inside, I'll be fine."

My mother yanked her sweater tight around her shoulders. Her head was in the stars. "You *won't*. I won't have you catching pneumonia just because you insist on, I don't know, returning to a state of nature. I think it's going to rain."

"Oh, for Christ's sake, Mom."

After a moment she said, "I suppose I'll have to get used to being sworn at, too."

"Mom, I'm sorry. Look—I'm fine, really." I had no intention of moving.

"Forget it." She turned and started back toward the house. Then, as if to herself: "You're fine, I'm fine, we're all *fine*. Goodnight." She got halfway to the house before she stopped. She spoke in a voice almost too low to be heard but which carried, like the layered wind off Lake Michigan, mixed tones, warm and cool. "Call me if you need anything."

I had already considered the possibility of rain and had a plan ready so that when, in the middle of my third night outdoors, I woke up with rain in my face, I quickly bundled up my bag and ran up the path to my mother's studio.

In the event of an earthquake, I reasoned, the shed would dance a little but would not collapse. Turning on the light, I surveyed the interior of the ten-by-twenty all-wood—therefore flexible—building.

Nailed to one of its long walls and framed by windows on either side was my mother's new painting, of Saint Matthew composing his gospel.

According to legend, Matthew was illiterate, and wrote his gospel under the tutelage of an angel. Most of the classical pictures show him puzzling over a piece of paper while a studious and obliging angel stands nearby, guiding his hand toward enlightenment.

But my mother's saint has dropped his paper and pen and stares in astonishment at the decidedly female angel who's sitting on his lap. Their mint-perfect profiled heads all but touch at the nose and a yellow light shimmers from their hair, which appears, at first glance, to be in flames. You sense that only one or two moments have passed since the angel's appearance. But Matthew has regained composure enough to hook one arm securely around her waist and twist his fingers into the braided gold of her belt, anchoring her; and her right arm is flung around his neck, her fingers are already interwoven with his hair. At the exact center of the picture, she touches his lips with the fingers of her other hand, daring him, with her eyes, to speak the truth.

I spread my bag on the floor in the dark and crawled inside. Listening to the rain's impatient fingers on the roof, I fell asleep thinking about the possible kinship of women and angels, about my mother's saint catching fire, and, briefly, about how and when I would return to my own bed.

My mother was not at all pleased that I'd spent the night in the studio.

"You were breathing turpentine fumes all night," she said. "Don't you know how dangerous that is?"

"I didn't even notice."

This wasn't true: I'd woken up at six with a sharp pain jimmying my ribs.

"You should have noticed."

It was Saturday. We were all sitting at the kitchen table.

"Carl, I have to agree with your mother," my father said.

"You're in there all day," I said, ignoring him.

"I keep the windows open."

"So did I."

There was a silence. I lowered my eyes, but not before I caught the glance that passed between them. I drank my coffee, breathing shallowly so as not to awaken the turpentine cough that lay coiled at the end of each inhalation.

"Carl." My father leaned forward. "Marian and I have talked this over—now, don't misunderstand me. We respect your feelings about the earthquake and we know you're apprehensive. Maybe—"

"Oh, you've talked it over. That's great," I said. To avoid their anxious eyes I looked at the window, running with California rain.

"Carl—"

"Just call me Chicken Little."

"Carl? Hon?" my mother said.

"Old Yeller," I said.

"Absolutely not," my father said. "You're being hard on yourself for no reason. What you're going through is by no means uncommon."

"I'm not one of your psycho patients, Dad."

"*Carl.*" My mother's incantation was a whisper.

"No, clearly not." My father stood up. "You're my son. Do what you have to do."

I stood up, too, but I didn't know where either of us was going. My mother remained seated. Her red flowery wrap with its deep, extravagantly cuffed sleeves gave her the appearance of a mandarin. She seemed about to pass sentence.

"The studio is off limits," she said.

"Okay."

"It's mine," she added. "Not yours, not ours. Mine."

"Fine."

"Just so you understand," she said, and rose from her chair. She began to pile the breakfast dishes deliberately and loudly into the sink, and my father and I went our separate ways.

As I exited Bauman's Outfitters that afternoon, I swerved to avoid running into Carolyn Wilson, who was entering.

"We meet again," she said. "Going camping?"

"Hi. Yes. Well, sort of."

She grinned and gestured widely with her dripping umbrella. "You've got the perfect day for it."

I shifted the bulky package containing my new tent to my other arm. An escaping pair of metal-tipped tent poles made a swipe at Carolyn and missed, then clattered onto the sidewalk. I bent to retrieve them, and several more fell out. Then they all fell out.

"Whoops," she said.

I gathered the poles together and stood up, dizzy with embarrassment, crushing the wet and disintegrating bag to my chest.

"Not really camping," I said. "Just—"

Carolyn was waiting, looking at me out of hazel eyes. Her eyebrows were brushed, like her hair, with red. Her smile was going to go, any minute now. She would vanish.

"My name is Carl," I said.

"*I* know. Carolyn," she said, putting out her hand and laughing. We shook hands.

"Would you like to go out sometime?"

"Sure. When?"

"I don't know." I really didn't know, but I had to keep talking. "I don't know," I said again, brilliantly. "But I'll call you."

"Great! I'm in the book."

I walked home slowly. The rain fell steadily, mildly, and I put my face into the sky and let it run into my eyes. I thought about nothing at all except how she had held her umbrella over both our heads the whole time we were talking.

I had used my tent only twice when my parents told me I had to begin sleeping indoors again. My father offered to pay for the tent, which I had bought out of my savings, and I refused the money.

"Carl," my mother said, "listen to me. Once you sleep indoors one night, just one night, you'll see, I'm certain, that nothing's going to happen. Nothing."

"No," I said. "This house is going to fall down and I'm not going to be inside it when it does."

My father whipped off his glasses—a spectacular effect, one that I had seen before, though not often. He stared at me with myopic intensity.

"Good Christ," he said. "Aren't there enough real problems in the world without adding to them? Your sleeping outdoors simply isn't tenable anymore. Now make up your mind to it and let's have an end to this."

"Oh, it's real," I said.

"It *isn't* real," my mother said. "You've been scared and we want to help you. But you've got to meet us halfway."

"I'll sleep in the car."

"You will NOT sleep in the car," my father thundered. "You will sleep in the goddamned house beginning TONIGHT."

That night I slept in the closet. I positioned myself so that my head and shoulders were within the shelter of the door frame. In order to accomplish this I kept the door open and slept on my side, contracting my body into a fetal position in the cramped space. I woke up feeling bruised and sore to find my mother standing over me.

"Oh, Carl, *Carl*," she said. "Breakfast is ready."

The following night I turned down my bed to discover that my mother had bought me new sheets: crisp, fresh-smelling, blue-striped cotton. Matching pillowcases.

I sat gingerly, reluctant to disturb the hotel-perfect fit. Doing so, I felt, would be an admission of some sort, a physical declaration of my intention to spend the night there. But it would force me, too, to face another fact: that I was no longer so afraid. I was now merely—and for some reason, shamefully—worried.

I rolled into bed fully dressed. Switching off the light, I closed my eyes for several minutes. When I opened them again my room's familiar features stood out in dim but ordinary relief. There, the window. There, the dresser. Up there, the crack.

A cool wind fluttered the curtains and I pulled the bedspread over me. My mind, strangely peaceful, ticked off my concerns in stately slow-motion as I turned over my worries:

I would never see my grandparents in Chicago again.

Carolyn, who seemed to like me, would suddenly cease to care.

My father would become chronically dissatisfied with his work and move us again and again.

I would be buried in an earthquake and die anonymously, needlessly, along with thousands of others who had gone on believing that everything was all right.

My mother, whom I loved, would also die.

I became aware of the silence in my room and of the noises darkly hidden within the silence: the *shush* of blood in my ears, the rhythmic thump of my heart when I placed my hands, one over the other, on my chest. Exhaustion and worry fell like twin pennies on my eyelids.

I dreamed that I was walking on a strange continent whose obelisk-shaped buildings poked their tiny upper stories through the clouds. I knew the buildings were empty because of the numbers of people walking over the grass in the oppressive, sunless heat. Everyone seemed to be talking at once and I couldn't make out individual words. But a needle of news threaded the heavy air, giving shape to a stifling rumor: I understood that an impending earthquake had sent everyone outdoors, and it further became clear that everyone's wish now was to escape the open areas that would fill with rubble when the skyscrapers collapsed. With a rising sense of confusion and panic, I fled into another dream:

I was on a road in a village at twilight. Bougainvillea vines climbed the walls of the adjacent houses; bunches of their blood-red, voluptuous leaves nearly overshadowed the road. At the end of the road stood a house with a single high, brightly lit window, and at the center of the window a woman stood framed. I ran toward the house with relief, shouting and waving, certain that the woman was my mother. But when I reached the house, I saw that the figure in the window was an angel—my mother's angel from the Saint Matthew painting—and that her eyes were brilliantly blue, and blind. She raised her hand in greeting or negation, then slowly drew the hand across her face.

I woke up before dawn and made my bed while light materialized in the room. My father looked in.

"You're up," he said with surprise. I finished dressing and followed him out to the kitchen.

"Coffee's ready. Marian's sleeping in." He sat down heavily, as if tired out by the effort of making these announcements.

"What's wrong?" I said.

Something wasn't right. He wasn't ready for work. He sat very still, his hands lying on the table like a pair of gardener's gloves.

"Did you sleep well," he said.

"Fine." I waited. "I'm going to sleep in my bed from now on. And I'm sorry for what I said, Dad, about your patients being psychos. I was out of line with that shit."

He nodded so slowly that I couldn't tell if he'd heard what I said. He seemed to be entranced. Then his hands came back to life and he waved one of them as if to clear the air.

"That's good," he said. "I know it was hard for you, Carl."

Heaving himself up, he went to the counter and poured a cup of coffee for me, then set it down on the counter and simply stared out the window.

"So, what's going on?" I said—and was suddenly afraid. "Dad, you didn't quit?"

"What?" He looked at me blankly. "Quit what? *Oh.* Quit my *job.*"

He began to laugh, one big explosion setting off the next, until he was leaning over the sink, shaking, his arms wrapped around his middle. Then, stopping as suddenly as he had begun, he ran the tap and washed his face. He lifted a fresh dishtowel from the drawer and wiped his face dry. His voice, when he spoke, was hoarse.

"That boy, the marine I told you about? The one who jumped from a window? He's dead. He killed himself in the hospital last night. Got into the dispensary and drank something—took something."

He folded the dishtowel into thirds as he spoke, smoothing it with the flat of his hand. "He had a second opportunity, and took it."

"God, Dad. I'm sorry."

He nodded. "So am I. Sorrier than I can say. I've been trying to figure out what I could have done." He brought his hands together, leaving a space between them that a face might have filled, or slipped through. "To prevent this. Eighteen," he said. "Good *Christ.*" He dropped his hands and turned from the counter. "Your mother will probably sleep for a while. We were up so late. I have to leave in a minute." He rubbed his cheeks. "I'm unshaven, Carl. I forgot to shave."

I went to my father and put my arms around him, and his heavy arms fell over my shoulders like a landslide.

After Dad drove off, I walked out through the early morning coolness of the backyard, let myself into my mother's studio, and stepped up to her painting. At first I could see nothing different. Then I observed the changes she had made since the last time I looked.

Although the angel still sat on his lap, Saint Matthew was now weeping. He continued to look astonished in spite of his troubled tears. And his angel, the original dare still alive in her expression, no longer touched his lips but instead reached a little higher with her outstretched finger—drawing out his tears in an effort, perhaps, to teach him a more fundamental language than he had bargained for.

It was still too early to go to school, so I wandered down to the ocean. Walking out onto the broad beach I pulled my jacket tighter around my shoulders, feeling the wind beat down on me in short, hard gusts.

There was no one else in sight. Only an occasional gull-screech cut through the steady roaring of the waves. The packed sand barely moved under the pounding of the surf, but as I walked farther out it loosened, melting as the retreating water slurred and sucked around my shoes.

The world was in constant, sometimes secret motion: I was moving—I hoped—toward Carolyn. My father was behind the wheel, freshly shaven, heading north. My mother, still asleep, traveled toward morning in a dream.

I stood in the surf until my shoes nearly disappeared, the heels digging in first, the toes tipping skyward. This was how I wanted to go: a little at a time in a slow rush, not all at once, not missing anything. Stumbling backward, I regained my balance and ran back up the beach with the wind beating around my head like giant wings.

2010

James Crews

Paradoxical Undressing

Investigators believe the couple died the same day they called
911 more than five times from a cell phone trying to explain
their pickup was stuck in the snow and they were lost in a rural
area southwest of Omaha.
ASSOCIATED PRESS

He made his girl a nest in the snow, took off his coat
and wrapped it around her thin shoulders. He had tried

to call 911, but the operator, like a slow child, could not
understand when he explained that passing cars were

no longer cars but the larger, looming bodies of talking
cattle and then wolves shooting across endless Nebraska.

They asked for an address, so he told them crystal falling.
Some trees. A billowing, starry sky like a blanket-tent

above them. He said they were two flashlights drifting off
to sleep and nearly out of battery. Soon, he began to shed

his scarf and flannel, and she too found she did not need
his coat or the rest of her clothing. They made a pile

next to the snow bank and climbed back into the hole
he had hollowed, dead leaves as soft as fur beneath them.

But the search team found them too late, still locked
in each other's arms and stark naked. *Paradoxical undressing,*

the coroner called it, when instinct kicks in and sends
signals like gifts to the faltering mind that say, *This*

is perfect warmth. That night, they must have believed
the moon blooming through clouds shone as blinding

and hot as any sun, soaking its glare into their bare skins
until the still-falling snow sifted into a fine white sand

on some desert island of the imagination and she stopped
shivering long enough for him to hold her silent face

with both stiff hands and kiss the salty, already bluing lips.

Metacognition

Neuroscientists insist it is the greatest gift
of being human, this ability to take a step back
and think about our own thinking, to abandon,
for instance, the insistent glare of a grocery aisle
a moment and climb the mind's Escher-like stairs
when faced with those endless shelves of bright
cereals, sprouted loaves, and pyramids of trucked-in
produce to ask ourselves: which one, what kind,
and how exactly did this basket get so full? But
I say any thought about decision can instantly
ruin it, mangles and shunts our wise neurons
until their instinctual paths run someplace else
entirely: a nowhere-door or useless brick wall.
Imagine colonies of bees for the first time
considering the theory of flight and tumbling
down, or the pollen powdering their wings,
pondering the shifting winds of the grand
scheme, the butterfly effect, its definitive part
in stirring up the most devastating of tsunamis.
And what if a blossom began to contemplate
pistils and stamens or inquired of the air: why
this wafting scent and then the falling away;
if the branch asked, why this weight, this bending
and ripening, and then the sudden rip of the
picking like a torn tendon? In short, what if
the rest of the world became more human?
Wouldn't the skin of this plum I have for some
reason chosen today simply shrivel and
collapse if the flesh started to analyze the nature
of all existence, all sweetness and mystery

surrendered to the far more grounded, pragmatic
pit? What if my hand measured its own shape
against this page, if the palm now cradling the plum
tried to read the lifelines of itself, if I wondered
why the knife, the teeth, or the juice now helplessly
finding my chin, if I stopped to ask myself,
how much do I actually want this delicious thing?
Sometimes I'm grateful the mouth just knows.

The Bees Have Not Yet Left Us

With a click, morning news pours heavy into the bedroom,
embedding itself with anchors' voices too syncopated and smooth
for the tangled math of troop buildups, the surge of death tolls
tallied daily now. Forgive me, distant wars and local heroes,
but I cannot listen. I can only sneak down to the boardwalk
and pick unlikely hyacinths on fire in rising light, can only
place them lance-like in last night's water glass as if this
one act could save a life or erase the reports of whole colonies
of bees lost on the wrong roads between our phone signals.
If apocalypse ever shows up, let us then eat only ashen bread
and bone-dry tubers. For now, I refuse to let another
second tick by, wasted, while he is waiting for me at the table
with dishes of fresh blueberries swaddled in cream.
I turn off the TV, throw open every window so we can taste
the faintly salted breeze filtering in from Humboldt Bay
and trembling the violet petals of these hyacinths I am now
holding out to him, until their pollen scatters violently
golden before us, this dust and air we are somehow
still breathing together.

Sagittarius

The land surrounding the house is state forest. A dirt road climbs farther up the mountain, where paint-stained bark indicates the direction of hiking trails and orange signs warn off hunters. It is into this wilderness that he has run away. Seven o'clock in the evening. While they were arguing (again) about the surgery, the baby vaulted over the rail of the playpen, as if it were a hurdle to be cleared. They heard his hooves scrabbling on the rubber mat but were too late to see him jump: tucking his forelegs up, hind legs flexing and thrusting, body tracing a parabola through the air; then the earthward reach of the forelegs, the tucking up of the rear hooves, the landing. They shouted his name in unison. When they reached the sunroom, they saw him bounding out the door. Upper half, human half, twisted in their direction; a look of joy and terror in the infant's eyes. But the equine part would not stop . . . Now he stands in the trees, hominid heart thundering in his chest. Though the twilight air is cold on the bare white skin of his torso, it can't touch him below the waist: his hindquarters are warm under a coat of dark hair. He hears his mother call. "Sebastian!" A flick of the tail, the shuffle of hooves. As he bounds deeper into the maze of trees, night's first star appears in the ecliptic.

~~~

The first fear blazing through her mind: someone with a rifle will mistake him, in the mist of dawn, for an animal. No, Isabel thinks. Dawn is ten hours away. We'll find him before then. We'll hear him crying long before that. We have to. Hardly April. The temperature still hypothermic at night. Even if he wanders for a mile, in this silence we'll hear him. Except that his cries, until today, have been so very faint . . . She herself can scarcely speak. When she calls for him, his name seems to catch on spikes in her throat and come out torn. She stops. Sweeps the flashlight through the trees. Listens. All she hears is her husband's voice. Much stronger, more certain than hers. Still, he sounds far away. Each time Martin calls Sebastian's name, he sounds a little more distant; and Isabel feels a little more alone in the dark. It seems very wrong to her, in these moments, to be frightened for herself. But she is. A sense of the future washes through her like the memory of a dream, vague and unreliable but sharp nonetheless—an impression of a place she will be one day. Dark, solitary, cut off from lovers and children. She is thinking only of her baby. Where he is, how to reach him. But every thought of him feels somehow like a thought about herself. As if there's still a cord strung between them, a useless cord that links them but doesn't keep them connected. She stops. Listens. Sweeps the beam through the trees. There's a burning in her chest as the light catches on two yellow eyes. Too big by far, this animal. But in the moment before it bounds across the road, darkness and hope conspire to let her see exactly what she wants. For one blessed moment, it's him. Then it's a fawn darting into the forest—with its mother chasing behind.

Martin could see, for a short time, the other beam sweeping up the dirt road and his wife's figure delineated in an auroral glow; but the space between them is widening—trees, darkness—and the light seems, from where he stands, to be going out. "Sebastian!" he shouts. He's careful to keep his voice free of anger so his son will not misinterpret his intentions. I don't want to punish you, I just want to help. He does not feel panicked. Worried, yes. Scared. But calm, clear enough to wonder if he might be succumbing to a state of shock. Probably he's been in shock for months already. He and Isabel both. Each in their own way. It's getting darker. Just since they've been out here (can't be more than four or five minutes), the sky has blackened enough to begin showing stars. The buds on the trees haven't opened yet, so the view to the firmament is clear. Martin only glances up; but that one glance is enough to remind him just how much space there is, in heaven and on earth, to get lost in. Again, he calls out. Hears only the clicking of crickets and the wind chime reverberations of traveling starlight. Then, noise from up the road, where he thinks his wife is.

"Is it him?" He waits for an answer. "Isabel?"

"A deer, I said."

She sounds shaken. Her voice already tinged with grief.

The boy sits on the couch watching the eyes of the cartoon characters bug out on the television and their tongues unfurl like party favors. Through the cotton of his pajamas, he tugs on his penis. He's three years old. He has never been alone in the house before. Although his parents sometimes threaten to leave him here (if he doesn't hurry up and get dressed or hurry up and get in the car), and though tears sometimes spring to his eyes at the thought, he always understands that the abandonment is not really going to occur. Yet here he is now. Left behind. At first, he was able to hear them calling his brother's name. Not anymore. He can't hear anything now. He has touched the remote control and made the voices on television go away. Now he can't hear anything but crickets marching closer and closer in the dark.

~~~

Night is nearly done falling. Isabel thinks momentarily of Kaden, back at the house. She has never left him alone, unless you count the time she accidentally locked him inside with all the keys. After breaking in through the bedroom window, she found him sitting on the kitchen floor playing with the salad spinner. She thinks: he can take care of himself. Then her mind returns to the woods and her fears to wild animals. Raccoons, owls, black bear. What is her baby to these creatures? A peer, a brother—or an unknown encroacher? Isn't it all about territory, the cruel mathematics of the food chain? It occurs to her suddenly that this is all her fault. If she hadn't refused after the ultrasound to believe what the screen showed them; if she'd consented to the operation after the birth (at which point she could no longer deny the truth); and if she hadn't brought him out here, just today—only hours ago, they'd climbed this very road. If she hadn't shown him the world in all its openness and wildness. What happened today, what's happening even now: doesn't it validate the position she took from the very beginning? Her mind flashes back to the first appointment with the orthopedic surgeon. They hadn't even left the hospital yet. The baby was in neonatal intensive care; and there she was in that waiting room, with the magazines fanned out on the tables, those airbrushed cover photos, those mirages of flawlessness. Back in his office, the doctor told them their son would never walk. To increase the slim chances of ambulation, but mostly for the sake of anatomical correctness, he advised the removal of the two forelegs . . .

You mean amputate?

Mmm.

Is that . . . necessary?

Depends, Mrs. Avery, on your definition of necessity.

Martin leans against a tree and feels that some balance is tipping inside him. He closes his eyes, opens them again. Sees plainly, as if it's something caught in the beam of his flashlight, the futility of what they're trying to do. The baby could be anywhere! Abruptly, he starts back toward the house (remembering, all at once, his elder son). He intends to call the police, report a missing person. Then decides, with equal impulsiveness, against the idea. What kind of description would he give? How can he explain when he himself does not understand? Even the doctors can't make up their minds. The diagnosis changes every week. Spina bifida, muscular dystrophy, cerebral palsy as the cause of the musculoskeletal deformity; the body hair most likely the result of a condition called congenital hypertrichosis; and the extra legs—they don't have a clue. A genetic mutation, or the vestiges of a twin who failed to fully form. The fact is, no one knows exactly what's wrong with his son. No one knows what he is.

"Sebastian!"

His voice sounds, to his ears, less controlled this time. It's a fact that he, the father, is the cause of this situation. Had he responded differently back at the house, the baby would never have leapt over the rail of his playpen, knocked the back door open, and run away. A knife blade twists in his stomach. Suddenly, sharply, Martin is aware of his conduct. Out here, under the stars, he isn't sure if it made any sense at all . . . My son stood today. My son walked today.

Kaden walks down the hall, crying. Saying, "Where are you, Mom?" He knows they went out the back door. Still, he looks for them in the house. He goes to the bedroom first and speaks into the darkness. Gets no answer. He doesn't know where they've gone, yet their absence is part of a pattern. Kaden let his brother out the back door. His brother ran outside. His father ran through the door, his mother ran through the door. They have all disappeared into the night.

I let them out, he thinks.

Me.

I wanted to see my brother run. My brother is a horse.

~~~

Isabel's foot slips. The ground is sloping upward. She realizes she's wearing sandals, and this pathetic detail pushes her to sob. She feels a surge of confusion. Not new. She's been feeling it—a dreamlike gap in logic, a page missing from the book—ever since the night he was born. There is a name for what he is. Why can't she think of it, why can't anyone think of it? After the delivery (which had been both easier and more difficult than Kaden's), she had not seen Sebastian right away. While she'd lain in the bed, her body light as a soul, a phalanx of nurses had spirited the newborn away. Nobody would answer her questions. Not the midwife. Not her own husband, who claimed to have seen nothing in the confusion. He sat beside her, worrying with his fingers the plastic wrist bracelet printed with his name and the name of their son. He took her hand, but wouldn't look at her. The lack of eye contact, though unnerving, allowed her to maintain a kind of distance. As if they were back in birthing class, watching a video about complications. As if the situation were purely hypothetical, a scenario invented for the purpose of instruction . . . Neonatal intensive care. First, a lobby with a nurses' station and a smaller room off to the side equipped with sinks. Isabel could not, for the life of her, figure out how to turn on the water. There were no handles on the faucet. She wondered then if she was dreaming, anaesthetized in the operating room; or still in the birthing suite, drugged even though she'd forsworn the drugs, and now she was hallucinating, succumbing to one of the adverse reactions that their birth-class instructor had warned them about: I can't breathe, I'm going into allergic shock, my heart is slowing, slowing, stopping. Suddenly, magically, water gushed from the faucet. Her husband's foot was depressing a pedal on the floor. Then they were going in. The unit was one large room, very quiet, full of incubators that made her think first of aquarium tanks, then display cases, then—because they were wheeled and curtained—of something else she couldn't quite put her finger on. The babies she could see were tiny, impossibly small, blue and mummified. Sebastian was not one of these. Not premature. Despite the debriefing with specialists, she didn't yet understand what he was. Was there no word for him, or simply no cute word, no word that didn't invoke a darker age? She was afraid, but relieved to feel, underneath the terror, crushed and barely breathing, but there, *there*, a desire to see him, a longing, whatever he might be. They neared his incubator. Positioned in a secluded corner of the room. The curtain was drawn. Monitors overhead displayed fluctuating numbers and jagged inscriptions. Under an impulse that upset her stomach and wrung her heart the way feelings of romance had when she was younger, Isabel moved closer. Yes, she had already fallen in love with him, with the idea of him. She'd made a space in her mind and heart, and now he would step into that shape and fit it perfectly, fill it perfectly. She reached out a hand and pulled open the curtain.

He thinks: my son walked today. Any other parent would be filled with a clear and simple happiness. For Martin, it is all too much. He had come home half an hour ago, with a bottle of red wine and the honest intention to start from scratch. No made-up minds, no sides. They would talk, really talk. Work things out together. Figure out what to do. Then he walked in the door and his older son grabbed him by the hand and pulled him back into the sunroom where his wife was waiting and beaming with joy; and then he saw the reason—the baby was standing, standing on all four feet—and he couldn't understand why, but his spirits simply collapsed, and all his hopes seemed like a fantasy compared to the concrete fact of the creature in the playpen.

He's standing, Dad.

I can see that.

Not only that, said his wife. He can walk. He got up in the meadow today, on the grass, and walked.

Like a foh-wul, Kaden said.

A what?

Dad, a foh-wul is a baby horse.

He's not a foal.

Isabel continued: He fell down at first. But then he did it, Martin, just like they said he wouldn't.

Martin looked again. No illusion. Surrounded by the trappings of any boy's infancy—a floppy blue teddy bear; a plush baseball with a jingle bell inside; a mobile of the solar system, its planets swaying in a lazy orbit—their disabled son was standing. Eyes wide, hands clapping, he bounced on his four legs, hooves scrabbling on the polyester mat. Martin walked over to him and placed a hand on his head, and said, We can't let him do this.

Why not?

He'll get used to it.

She smiled uncertainly. I don't see what you mean, she said.

Yes, you do.

I don't actually.

He'll get used to standing like this. We won't be able to break him of the habit.

Standing isn't a habit.

Okay.

Nose picking is a habit. Thumb sucking, she said, tears coming into her eyes. Christ, even today? Even this? I don't understand you.

No kidding.

How can this be anything but wonderful?

It's only going to make everything harder. The longer we wait, the harder it's going to be. For all of us.

He slipped past her, taking pains to avoid brushing any part of his body against hers. She followed him down the hallway to the stairs. Leaving the two children behind.

You just wish he'd go away, she said too loudly.

Untrue.

Not just half of him. All of him.

Kaden remembers the back door. Wonders what he's doing here, at home, when the rest of them have run away. Back in the sunroom, he stares at the empty playpen. The mobile of the solar system hangs frozen in the darkness. His brother had set it whirling when he jumped. Jump, Kaden had whispered. Down the hall, they'd been saying, Go away. All of him. Kaden opened the back door. Go, brother. Now the boy feels a heat, like a candle burning in his belly. He feels for his sneakers in the pile of shoes beside the door. Pulls them on the wrong feet. Steps into the starry night and onto the road.

~~~

Suddenly, she thinks, The meadow! Of course. That's where he went. Is now. A realization so sharp, so visual—she can *see* him, a four-legged shadow tracing a lazy path through the grass—as to make her feel clairvoyant. Isabel starts to reach for her cell phone, to speed-dial her husband and tell him where to meet her: she's confident enough now in a happy ending to laugh at the impulse. She runs back down the road. Seeking out the trailhead with the flashlight beam. The memory of the afternoon speeding a dizzy spin in her head.

She hadn't been sure, earlier in the day, if the ground of the meadow would be dry (the last of the snow had melted only recently), yet the world wore the beckoning look of spring. She packed a blanket in the backpack and managed to get him into the front pouch, his forelegs through the two extra holes she'd cut in the padding. All through the winter, Sebastian had confirmed his doctors' expectations—sleeping excessively, communicating only through weak cries, showing little interest in his surroundings—but now, in the outdoors, he observed everything with wide eyes and squawked like a tropical bird. How beautiful to hear! Isabel felt a strength bubble up from deep inside her. We can get through this, she thought. All of us together. As she carried him through the woods, she felt strangely blessed. As if this improbable child, as he appeared right now, was the fulfillment of some secret wish. They found the meadow golden with sun. The flaxen grass long and dry enough. Isabel freed the baby from the carrier, laid him down on the blanket. Immediately he started struggling. A seizure, an allergic reaction? She was about to sweep him up again and rush down the trail, back to the house and the telephone, when she realized there was something methodical, something conscious about his move-ments. The knobby, hairy legs stretched and slipped, stretched and slipped. Then the bones momentarily straightened and locked, and his body almost lifted from the ground. He tried again. Again and again. To hoist himself up. To balance. The closer he got, the more violently his legs trembled. So frail, she thought. Like they might snap under his weight. Scary; but she gently urged him on, support-ing his underbelly with a hand. She shaking too—and feeling, too, that she was rising somehow. It took an hour, maybe more; yet the day was far from over, the sun still warm and high overhead when she heard herself say, in a broken whisper, Look at you, little man. Look at you standing up.

Now, searching for the trailhead, she again feels weightless with thanks. Yes, everything's going to be alright. She calls out to her husband. "Martin! Can you hear me?" But a vehicle, a pickup truck, is coming down the mountain, tires rasping against the dirt road, columns of halogen light careering through the trees and blinding her as she moves out of the way.

Martin can barely admit it to himself, but his wife is right. He does sometimes wish the baby would disappear. Not half of him. All of him. Now it's happening. And if they don't find him—if they do and it's too late . . . His mind projects a scene: his return to the house in the gray light of dawn, exhausted and empty-handed. It comes to him like a psychic flash, crisp and definite, this picture of himself. Followed by another that's simply unbearable: their second child dead on a carpet of last autumn's rust-colored leaves. Not the first time he has imagined such a thing. Ever since the doctors started talking about life expectancy, Martin has been fighting off dark imagery. We can't be sure (they say), we need more neuromotor assessment, and intelligence tests are a year away, but physical deformities this severe suggest associated malformations of the brain; and if the muscle disease is degenerative, as it almost certainly is—well, it's only a matter of time before it reaches the heart, which is, in the end, just another muscle . . . What would be worse? Losing the boy tonight (just a baby, five months in the world and already gone from it) or losing him thirteen years from now? No, he doesn't want his son to vanish. He just wants him to be normal. He wants fatherhood to be free of pain and paradox.

Suddenly, his hands are breaking a fall. Fucking rock, fucking root of a tree. He hits the ground, pant leg tearing on something. Kneeling now on the forest floor, ankle possibly sprained, he becomes aware of an open space ahead. Dark, but lighter than the woods.

The meadow.

For a moment, the father can hear something in the grass. A tiny voice. Musical and human. Very small, very clear. There—then gone. Cancelled by the sound of a car or truck bounding down the mountain road.

Kaden feels his way along the road. For a few yards, before the trees get thick, the night is like a picture in a storybook: the road faintly glows, but on every page it gets a little blacker. The boy stops, looks back. Focuses on a window of the house pulsing with television light. Figures out, finally, why his feet are hurting. He sits on the rocky dirt. Taking sneakers off is one thing; trying to put them back on in the dark is another. He remembers one time in the car (he had no brother yet and his seat faced backward) seeing through the window a girl with dark glasses and a long silver wand that showed her where to go. He needs a wand. Without a wand, he will never, ever find them. He holds a sneaker up to the sky, eyes squinting and blinking. Slowly, the object comes clear to him. The red stripes, the contour of the toe. Not until the light grows bright enough to reveal the terrain of the road and to make the trunks of trees leap out from the forest does Kaden wonder about the source of it, turning his head, imagining that such radiance could only come from a friendly, enchanted star.

~~~

She glimpses the trailhead (the little tin marker, stick figure with walking stick, nailed to the tree) and hears, at the very same moment, the panic of wheels going into a skid, treads clawing violently at dirt and rock, then the collision—crush of metal, bleat of a horn—and the harmonics of breaking glass. Isabel freezes. Same as when she wakes in her bed, having heard something that may have been nothing. Running down the road now is like all the times she has moved through her home in the dead of night. This is something, this is nothing . . . Isn't that also what she told herself in the days after the ultrasound? On that screen, they had seen the ghost of an impossible fetus. Six limbs. Two arms and four legs, each foot badly twisted and missing toes. She saw the images with her own eyes (the technician had printed enough pictures to fill a scrapbook). She heard everything the doctors said in the days afterward about how and why and what to do about it. Still, a patchy fog obscured her vision. Static broke on her eardrums like ocean waves. A few months later she reached for that curtain in the NICU, fearing suddenly that she might be about to suffer a crippling blow. But no. As she pulled the curtain aside, her body felt no shock from without, only a sweet confirmation from within. Not like other boys. And not entirely human. But why all this grave talk of abnormalities and deformities, when anyone can see he is exquisitely formed? A beautiful boy from the waist up, and from the waist down, a beautiful horse . . . Now she runs, as on a tightrope. Each time she blinks, a film of tears spreads evenly over the surface of her eyes, and through this aqueous medium, the light down below (dim; one headlight bulb must have burst on impact) looks like an aura suffusing the scene of the accident. No, no, no. A voice in her head, hers but not hers, keeps saying the word, as if refusing to find something horrible is to omit it from reality. When she reaches the foot of the hill, feet skidding, her lungs crumple and contract. No room for air. The truck is sunk front-first in a ditch at a forty-five-degree angle, rear wheels in the air, hood reshaped by a tree trunk. The driver, ejected from his seat and halfway through the windshield—lower body in the cab, upper on the glass-spangled hood—isn't moving. "Oh God," the mother says aloud. Then starts calling for her baby. Shining the light into the ditch; into the trees; finally onto the road, where it finds first a tiny red-striped sneaker, then her other son, her human son, sitting in the dirt, staring, mesmerized by the wreck.

Though Martin hears the crash, he is also deaf to it. In the peace that follows, there seems to be only one sound in the universe: it comes from the heart of the meadow. "Uh-boo-boo-bah. Uh-voo.

Uh-bah-bah-bah-bah-bah." Martin can see him—a four-legged shadow moving through the grass—and as the father emerges from the trees, the sky above the child expands. Not the first time he's been out here after dark. Last summer he made love with his wife under this blown-glass sky. Still, the place feels like a new discovery to him. Never has he seen a thicker spread of stars. Beneath all those dots of light, the baby continues to murmur in a private dialect. When Martin comes within a few yards, he stops and whispers:

"Sebastian."

The boy turns—neither startles and runs off, nor comes rushing into his daddy's arms. It's as if the parent has been present all along, as if there's nothing extraordinary about the situation. Again, he thinks, My son is walking. Only this time, the idea, the sight of it, gives him a shiver of amazement. He crouches down and watches. He watches his strange son walk. Emotion twists once more like a knife in his belly. If up to Martin alone, the surgery would have been performed long ago. The forelegs lopped off. After that, an operation to alter the angle of the femur and another (involving the imbedding of metal hooks and wires) to straighten the spine. Six weeks in a cast. Then laser hair removal. Genital reconstruction. The doctors call it medical necessity. He can't stay like this. He will never walk. He never will—But he is. Ever since the birth, Martin has been praying he'll wake up. Wake up to find that the world is really a mundane place. Now, under the zodiac sky with this infant, he sees the absurdity of the notion; and with a trembling inside, he thinks to turn away from it. The insight seems part of the night, part winter and part spring, something he can breathe in and keep breathing in. Very slowly, he stands and moves closer. Places a hand on the boy's body, on his bare back, the root of his spine, where soft white skin grades into a coat of hair.

~~~

He will fall asleep now: here, in his father's arms, long before they reach the house, before they come upon the accident. Breathing the sweet fumes of pine needles. Feeling through the father's flesh the warmth of flowing blood, which is his blood too. When Martin starts to run, Sebastian's eyes will flutter open. He will glimpse the light, the vehicle, the body slumped over the hood. But he won't remember. He won't remember and he'll never forget the night he ran away and his father brought him home. It's the kind of impossible story that holds a family together. You tell it over and over again; and with the passage of time, the tale becomes more unbelievable and at the same time increasingly difficult to disprove, a myth about the life you carry.

2011

Susan Blackwell Ramsey

Boliche

All through high school Paul's nickname was Boliche
    because in seventh grade Spanish class he bragged
"*Yo soy más boliche!*" which translates to
    "I am more bowling!" It made a certain sense

when you remember the fad in language teaching
    for immersion: conversation, vocabulary,
but never grammar, never a hint that Spanish
    was a different building, not just repainted English;

so if the book said that "I like bowling better"
    in Spanish goes, "*Me gusta más el boliche,*"
then *boliche* must mean "better." We had to learn
    that no one ever likes anything in Spanish;

things are pleasing to you, a small stone wall
    we tripped over, and getting up looked back
at our own house, yard, from a different angle.
    It was a first attempt to fit our thinking

in another's, like empathy or ballroom dancing.
    It felt perverse, a deliberate obstacle,
like the Swiss building railroads a smaller gauge
    than every other country's to thwart invasion,

which forced us to wake and reluctantly stumble
    across the border lugging packs and passports,
to walk fifty feet, climb on, and start again,
    learning new words just so they could give us grades.

I hope old Boliche got an A.
    While the rest of us slumped in language lab,
going through the motions, lockstepping our way
    from one unconsidered language to another,

Boliche grabbed a flag, wrapped it around his neck,
    ran off into the trees, picked a bowling ball,
and took a big bite. Of course he got it wrong,
    but he got it wrong the right way. When I skip

tourist attractions because they're a cliché,
    don't dance when Los Bandits are playing in the park,
decline to sing along, every time I blink
    instead of winking, wear black instead of red,

I'm back in language lab, back in junior high,
    for which the translation is "*purgatorio*,"
but a place for learning, where learning may get you out,
    out, and if you're lucky, *más Boliche*.

Knitting Lace

Like any widow, any amputee,
   lace is defined by absence,
by what is missing, lack.
   There is no such thing
     as solid lace.

It's possible
   to churn out lace by rote,
each row executed, crossed off, mere
   mechanics of fingers, thread.
     But lace craves

full engagement, the moment
   that you grasp
its particular logic, spot
   the error in the row below, know
     how to fix it,

not ripping out whole rows,
   but dropping down
one stitch, amending, climbing back up
   to go on waltzing, stitch, space, stitch,
     counting with the body, not the brain.

Lace makes you concentrate.
   No coasting, cruising,
mind in neutral, fingers ticking off
   a rosary of repetitious stitches.
     Lace takes

your best attention,
　　the park bench in your brain
where math and language hunch
　　over a chessboard, leaves blowing
　　　past their ankles.

Karen Brown

Little Sinners

We weren't bad girls. When we were little we played church, flattening soft bread into disks, singing the hymns from stolen paper missals: *Our Fathers chained in prisons dark, were still in heart and conscience free; how sweet would be their children's fate, if they, like them, could die for Thee.* We set up carnivals and lemonade stands, and collected pennies for UNICEF on Halloween. We bought trees to be planted in our names in forests purged by fire. We drew elaborate peace signs on our notebooks, and watched the Vietnam War on television every night, scanning the faces of the soldiers for our babysitters' boyfriends. We included everyone in our neighborhood games, even our irritating younger siblings, even the girl, Sally Moore, who was clearly a boy, and the boy, Simon Schuster, who was clearly schizophrenic. They were cast as the frog in our production of *The Frog Prince*, or played the dead boy in our Haunted Woods. We would grow up to understand, perfectly, what was expected of us—and still, when it came to you, none of this applied. We were feral, unequivocally vicious, like girls raised by the mountain lions that occasionally slunk out of the wilderness of Massacoe State Forest, between the swing sets and the lawn furniture, into our tended backyards.

It was May when it all started, and the air was still sharp and the forsythia waved its long arms of bright flowers. My friend Valerie Empson and I had been stealing our parents' Pall Malls and Vantages, hiding them in clever places in our bedrooms. I'd taken off one brass finial and slipped the cigarettes into my curtain rod. At prearranged times we'd retrieve them to smoke in the woods, and one day we put on clothes we found in my basement first: my mother's pleated plaid high school skirt (Drama Club, *The Tattler*, 1958), a cocktail dress (Wampanoag Country Club, 1971). We put on her old winter coats, camel hair and cashmere smelling of mothballs, her satin pumps, and black patent-leather slingbacks. We went out walking about in the woods behind my house, pretending we were someone else. We were too old for dress-up—this was our last fling. We put on the clothes and assumed other personalities with accents.

"Blimey, this is a steep path, I say."

"Where are we headed? Isn't that the clearing, darling?"

The woods were composed of young growth—birch, maple, and pine saplings, a thicket suitable for cottontails. A brook ran through it parallel to the houses, filled with brownish-looking foam that may have been the result of the DDT misted over us each summer. The planes would drone overhead while our parents sipped whiskey sours, and we lay on our backs in the front-yard grass like unsuspecting sacrifices.

"Oh lovely, I've gotten my shoe wet."

"Look at that, the hem of your skirt is muddy."

"Jesus, Mary, and Joseph."

We walked along the brook's bank, and I slid down the side in the high-heeled shoes and toppled into the water. The brook wasn't very deep, but it was fast-moving, its bottom a variety of stones, and I struggled to stand. Valerie watched from the bank, doubled over laughing with her hand between her legs. Pee streamed down onto the trampled Jack-in-the-pulpit, wetting her chiffon skirt, probably dribbling into her pumps. I felt the icy water soak into my coat. We were too busy laughing and peeing to notice anyone nearby. If it had been a boy we'd have been embarrassed. But it was only you, the weird neighbor girl, with your doughy cheeks, and your intelligent eyes. You looked at us laughing, and I sensed a sort of yearning in your face. That you were watching only made us laugh harder.

"You're going to catch something from that water," you said, matter-of-factly.

We'd met you years ago in elementary school. You were younger, consigned to the kindergarten playground. You carried a blue leather purse and were always alone. Drawn to your oddness, we broke the rules to sneak over to talk to you.

"What's in your purse?" Valerie said.

Your lips tightened with wariness. "None of your business." Your hair was cut short, in the pixie style my mother once foisted on my younger sister. You were thinner then, almost tiny, a dollish-looking girl. We laughed at nearly everything you said, most of it mimicked from a grown-up and strange coming from your mouth.

"Why can't you just be nice and show us?" I said.

You knew that you should be nice, and you did like the attention from us. Finally, one day you undid the snap of the purse and opened it up. We looked into its depths. There was a small change purse, the kind we made summers in craft class at Recreation when we were little—imitation leather, stitched together with plastic. Yours was blue to match your purse. You also had a handkerchief, a tiny pink one, and a bottle of Tinkerbell perfume. Valerie reached her hand in quickly and grabbed the change purse before you could snap the purse shut. Your face hardened like your mother's probably would when someone did something wrong at your house.

"Give it back," you said.

"I'm not taking it," Valerie said, dancing off a ways. "I'm just looking. I'll give it back in a minute." She opened it up and looked inside. You had quite a bit of change in the purse—silver, not all pennies. We glanced at each other. This would buy a few packs of gum, or the little round tin of candies we loved, La Vie Pastillines, in raspberry or lemon.

If you hadn't seen me fall into the brook, spring would have progressed into summer, and nothing of the business would have transpired. Maybe I'd have seen you riding your purple bike in lazy circles at the end of the street, but that shapeless figure of you wobbling on your Schwinn, those annoying plastic streamers spraying from each handlebar grip, wouldn't have prompted it. That you occasioned to show yourself, that this triggered my thinking of a way to involve you in some deviousness, was purely accidental. I'd climbed out of the brook and stood dripping on the bank.

"Go away," I said. "We're meeting someone and we don't want you around."

I took out the cigarette I'd hidden in my coat pocket and lit it up. Valerie did the same.

Your eyes widened. "Who are you meeting?" You took a careful step closer, pretending our smoking wasn't anything out of the ordinary.

Valerie put her hands on her hips. Her coat opened, revealing the shape of her new breasts beneath the dress's bodice. "A boy," she said. "Charlie."

We held the cigarettes out in the *V*s of our fingers.

"Charlie who?" you asked me, suddenly wary. There wasn't a neighborhood boy named Charlie, and this meant that he must be a stranger, someone from beyond our subdivision.

"He lives on the farm there, over the hill."

Your eyes narrowed to where I pointed beyond Foot Hills Road, to the rise of a local dairy farmer's pasture. "How did he tell you to meet him?"

"In his letter," I said.

"What letter?"

"The one he left for us."

"Where did he leave a *letter*?" you asked, well aware that a letter was something mailed from one house to another with the proper postage. It could even be placed secretly in someone's mailbox. A note was passed between popular girls in the dull hour of American History. And then I told you it was none of your business, that I'd heard your mother calling. You didn't give up, or suspect that we were lying. You wanted to believe what we told you was true.

I don't have to emphasize how often this happens, how typical of human behavior. The UFOs that circled our neighborhood one summer evening, flashes of silver and iridescent violet panning across the night sky, bringing us out of our houses to marvel—parents with drinks and cigarettes, children in cotton pajamas, all of us poised on our own wide sweep of perfect grass. The ghosts we've claimed to have seen in our lifetimes—nuns in barns, men with handlebar mustaches appearing in old medicine chest mirrors, the footsteps on the stairs, the "Light as a Feather" game, where girls levitate each other with only their pinky fingers, the mystery of blood and wine, the Holy Ghost we'd speak of when we crossed ourselves. You bought it all. You crept behind us and we pretended we didn't know. We put out our cigarettes on a rock, and we saw you bend down and retrieve the butts, like evidence, or talismans. You followed us up to the next road, and then to the dead end where a strip of old barbed wire separated our neighborhood from the farmer's field, where beyond the asphalt curb Queen Anne's lace bloomed and twirled its white head, and cows lowed and hoofed through muddy grass, around stones covered with lichen. There at the foot of the cedar post was one of these stones, and I pretended to lift it, to pocket something in my mother's heavy coat that I carried slung over my arm. You took it all in at a distance, your white face round with pleasure, while we pretended we didn't see you.

That night Valerie and I wrote the first letter. *Dear Francine*, I wrote. *Can I call you "Francie"? I heard your mother calling you in for supper. I saw you on your bike stop and turn to answer her.* Who can say what it is that makes us revel in deceit? I liken it to something pagan and impish. Weren't the fields and woods surrounding us a sort of pastoral landscape? There was the farmer riding his tractor, the newly planted corn emerging to shake its tassels, all pleasant and bountiful, the smell of manure seeping through window screens into kitchens and bedrooms, awakening in us a sort of misplaced disgust.

And it was easy because I wanted it myself. I wanted there to be some mysterious boy who had been watching me, in love with me from a distance. I'd imagine that out beyond the bay window, on the street that winds higher up the hill than mine, a boy with sweet wispy hair and lips that are always half-smiling was watching. He saw me walk up the driveway to catch the school bus. He saw through the new spring growth of fox glove and pokeweed and fern, through those bright little shoots on the elms. From the Talcott View dairy's fallow fields, white-sprayed with bluets, I could almost hear his sigh and his gentle breathing. I could smell his sweat—coppery, the mineral smell of turned earth.

We left the note under the stone. We didn't actually see it happen, but two days later, after school, a hazy day warming up to be summer, we slipped back and there was a note to the boy from you. *Dear Charles*, it said. *You seem very nice*. It revealed aspects of your family life—your mother sleeping all afternoon on the couch, your father and his woodworking hobby. *He carves puns out of wood*, you wrote. *Shoe tree, water gun, bookworm. He is now making a train track that one day will run through the entire house, upstairs and down.* Valerie and I read the note in the upstairs bathroom at my house. This was the only room with a lock. We both sat on the closed toilet lid. The bathroom smelled of my father's Old Spice. This is where we sat together to read the *Playboys* and *Penthouses* he had hidden in the vanity drawer. Once, as little girls, we mixed up potions in paper Dixie cups on the counter—toothpaste, shaving cream, Bay Rum.

"They're all crazy," Valerie said. Her eyes feigned shock beneath her bangs.

"Tell her he loves her anyway," I said. "He doesn't care about her family. She's different. She's the one his heart is aching for."

My mother was downstairs on the phone, her voice lulling. It was a weekday, and my father was at the office. My sister was outside with her friends, watching the boys construct a go-cart out of a large sheet of plywood they'd stolen from the new subdivision. They were hammering on two sets of old training wheels. They would ride the thing down the hill, the girls watching, envious, waiting for a turn, and up-end it on the curb. This would result in Valerie's brother's broken arm, and a rush to the hospital in her father's Bonneville, her brother shrieking, his face white behind the passenger window. Her mother drove because her father had already started the cocktail hour. She had her lit cigarette, and she backed out of the driveway with a chirp, and took off with a squeal of tires. I remember watching them drive off, and then Valerie came home with me for supper, and she got to spend the night since it was a Friday, and her parents didn't return until long after bedtime.

We wrote the second note and said, *I think I love you*. We laughed until we cried at this, a Partridge Family lyric. Valerie said to write, *But what am I so afraid of?* But I wouldn't. Too much, I told her. We sprinkled my father's Bay Rum on the envelope. We'd used one of his old *Playboy*s to write on, July 1969, Nancy McNeil topless on a blanket in the sand. And then we slipped out to the dead end. No one knew where we were headed. No one followed us. We had our cigarettes, and after we left the note we lifted the barbed wire and kept walking through the field's tall grass, its black-eyed Susans, dame's rocket, and chicory, the kinds of flowers we used to bring back in damp fists to our mothers on their birthdays. We sat down in the middle of the field, and no one could see us smoking.

"She'll look today," I said, predicting what would happen next.

Val practiced smoke rings. In a year she would be caught making out with Ritchie Merrill on the Schusters' bed while babysitting. The news would spread, and she would suddenly become popular in school, and we would no longer be friends. Neither of us could have known that this would happen. In our bliss we believed we were forever bound in our conspiracy against you. We would always press our foreheads together, and stare into each other's eyes, and know exactly what the other was thinking. It was the beginning of summer, and the possibility of days of endless letter writing, and grape-flavored ice cubes, and gum-wrapper chains, and a new attraction to plan—a circus in the backyard, where I would construct a trapeze and practice on it, flipping upside down, dreaming about being watched and applauded. We would have our stack of books from the library to read—*Flambards*, and *Flambards in Summer*. Boys our age would continue to keep clear of us. We would find evidence of them—murdered robins riddled with silver BBS, muddy trails in the woods littered with potato chip bags, and soft drink cans, and trampled violets—but they remained elusive that summer, and we were perfectly happy to invent a boy all our own.

We'd orchestrate moments to slip away to the dead end. Old Mrs. Waddams lived in the house at the end of the street, and once she came out and stood at the foot of her driveway with her hands on her hips. "What are you doing over there?" she called.

Val explained that we were working on a science project for school. "We're testing the rate of decay on varying thicknesses of paper," she said.

Mrs. Waddams pulled her cotton cardigan around her shoulders. You could almost smell the mothballs, the lilac powder she fluffed between her breasts. Her hands were gnarled like the branches of her crabapple. She made a noise as if she didn't believe us, and turned away and shuffled into her house. As a teenager, after we'd moved away from the neighborhood, I would bring boys to the dead end to have sex, and sometimes we'd fall asleep in the car. The next morning old Mrs. Waddams, still vigilant, would come to the fogged-over car window and rap her bony fist. "You in there," she'd say. "Are you alive? Wake up!" She would see us scramble to rearrange our clothes, embarrassed by our bodies, as if what we had done with them had nothing to do with the pale skin showing in the morning light, the sex a ritual, and empty after, like the one thing we had hoped for had died, and we were dead along with it.

The farmer boy didn't need to write much in his letters to convince you. We created his messy cursive. He said he had chores on the farm, and he hunted and fished in the little pond we'd seen when we went on our explorations as children, choosing a swath of a green hillside showing over the trees in the distance, and heading out with Scout canteens and peanut butter crackers. You had plenty to write about, your letters growing longer, written in colored ink on lined notebook paper. You drew designs along the borders—swirling paisley, hearts and moons and stars and clusters of grapes. You filled the pages with clever stories about your family and your pet gerbils, Hansel and Gretel. *Today we had an adventure!* you'd written. *Gretel escaped and is currently unaccounted for. The King and Queen are beside themselves thinking they will put a foot into a shoe where she is hiding and crush her.* And *Oh, the plight of a lost gerbil is one we will never have to endure. So small! And the world so large!*

It didn't matter what we wrote back. Any sort of acknowledgment seemed enough to keep you writing. When you were punished for some small household infraction: *My bedroom is a tower, and I will forever watch the world from it.* And *I am thrown into the dungeon and the blackness is deep and desolate. Then I remember you, writing from your sunny field, waiting in the woods to retrieve my letter. You are Lancelot, Tirra lira.* Your letters cast a pall over that summer. We came to know all of your flourishes and games, your mundane details: what color you painted your nails (*skinny dip*), how much money you'd saved watering the vacationing neighbor's philodendron, and what you intended to do with it (*buy a ticket to France to meet my pen pal Chantal*). We learned of your disappointment in never knowing where the balloon you released in science class ended up (*Oh, where oh where? Zimbabwe? Tahiti? Scranton?*). You described your weeklong beach vacation (*seaside manse*), your father in his swimsuit (*hairy thighs, and the conspicuous lump, like something alive stuffed in his skimpy trunks*).

We never knew exactly what to make of your revelations. They became things Val and I thought we should not know, like the questions and answers in the *Penthouse* forum. *The King is on a rampage this morning. The Queen has spent too much money on summer clothes and groceries and other means of existence. Meanwhile the King is busy with his hobbies, and refuses to seek another position in the kingdom. Tonight we dine on canned Beeferoni. The Queen puts it on the Royal Doulton.* "*Don't be a cunt,*" *the King says, in the foulest of humors.* Charlie, the farmer boy, was boring, his domain limited. We couldn't imagine anything else to fill his life. Faced with your letters, growing longer and more intimate, his became brief, like jotted-down lists. *Work to do today*, he'd write. *Build the fence down by the road. Caught some nice perch this morning.* His only allure was his mysteriousness.

Finally, it seemed you were tapped. It was late July, a heat wave. We hunkered down in my basement and played naked Barbies. *Show yourself to me*, you wrote. Years later I would have a letter-writing affair with a man. It was thrilling at first, to see his slanted script, to learn who he was, or who he wanted me to believe he was. I imagine, with writing, the words on the page unfurling like little banners, their meanings cryptic, that we can never know what anyone intended. I put off meeting him, despite his numerous attempts and arrangements. I could never be sure, in the end, if the feelings he revealed were authentic, or just a guise to lure me into having sex. He tired of just the writing, and getting nothing, and that summer we grew tired of it as well.

We became careless and silly. We asked you to leave a pair of your underwear under the stone. *If you do*, Charlie wrote, *I'll meet you.* It was so ridiculous we didn't believe you would do it. We thought that would be the end of it, that you would know the truth. I remember the day Val went up to the dead end to check. We'd begun doing it separately, to avoid detection. She'd come to my door and my mother let her in.

"*Vite! Vite!*" she cried, tugging on my arm. Her breath smelled of cigarettes.

My mother was in the middle of something—folding laundry, or making lunch, or swiping the tables with Pledge. She never knew. Parents don't, even when they think they do. I expected Val to pull the underwear out of her pocket, but she said, no, she wouldn't touch it. So the two of us headed up the street. Of course, we were spotted by some of the younger neighborhood kids who'd been suspicious of us from the beginning. It was a small gang of us watching as Val lifted the underwear up in the air with a stick, holding it there like a flag. It was a simple pair, pale and slightly grayed from washing, a small flower attached to the elastic waistband. Soon, for all of us, there would be that splash of bright blood, and we knew it then, and it terrified us. I imagined my own underwear, tucked in the darkness of my top bureau drawer, exposed against the contrast of sunlight and waving grass, the starkness of the stone, the asphalt, the barbed wire tines, the decaying cedar post.

We were done with the letter writing, with the whole game. We didn't care what happened next, or who knew. I can't remember if we told everyone, or if the boy who grabbed the stick and the underwear and raced off on his bike knew who they belonged to. I didn't think it mattered. I see the group of us parading back down our street, the boy at the lead, looking like the benign children depicted in Joan Walsh Anglund prints, with their chunky limbs, large foreheads, heavy bangs, eyes like dark pinpricks.

That night we stayed out late, organizing yard games for the neighborhood kids: Freeze Tag, Red Rover, Mother-May-I, What Time Is It? We played until we could no longer see each other in the darkness, until the fireflies began their heated blinking, bobbing and elusive along the edge of the woods, until the mothers, standing in clusters with their cigarettes and drinks, called everyone in. We went to bed with grass-stained feet, our hair smelling like sun and sweat. And the next morning you were gone. The phone rang and the news came from the Schusters. The police parked in front of your house. Val and I stood with everyone at the end of your driveway, waiting for word. Your mother was there, roused from her couch, her eyes red-rimmed, her hands large and veined and clutching something we learned was the baby blanket you still slept with. Your father was there, an older-looking man, hunched over in a sports shirt.

"Geppetto," Val whispered. We both laughed, nervous laughter you might have forgiven us for.

Your bike was found at the dead end. And it wouldn't take long for some of the story to come out, but just part of it about a boy writing you notes. No one knew who the boy was, or where he lived, and all of the neighborhood boys were questioned, the police going house to house. Val and I said it was like "Cinderella," when the prince goes through the village trying to ferret out the young woman whose foot fit the slipper. We stuck together all that day, waiting for the letters we'd written to be discovered, but they were not. We imagined you'd hidden them in some old book, Lord Alfred Tennyson's *Poems*, the pages carved out beneath the mildewed cover. We thought we knew you then, as well as we knew ourselves. Still, we said nothing, our hearts soft and quick like the robins we'd find near death. Search parties were organized—neighborhood people, volunteer firemen from the town over. Mothers made sandwiches. The men combed the woods along the little brook, climbed over barbed wire and waded into the maze of cornfields. *Francie! Francie!* The sound of your name became a refrain. Long into the evening hours we listened to the way it went, back and forth, from all sides surrounding our neighborhood, echoing back off the rows of houses, the shake shingles and the aluminum siding.

There was a fear of abduction. There'd been little Janice Pockett on the news the summer before, who'd gone out on her bike to retrieve a butterfly and never returned. We'd seen the photos of her on flyers—blond hair and freckles and blue eyes, slightly crooked teeth—the newspaper articles documenting the search, and the giving up on searching, until she became just someone missing, a girl whose mother continued to "hold out hope." I am still plagued by that girl's eyes staring out from some third-grade school portrait, the way life shines in them, alert and potent, waiting to be lived. Val and I stayed together, consigned to our yards. The general fear of the unknown took over, and we gathered in hushed groups to imagine what might have happened to you. No one mentioned the underwear, tossed over the fence into the pasture, trampled into the grass by the farmer's cows. But they were found by the searchers, and cataloged as grim evidence. Val was called home earlier than usual, and we separated, worrying what the other might, in a moment of weakness, confess. At night every deadbolt turned. I lay in bed listening to the crickets, the frogs in the brook, the pinging of beetles against the metal window screen, sounds that I can still imagine, that make me think of the child I was, and the woman I am now, and how little I understood of my life, and how little I still understand.

You weren't taken away by a stranger. A maroon car didn't pull over and scoop you into its dank upholstered depths. Near morning they found you nestled at the base of a pine tree a mile away. You suffered from mosquito bites and dehydration. They brought you back wrapped in a pink blanket, your hair disheveled and stuck with pine needles. We watched from the safety of someone else's front lawn. The police were there, and the fireman who found you, and your parents. Your mother swooned onto the dewy grass and the fireman caught her. Your father stood apart, shaking his head, his hands on his hips, as if to chastise the two of you. I imagined wood shavings were caught in his gray curls. I remembered the word he called your mother. No one could fathom your resolve to stay hidden, to avoid the comfort of your own bed, the stuffed animals and porcelain figurines that lined your bedroom shelves, staring down at you with their frozen, wise looks. I watched you brought home and I felt, even then, the widening rift between myself and that world of mown grass and tree canopies, the race of years, their rush to overwhelm me.

You never told. But I remember the story you wrote to the boy you may have known all along was pretend. Someone came into your room, you'd written. *His breath smelled of crème de menthe. His hands were furry, like a wild beast's.* You told the searchers that you'd fallen asleep in the woods. You didn't expect them to believe you, but they could come up with no other alternative. We never checked under the stone again, but one night with a boy at the dead end I lifted it one last time and sifted through the dirt. I imagined I saw the decaying pieces of what may have been your last installment. In all stories are the seeds of what we cannot say out loud—that we are corporeal, left to the mercy of the body's urges. You never married.

Your mother died of breast cancer, and you fought for years, seeking to lay blame on our corrupted well water, citing the incidences of cancer in our neighbors. My sister sent me the article you wrote, and your picture—a taller version of you than I remembered, standing in the doorway of your mother's split-level. I imagined your father doddering about in the dim interior. You have one arm held across your chest like a shield, stalwart with your secret. Nothing ever came of your fury, your petitions. Today I discovered that you succumbed, too, of the same disease as your mother.

That night you disappeared, I'd lain in bed and imagined you in the arms of a boy I'd invented, his hair a shock of blond over his eyes, from his mouth a hum like the drone of hornets nesting in the garage. I see your face, rounded with joy, the way it looked retrieving the letter from under the stone. This is the way I like to recall it. The neighborhood remains, the farm and the farmer's fields. In summer the corn does its fine green swaying dance. In thunderstorms the lightning arcs and cleaves and the air fills with ozone. The houses still line the street in their same order. How much stays the same is undeniable, but I am unsure how much this reassures anyone. I no longer go back. What would be the point of revisiting it? We are all alone with the stories we have never told, and even now, given your death, there is no real forgiveness. Just this acknowledgment, whatever it is worth, of all the little deaths that came before it.

2012

Orlando Ricardo Menes

Elegy for Great-Uncle Julio, Cane Cutter

Martí Sugar Mill, Matanzas, Cuba, 1998

Growing up in Miami I never heard his name,
my aunts hissing *communista*, his image cut
from photos, his letters torn. "Fool, let him eat swill
in paradise," Uncle Manny would say as he
bit ripe tomatoes like apples, dimple dripping.

I wait in darkness, sitting on an oxhide chair,
smell of sinew, tallow. Tío Julio's *bohío*,
palm thatched, tobacco leaves like animal skins
nailed to walls of peeled bark; cradled by a rag
doll, the radio gargles sugar-harvest statistics.

Wakened from his nap, Tío Julio shuffles
on *bagasso* slippers, sputters when I say
I'm Cuca's grandson, sister he hasn't seen since
New Year's '59, day a triumphant Fidel
entered La Habana like Hannibal on a Sherman tank.
Cowrie shells augured exile. Few listened.

Knees buckle, fingers claw my wrist.
I lay him on a mattress stained by urine,
wilted clippings of Fidel glued to bedposts.
Stroke scarred hands, arms as if touch
could heal a lifetime cutting cane in the sun.

Tío's wife rejoices when I give her fat pork
brought from a butcher pushing a broken bicycle,
pig guts like eels in brine. Brings *cafecito*,
chicory coffee, tepid, bilgy water, raspy dregs.
I swallow to be polite. Opening a cigar box,
he shows me freckled photos of ancestors:

men who tilled with wood plows, slow oxen
fields that withered early in the planting season,
arroyos and ditches evaporating to molasses.
One sepia print shows a girl switching a mule,
Cuca at twelve, looking stern because teeth
had grown crooked on the cobs. Voice crackles

when I promise to tell Abuela how ill he is,
that his nieces will write soon. "Politics
should never divide family," Amelia says,
and I give her $20, press the bill into her hand.
"So soon, stay for dinner." "*No puedo*," I say,
fib that the last mill-train leaves at dusk.

Tall as royal palms, smokestacks spew ghosts
of the sugar harvest; dismembered,
Soviet tractors rot in sheds, corrugated tin.
Boys playing baseball chase me across
the yuca thickets. *Cuoras, chocolate, chicle*,

they plead, hurling rocks when I say no.
On these rutted canefields I trip over pits
of memory, red dust stinging my eyes,
I, bearer of dollars, false promises.

Television, a Patient Teacher

Never a nag, mean word, our color Quasar in the sunroom
where Mr. Rogers purled droplets of praise, and I could forget
the clang of Miss Dorn's burro bell when I said *shadow*
like *chado*, stretched the *O*s of wood and good into a *U*.
Mamá's gleaming bathroom, a language lab, where I stood
before the gold mirror to chew in Cronkite monotones,
pop like bazooka gum those plosive *P*s, *B*s that pummeled
Batman's foes. After a hot bath, I'd practice the tidal schwas
of Captain Kangaroo, my vaporous face breaking up,
drips and streaks on cold glass, the mouth swollen, rubbery,
a cephalopod in eddies. Within three years, I could pass
for a Hoosier or a Buckeye, Mamá proud I'd mastered a tongue
that to her sounded like a sick dog. *El castellano* retreated
into memory, dreams, the once proud hidalgo humbled
to chatter. No quitter, it began to lurk, mind's liminal wilds,
borderlands between the conscious and unconscious,
a *guerrillero*, a trickster, resisting English, his usurper.
As in a game of musical chairs, *El Padre Nuestro* lost
his throne to the Lord's Prayer, but any requests, my talk
with God, in sovereign *castizo*. To break writer's block,
think like a child, I free-write *en español*, squelching any intrusions
by Lord English. After an argument with my wife,
those words I regret are hard nasals, caustic fricatives,
but *cariñito* cloys like *guayaba* paste on a sticky afternoon.
Colleagues call me *cubano*, rounding out vowels like smoke,
which pleases me enough to wear *guayabera*, pestle cumin
with garlic, fix saints to the dash, let rice boil over the pot.

Xhenet Aliu

Flipping Property

1. What is pre-foreclosure and how can you make it work to your advantage? In the next half-hour, world-renowned real estate guru Truman Evans will show you with his patented *No Money Down Deal-Sealer's System.*

The way I understood it was like this: most people hoard more than they'll ever need in this life like it's going to give them a head start on the next one. You know, the two-for-one, the family size, the value size, the free six-inch sub with the purchase of a footlong and medium soda IN-STORE ONLY COUPON MUST BE PRESENTED AT TIME OF ORDER, the six-CD stereo upgrade for a limited time only with a 48-month lease at your friendly neighborhood Ford dealer NOT ALL LESSEES WILL QUALIFY, the Unlimited Nights & Weekends Families Talk for Free plan WITH THE PURCHASE OF FOUR (4) V600 CAMERA PHONES, the $3,000 Home Depot gift card with your down payment on a new prefabricated home at Gardenia Gardens MINIMUM 1800SQ FT PLAN WITH FINANCING THROUGH FIRST UNITED BANK MEMBER FDIC, the people die every day doesn't your family deserve more coverage you automatically qualify if you're a non-smoker, etcetera and so forth.

But some people can't even keep their hands on the barest needs. Terrell Berm, for example, barely keeping the roof over his pockmarked little head after the divorce and the bankruptcy and probably a stint or two at the Who Owns You Now rehab facility down on West Main. I didn't know Terrell Berm from any of the other guys living in any of the other gutted-up modular homes up and down the gutted-up modular streets down in the Valley, but I knew the type. I figured someone like Terrell Berm would want rid of his pre-foreclosed property, his pre-foreclosed goddamned life, so bad he'd pay the closing cost and send me a greeting card in the mail afterward. That's why I was feeling alright when I pulled the Tempo over and slipped that envelope into Mr. Terrell Berm's mailbox. Inside was the Magnetic Marketing Letter I'd printed up on the Deskjet at work: *I buy houses in any condition! Quick closings! Turn your undesirable property into* DESIRABLE CASH*!!!* Everything was red and blue on white, because cash is American is good. That's what Truman Evans said, to identify yourself with something positive, something that doesn't say, *You poor, losing bastard, I will take from you the last thing in this life that is yours.* A nicotine-beige curtain fluttered but I missed the face behind it. Enjoy your magnet, Mr. Terrell Berm, I thought. Seal your bills to the refrigerator with it, or if the bills don't make it that far then the Chinese takeout menu or a coupon for a dollar off two rolls of Pillsbury biscuits. Just maybe pause a minute at the name in red caps: LIZA BUSHKA, your friend in finance, or just CASH!!!, whatever's prettier.

Mr. Terrell Berm owned, or at least used to pay the mortgage on, a double-wide in Naugatuck set just down a ways from that business park filled with empty warehouses which every once in a while host a traveling discount book sale. I knew that because I work at the bank that owns his re-mortgaged mortgage, dialing the phone numbers that the recordings are sorry are no longer in service, licking the envelopes for those pre-foreclosure letters that go straight into the trash. 99 N. N St. More like a stutter than an address, or a candy bar you'd buy at the Dollar Value—like, the N&Ns right next to the Snuckers and Three Nougateers, that chocolate that's so cheap your mouth ulcers if you eat it. Even my kids don't beg for that crap. That's what the house was, too, a knock-off of a home, an ugly 2/1 in a puke-green color that's only used for cheap siding and Tupperware. And that was the only green there. It's funny—you think grass is free, I mean it's everywhere, some states and countries are nothing but grass, people mow it down for Cris-sakes, but some poor bastards just can't get any in to grow in their 40' x 50' lots. It's like some kind of scarlet letter, only shit brown. The kind of shit-brown yard with a busted bicycle plopped right in the middle like the topper on a birthday cake.

The Magnetic Marketing Letter didn't list my address two exits further down Route 8: 97 Harpers Ferry Road in Waterbury, the city that people in Naugatuck use to remind them that things could be worse. Terrell Berm didn't need to know I don't even have the down payment for a house of my own yet. Real estate negotiation is all in presentation, in confidence, and he didn't need to know I don't have that either. Because according to Truman Evans's patented *No Money Down Deal-Sealers System*, you don't really need money to make money. You just need a little creative self-marketing, a hard-money loan, and some carpeting to slap into a distressed property before you sell it, flip it, for market value without a single mortgage payment due. So I pulled away from the house with my sunglasses on because I thought maybe things were changing. Maybe I could be someone who could wear sunglasses without feeling like a jerk.

True, Truman Evans's *No Money Down Deal-Sealer's System* didn't include a chapter on how to make your kids' feet stop growing long enough for you to buy the decorative ficuses you can't even afford for your own home, or how to live off the life insurance policy your dead husband would've left behind if you hadn't insisted there wasn't any point in getting married, or how to stop Caleb's night terrors that set him off screaming at least three times a night and start Jenna crying right along with him when Jesus your head this is the only time you get to study the *No Money Down Deal-Sealer's System* can't you just be a big boy and sleep through one freaking night. I'm not stupid, I could see the holes. But the infomercial had offered a thirty-day introductory trial of the entire system for just the cost of shipping and handling, and then they'd asked, *What do you have to lose?* Right up until then I'd been laughing at all the fools in the commercial, their stiff hair blowing in one Dippity-Do as they were interviewed in front of their new motorboats, but that question brought me right back down. What do you have to lose, Liza? I tell you, I thought a long time about that question, and to this day I haven't come up with an answer.

2. Truman Evans first began investing in pre-foreclosures as a penniless undergraduate at the University of Illinois. By the time he earned his degree, he'd already made his first million. Now, Truman will show you how to take control of your own lives, your finances, your destinies, with his patented *No Money Down Deal-Sealer's System* and optional seminars.

I was nineteen. I wanted a dog but the complex we were living in wouldn't allow them, and even if they did Scotty wouldn't. "I don't want to share you with a dog," he'd say. So I'd visit pounds and shelters with a bundle of Milk-Bones wrapped up in my pocket and slip them between the wires on the cages. I'm sorry I can't take you home, I'd tell them, but I'm sure you'll find a fine one eventually.

I also wanted cancer. Not to die from it, but to survive it. Any idiot with the money for tuition could get a degree, but to beat malignancy and hardly even miss a day at the call center—that was something worth trying. So I took up smoking and tanning and eventually went to Dr. Sizemore with my symptoms: fatigue, night sweats, nausea, constipation.

"Well, you've got great iron in your blood," Dr. Sizemore told me. "I'd say you're feeling exactly how you're supposed to be feeling." He flipped through the chart, then looked up at me funny like there was grape jelly crusted all over my face. "You do know you're pregnant, don't you?"

"Um, I guess so," I answered. And the sickness hit hard right then, and all at once I had to puke and pee and who was going to buy the formula and diapers and Diaper Genies and the little outfits with little pink gingham ruffles on the ass? But it was like drinking too much—after I threw up into the trash can I didn't feel so bad anymore. I still wanted a dog, but I knew Scotty would at least agree to a baby since he was one of twelve himself. That kind of stuff just made sense to him. A baby seemed less like sharing me than getting more of me, only thinking that made me sick all over again. Goddamned hormones.

I told my mother first. "Ah, crap," she said. "You know you don't have to marry him."

"I know," I answered.

Then I told Scotty. "How about that," he said. "You know we have to get married."

"I know," I answered.

Scotty came home the next day with a quarter-carat ring and a pair of tiny white booties. My mother didn't counteroffer, so I took the ring and strung it onto a gold-plated chain—since it was too small even for my pinky—and I wore it for special occasions like pig roasts and wakes. It was pretty and all, don't get me wrong, but I don't know who it was he was thinking of when he bought something that tiny. Maybe it was for his first girlfriend, the tiny Puerto Rican he brought to junior prom, or maybe he was just trying wish me into something easier to manage.

3. With the help of Truman Evans's patented *No Money Down Deal-Sealer's System*, you'll learn how to hone in sellers who aren't even aware that their properties are on the market! In the end, your sellers will be thanking you for saving their ravaged credit, and your bank account will be thanking them for the fat profits!

Mom smeared some more peanut butter on the toast she eats for dinner every night.

"You're wasting your money on that, you know," she said.

I'd spread out two days' worth of newspapers and three months' worth of junk mail to camouflage the *Deal-Sealer*'s binder, although really, I knew better.

"I'm not wasting any money except $9.99 shipping and handling,"

I told her. "It's a thirty-day trial and I'm sending it back after I finish it."

"You spent $9.99 on that?" she asked, like it was even worse than she expected.

In the pauses between the thumps and screams coming from the living room, a mind-murdering cartoon chanted a chorus to a song that gets stuck in my head for days, a whole string of gibberish that means nothing except that an overpaid Disney songwriter was too lazy to think of actual words. Someone probably earned six figures for that song, and yeah, I spent ten dollars on a white binder that was supposed to tell me how to buy a house even I wouldn't live in and maybe, by some act of God and legal fine print, I might've made a thousand dollars profit so I could invest in my next slum. And yeah, maybe I did have a better chance of writing one of those Disney songs than making this thing work, but I had three days left with the system and damn if I wasn't going to try and make at least the $9.99 back.

Mom pushed the toast crumbs over the edge of the table and onto the floor. "I'll sweep tomorrow," she said. "I have to get to work. Jenna had a little bit of a fever today so you might want to put her to bed early. And Caleb's probably going to catch it so you might as well put him to bed, too."

I nodded. I guess the fever didn't weaken their pile-driving muscles, but hey, I planned on putting them to bed early anyway, get in some good study time in my last three nights with that binder. I scanned Tuesday's paper while Mom gathered up her work smock and pocketbook, which seemed to take about ten minutes if I were counting.

Finally she mumbled goodnight and I pulled out the *Deal-Sealer's System* before the door closed all the way behind her. I had some work to do. See, Truman Evans said the Magnetic Marketing Letters just plant an idea in, say, a Terrell Berm's head. Selling them on the idea was up to us. So I opened up to page seventy-three, to the script Truman Evans gave us to follow more or less when contacting a potential seller. The script didn't call for a five- and three-year-old, so I walked into the living room.

"Hey guys," I said, "we're going to play a game. You guys get to be really, really quiet while I'm on the phone. Whoever's quiet the whole time gets a Toaster Strudel."

Caleb rolled off the couch right on top of Jenna. "We hate this game, Mom," and like usual Jenna followed up with, "Yeah."

"Well, it can be a game and you get a Toaster Strudel or it can be an order and you get a swift kick in the butt. Your choice."

I walked away there because they might actually have considered it a choice, and whichever one they went with there was still only maybe a 30/70 chance of ten minutes of quiet. I picked up the phone and dialed the number I wrote on one of the pieces of junk mail, a credit card offer that was obviously an oversight in their credit check process or else a downright taunt. The line rang and I stared down into the script, wishing I'd memorized it like I memorized the role of Rizzo that I didn't get in my high school's production of *Grease*. It was on three rings, four, then finally,

"Uhnn?" a voice on the other end said. I recognized that voice, a Pall Mall and Crystal Light voice.

"Yes, hello? Is Mr. Terrell Berm available?"

"Who's this?" he said.

"Hi, I'm Liza Bushka. I'm an independent real estate investor and I'm interested in talking to you about your real estate house or property located at 99 N. N St."

"What about it?" he said.

"Well, I understand that you've had some trouble making payments lately, and I'm prepared to offer what I hope is a solution that—"

"Are you from the bank?" he asked.

"Um, no, not really," I said.

"Then what the hell are you calling about?"

"It's . . . I'm interested in perhaps talking to you about potentially purchasing your home for a fair and reasonable—"

"You got the wrong number, lady. My house isn't for sale."

"Well, I understand that it isn't currently on the market, but I was hoping perhaps that we might discuss the possibility of possibly considering a sale, which would," I checked the script, "perhaps circumvent the possibility of foreclosure which you are now currently facing."

"What in the hell are you talking about? This house isn't for sale," he said.

"Yes, I understand that it isn't *now* for sale," I said.

"It isn't ever for sale. What in the hell are you talking about?" He choked out in a coarser voice. "Where the hell do you think I'm going to live? Are you that magnet?"

"Um, well," I said. It might as well have been *Grease* in front of me by then. "By clearing the burden of a mortgage, you could possibly find another—"

"No, lady, you possibly find yourself another shithead to steal a house from." He was screaming then, and let me tell you that voice didn't sound any prettier the louder it blew. "You want to take away a man's home? What do you even know about a home? You're probably some kind of dyke, right, don't want a man to have a home of his own?"

"Um, no, I'm not a dyke, I'm an independent real estate—"

"If you're not a dyke you're a slut. I bet you're a whore and a whore needs a whorehouse, don't she."

I hung up the phone and shook a couple of Toaster Strudels from their box in the freezer. "You guys were good," I called out to Caleb and Jenna, though I guess not loud enough for them to hear.

4. You might be asking by now if flipping is legal and if you can do it with no cash or credit. The answer is yes and yes!

I admit that Scotty was good. He worked hard, I mean legendary hard, down at Browman Bros., so hard that they broke the rules and put him on the concrete pumps at full union scale within six months of his starting there. I can tell you that because Mr. Browman and everybody at the company tells me that still if I run into one of them at PathMark, and it's like they're trying to convince me to think good of him when they see my carriage full of PathMark's Peanut Butter and PathMark's Tuna Fish and PathMark's Everything instead of Name Brand Anything. But I know he worked hard. $17.00 an hour on site days, plenty of time and a half. By the time Jenna came two years after Caleb we had the health insurance to pay for her to be born. I just worked part-time at the florist, which smelled nice and wasn't so bad, really.

And he was a good father. Our kids had nice clothes and nice toys. "Too many toys," my mother said. "You never had that many toys," as if that means something, as if I'm what I want my kids to grow up to be. The man was down on his knees every night building Lincoln Log cabins with them before he even took his boots off. That's what made hating him so hard. The World's Greatest Dad cap me and the kids gave him last Father's Day, that wasn't just a cheap novelty. He could've won that contest. But when he got me the matching Mom cap, I thought it was a practical joke. Because really, I was still thinking about that dog. Dry food in a bowl, some newspapers on the floor, a rubber bone and a tie outside—that I could handle. But watching Scotty watch *Pocahontas* for the eighteenth time that week with Caleb and Jenna made me want to walk out into the winter, leave a trail of footprints to the Mad River that'd be long snowed over by the time anyone realized I was gone.

Instead I told Scotty that I wanted to take some classes at Mattatuck Community College.

"You're going to drive all the way across town every day, and all the way back, probably quit your job that you barely work at as it is, suck up half my paycheck into tuition and half dumping the kids into daycare, so that you can 'better yourself'? Better your kids, babe," he said.

Then I told him I wanted to take karate, get strong, get out of the house a couple of nights a week.

"Karate? You? Babe, you cry when you stub your toe. You never even did that Tae Bo video I got you last year."

Then I told him I wanted to leave him.

"Liza, you can't." He said it once, twice, over and over again, and his voice broke down like a truck, and the tears fell so hard I swear they stripped his face away, and I saw past his flesh to the chasm right in the center of him, and I knew what he said was right. Liza, you can't. Because maybe the kind of need we had for each other was like drowning people who pull the other one down and ride them like a raft to shore, but it was need nonetheless.

5. Truman Evans's course details his exclusive step-by-step process for revitalizing distressed properties. Turn real estate lemons into lemonade with the *No Money Down Deal-Sealer's System!*

Truman Evans sold my name to about a thousand mailing lists, the son of a bitch.

"I told you that was a waste of money," Mom said. "And a waste of time."

"You never said it was a waste of time," I said, but really I just called her on a technicality since waste of time is pretty much built into everything I do.

Used car ad. Another credit card offer. Sewage bill. Electric bill. Letter.

But not really. No stamp, no address, just Liza Bushka printed in block letters like Caleb uses. I don't know if you understand this, but people like me don't get letters. If I was an army wife, I wouldn't get letters. Even the Austrian pen-pal I wrote to in the fifth grade never wrote one back. So I didn't need to know what was inside to know what was inside, but I opened it anyway because it was that or the electric bill.

The magnet tumbled out when I unfolded the page, a red ink scrawl on lined Highland Manufacturing memo paper.

Dear Liza,

I don't want your whore magnat. Your not getting my house and neither is anybody. Your a whore and that's why your man didn't marry you.

From,

Terrell Berm

"Jesus Christ," I yelled, and I wanted forceful but it came out a wobble instead. "Crazy son of a bitch, Jesus Christ." I hopped up and locked the doors even though I didn't want to be near them and I didn't want to walk past the windows with that crazy son of a bitch a few miles away or maybe right outside, who the hell even knew.

"Caleb and Jenna, come in here," I called, even though I don't know why they needed to be in there or what I was going to tell them.

"What's your problem?" Mom asked, still smearing that peanut butter on her toast.

"*This* is my problem," and I showed her the letter.

She read it over and handed it back to me. "Well what do you expect, going around trying to buy houses you can't afford from people who can't afford to give one up?"

"I don't expect to be stalked," I said.

"What do you want?" Caleb said, Jenna trailing right behind him like his security blanket.

"Nothing. Just play in here for a little bit, okay?"

"But you never let us play in the kitchen," he said.

"Yeah, well, happy birthday."

"It's not my birfday," Jenna said, but Caleb, he got it even though he shouldn't have, and he glared right into me.

Mom started back up. "You're not being stalked, you're being put back in your place. It's insulting to people, acting like you're better than them. Plus, why're you giving out our address?"

"Hello, the phonebook, the goddamned *newspaper* printed my personal business all over this goddamned town, remember? Freaking hell, I'm just trying to act better than I am. What the hell am I supposed to do, live in this hole forever? Lick envelopes forever? I mean," and it came out too quick, "don't you ever regret having me so young?"

She thought for a minute. "Nah. I wasn't doing anything better with myself. I mean, could you imagine life without these guys?"

Sometimes I cry thinking that this woman will someday die, and that the last thing that makes sense on this earth will die with her. Why couldn't I have inherited that sense, that pure logic that no science or religion could possibly stand up against, instead of these freckles on my shoulders? See, life without them goes like this:

I went through Mattatuck, got licensed as an LPN, and signed up with one of those traveling nursing agencies that sends me to Arizona or New Mexico or I don't know, just someplace warm, Hawaii even. Or I stayed on singing in that band I joined for three weeks in high school, and we're not famous or anything, but we do weddings and high school reunions, the occasional county fair. Or I'm really fit, a runner, a cyclist.

But the Department of Children and Families listens in outside triplexes, waiting for the chance to swoop down and prove you don't love your babies, so I just said, "Nope."

But it still scares me, sometimes, to look at my children. Jenna is so pretty that I want to take her to the doctor to fix it. There's no good to come out of that kind of pretty. And Caleb—Caleb is the kind of smart they call precocious but I call unnerving. He was looking at me there in the kitchen, and I knew he knew that I make everything up on the spot. And I could only look back at him and think, *Where did I come up with a name like Caleb?*

6. Truman Evans's *No Money Down Deal-Sealer's System* isn't the cheapest real estate course out there, but then again, the best never comes cheap.

What you need to know, what Terrell Berm and everybody needs to know, is that Scotty isn't better off. No way, no heaven in any religion could match what he wanted on earth. Caleb and Jenna sure as hell aren't better off. I'm not even better off. Maybe I wouldn't get that ring resized, maybe I told him once or twice that it was because I had to get out there and live some first, but I know now it was just to hear him say, *Liza, you can't.* Liza, you can't leave. Liza, you can't possibly understand how deep you're in. You can't love them alone the way that I can.

And it was his love that killed him, so big it just popped him right open. Except he got a little help from a die-cast fire truck and some cement basement stairs. Since we were on the first floor we were lucky enough to get use of the cellar, which meant more room for more stuff we didn't really need. And listen, I was always telling Caleb not to leave that stuff around the house like that, and I was always telling Scotty to back me up on it. They never listened, never. So when me and the kids came home one day and the door to the cellar was open outside and we couldn't find Daddy anywhere, even with all of us calling out for ten minutes, I knew I should've sent them to their rooms before I did anything else but I was scared. And I don't know what they saw when I pulled the door open wide, but I saw first the dollhouse half-finished and I thought you fool, you stupid goddamned idiot, why was the one you bought for Jenna a year ago not good enough? But when I dropped down to my knees and put his head on my lap and soaked up that blood on his hair, that blood that sank into my own skin and colored it for days, I understood finally the kind of love that Scotty felt, and I understood that I'd never feel it, and I told him Scotty, Scotty, I wish I could, Scotty.

7. If at any point within the thirty-day trial period you're unsatisfied with Truman Evans's *Deal-Sealer's System*, simply return it no questions asked SORRY, SHIPPING & HANDLING NON-REFUNDABLE.

Mom was on her way out the door when the phone rang.

"I got a dick you can suck if you need the money," Terrell Berm said.

I pulled a big stream of air into my lungs so I could yell, but suddenly I was crying instead, crying which I hadn't done in three months, and that bastard made me remember it and he could die himself for that. "Go to hell, you motherfucker," I said.

"What's the matter, whore? Don't you want my property no more?"

"I don't care about the fucking property," I screamed into the phone, and then hung up, and then whipped the receiver across the room into the cereal cabinet, and then Jenna was crying, and then Caleb looked up at me with the kind of disappointed eyes that no five year old should have earned yet.

"Mommy," he said.

"She meant flipping property, Caleb," my mother said.

"No I didn't," I said. "Mommy's mad and she shouldn't say things like that around you but that's how mad she is. She's sorry you had to hear it but sometimes life just isn't good and she's sorry you have to hear that, too."

Caleb stared up with those caramel eyes that came straight from his father, a whole face that came straight from his father, and I wished I could have seen right through to his insides so I'd know where they came from, if there was any chance at all, because my children, oh my children I am sorry.

Source Acknowledgments

All selections in this volume are reprinted by
permission of the University of Nebraska Press.

"Flipping Property," from *Domesticated Wild Things* by Xhenet Aliu ©
2013 by Xhenet Aliu.

"Dust," from *Ceiling of Sticks* by Shane Book © 2010 by the Board of
Regents of the University of Nebraska.

"Little Sinners," from *Little Sinners, and Other Stories* by Karen Brown
© 2012 by Karen Brown.

"Self-Portrait with an Ice Pick" and "Carnivale, 1934," from *Taste of
Cherry* by Kara Candito © 2009 by the Board of Regents of the
University of Nebraska.

"The Fund-Raiser's Dance Card," from *Carrying the Torch: Stories* by
Brock Clarke © 2005 by the Board of Regents of the University of
Nebraska.

"Last Call," from *Last Call* by K. L. Cook © 2004 by K. L. Cook.

"Paradoxical Undressing," "Metacognition," and "The Bees Have Not
Yet Left Us," from *The Book of What Stays* by James Crews © 2011
by the Board of Regents of the University of Nebraska.

"Leopold's Maneuvers" and "March 28, 2001 / March 28, 1945," from
Leopold's Maneuvers by Cortney Davis © 2004 by the Board of Regents
of the University of Nebraska.

"Vincent," from *Call Me Ahab: A Short Story Collection* by Anne Finger
© 2009 by Anne Finger.

"Preservation" and "Murder Mysteries," from *Famous* by Kathleen Flen-
niken © 2006 by the Board of Regents of the University of Nebraska.

"Physical Wisdom," from *Bliss and Other Short Stories* by Ted Gilley ©
2010 by the Board of Regents of the University of Nebraska.

"Elba," and "These Arms of Mine," from *Notes for My Body Double* by Paul
Guest © 2007 by the Board of Regents of the University of Nebraska.

Contributors

Xhenet Aliu received her MFA from the University of North Carolina–Wilmington in 2007. Her fiction has appeared in such journals as *Glimmer Train, Hobart,* and *The Barcelona Review.* She has received scholarships from the Bread Loaf Writers' Conference and a grant from The Elizabeth George Foundation. Her first book, *Domesticated Wild Things,* is the 2012 winner of the Prairie Schooner Book Prize in Fiction.

Shane Book's first collection, *Ceiling of Sticks,* won the Prairie Schooner Book Prize in Poetry (2009) and the Great Lakes Colleges Association New Writers Award and was a Poetry Society of America New American Poet selection. He is a graduate of New York University and the Iowa Writers' Workshop and was a Wallace Stegner Fellow at Stanford University. His work has appeared in seventeen anthologies and over forty-five magazines in the United States, the United Kingdom, and Canada and on film. His honors include a New York Times Fellowship in poetry, fellowships to the Flaherty Film Seminar and the Telluride Film Festival, an Academy of American Poets Prize, and a National Magazine Award.

Karen Brown received her PhD from the University of South Florida and is a short story writer. Her first collection of short stories, *Pins and Needles,* won the Grace Paley Prize for Short Fiction, and her stories have been chosen twice for inclusion in *The PEN/O. Henry Prize Stories* and have appeared in *Best American Short Stories 2008.* Brown's *Little Sinners, and Other Stories* is the 2011 winner of the Prairie Schooner Book Prize in Fiction.

Kara Candito is the author of *Taste of Cherry,* winner of the 2008 Prairie Schooner Book Prize in Poetry. Her work has appeared in such journals and anthologies as *Blackbird, AGNI, Prairie Schooner,* the *Kenyon Review, Gulf Coast,* the *Rumpus, Best New Poets 2007,* and *A Face to Meet the Faces: An Anthology of Contemporary Persona Poetry.* A recipient of scholarships from the Bread Loaf Writers' Conference, the Vermont Studio Center, and the Santa Fe Arts Institute, Candito is an assistant professor of creative writing at the University of Wisconsin, Platteville.

Brock Clarke is the author of five books of fiction, most recently the novels *Exley* and *An Arsonist's Guide to Writers' Homes in New England* and the short story collection *Carrying the Torch*. His work has been published in many magazines, newspapers, and anthologies, and he is the winner of the Mary McCarthy Prize, the 2004 Prairie Schooner Book Prize in Fiction, a National Endowment for the Arts fellowship, and two Pushcart Prizes. He currently teaches at Bowdoin College and lives in Portland, Maine.

K. L. Cook is the author of three award-winning books of fiction: *Last Call*, winner of the inaugural Prairie Schooner Book Prize in Fiction (2003); *The Girl from Charnelle*, winner of the Willa Award for Contemporary Fiction and an Editor's Choice selection of the Historical Novel Society; and *Love Song for the Quarantined*, winner of the Spokane Prize for Short Fiction. His Stories have been published widely, including in such journals and anthologies as *Glimmer Train*, *One Story*, *Best of the West 2011*, and *Best American Mystery Stories 2012*. He teaches at Prescott College and in Spalding University's low-residency MFA in Writing Program.

James Crews was born and raised in St. Louis, Missouri. His work has appeared in *Crab Orchard Review*, *Best New Poets 2006* and *2009*, *Columbia*, *Prairie Schooner*, and other journals. He is the author of three chapbooks: *Bending the Knot* (winner of the 2008 Gertrude Press Poetry Chapbook Contest), *One Hundred Small Yellow Envelopes*, and *What Has Not Yet Left* (winner of the 2010 Copperdome Prize). His collection *The Book of What Stays* won the 2010 Prairie Schooner Book Prize in Poetry. In his free time, Crews writes reviews and articles for *basalt magazine*, which he coedits, and he regularly contributes to the *Times Literary Supplement*. He has worked as a salesman of bespoke wallpaper, an AmeriCorps VISTA volunteer, and an English teacher in rural Oregon. He is now living and teaching in Lincoln, Nebraska, where he is working on a PhD.

Cortney Davis, a nurse practitioner, is the author of five poetry collections, including *Leopold's Maneuvers*, winner of the first Prairie Schooner Book Prize in Poetry in 2003. Her nonfiction titles include *I Knew a Woman: The Experience of the Female Body* and *The Heart's Truth: Essays on the Art of Nursing*. She is the coeditor of two anthologies of nurses' poetry and prose, *Between the Heartbeats* and *Intensive Care*. Honors for Davis's writing include an National Endowment for the Arts Poetry Fellowship, three Connecticut Commission on the Arts poetry grants, an Independent Publisher Book Awards silver medal in nonfiction, and the Connecticut Center for the Book's nonfiction prize. Davis is the poetry editor of the journal *Alimentum: The Literature of Food*.

Anne Finger has taught creative writing at Wayne State University in Detroit and at the University of Texas at Austin. She is the author of several books, including the memoir *Elegy for a Disease: A Personal and Cultural History of Polio*, *Bone Truth: A Novel*, and *Basic Skills: A Short Story Collection*. Finger's *Call Me Ahab* is the winner of the 2008 Prairie Schooner Book Prize in Fiction.

Kathleen Flenniken's first book, *Famous*, won the 2005 Prairie Schooner Book Prize in Poetry. *Famous* was named a Notable Book by the American Library Association and a was a finalist for the Washington State Book Award. Her second collection, *Plume*, is an examination of the Hanford Nuclear Site in Washington State. Flenniken's awards include a Pushcart Prize and fellowships from the National Endowment for the Arts and Artist Trust. She is the 2012–14 Poet Laureate of Washington State.

Ted Gilley is a writer and editor whose work has appeared in a score of magazines and anthologies, including *Northwest Review*, *Poetry Northwest*, *Malahat* (British Columbia) and *New England Review*. His nonfiction pieces, stories, and poems have won several prizes, including the 2008 Alehouse Press (San Francisco) national poetry competition. Gilley's *Bliss and Other Short Stories* is the 2009 recipient of the Prairie Schooner Book Prize in Fiction.

Paul Guest is the author of three volumes of poetry: *The Resurrection of the Body and the Ruin of the World*, *Notes for My Body Double* (winner of the 2006 Prairie Schooner Book Prize in Poetry), and *My Index of Slightly Horrifying Knowledge*. He is also the author of a memoir, *One More Theory About Happiness*, and his poems have appeared in the *Paris Review*, *Poetry*, *Tin House*, and the *Kenyon Review*.

Greg Hrbek received his MFA from the University of Iowa and is a writer of novels and short fiction. While working on his first novel, *The Hindenburg Crashes Nightly*, Hrbek won the James Jones First Novel Award. His collection of short fiction, *Destroy All Monsters, and Other*

Stories, won the 2010 Prairie Schooner Book Prize in Fiction. Hrbek's stories have appeared in *Harper's Magazine, Salmagundi, Conjunctions*, and *Black Warrior Review*. "Sagittarius," from *Destroy All Monsters, and Other Stories*, appeared in *The Best American Short Fiction 2009*.

John Keeble's collection of stories, *Nocturnal America*, received the 2005 Prairie Schooner Book Prize in Fiction. He is also the author of four novels, including *Yellowfish* and *Broken Ground*. His work has appeared in *Outside*, the *Village Voice, American Short Fiction, Prairie Schooner, Northwest Review, Zyzzyva, Idaho Review*, and *Best American Short Stories*. A longstanding member of the MFA faculty at Eastern Washington University and now professor emeritus, he also served as the Visiting Chair in Creative Writing at the University of Alabama. He is the recipient of a Guggenheim Fellowship.

Jesse Lee Kercheval received her MFA from the University of Iowa and is the founding director of the MFA program at the University of Wisconsin, where she is the Sally Mead Hands Professor of English. She is the author of eleven books of poetry, fiction, and memoir, including *Brazil*, winner of the Ruthanne Wiley Memorial Novella Contest; the poetry collection *Cinema Muto*, winner of the Crab Orchard Open Selection Award; and the memoir *Space*, winner of an Alex Award from the American Library Association. Her individual stories and poems appear regularly in magazines in the United States, the United Kingdom, Canada, and Australia. Kercheval's *The Alice Stories* is the 2006 recipient of the Prairie Schooner Book Prize in Fiction.

Mari L'Esperance was born in Kobe, Japan, to a Japanese mother and a French Canadian–American father and raised in California, Micronesia, and Japan. Her poems and prose have appeared in *Beloit Poetry Journal, Connotation Press: An Online Artifact, Many Mountains Moving, Poetry Kanto, Prairie Schooner, Salamander, Zocalo Public Square*, and elsewhere. An earlier collection *Begin Here* was awarded a Sarasota Poetry Theatre Press Chapbook Prize. A graduate of the creative writing program at New York University and the recipient of fellowships and grants from the New York Times Company Foundation, New York University, Hedgebrook, and Dorland Mountain Arts Colony, L'Esperance currently lives in the San Francisco Bay Area, where she works in the mental health field and teaches occasionally. Her poetry collection *The Darkened Temple* received the 2007 Prairie Schooner Book Prize in Poetry.

Orlando Ricardo Menes received his PhD from the University of Illinois at Chicago and is an associate professor of English and Faculty Fellow of the Institute for Latino Studies at the University of Notre Dame. His poetry collections include, among others, *Furia: Poems*, *Rumba Atop the Stones*, and *Fetish*, the 2012 winner of the Prairie Schooner Book Prize in Poetry.

Susan Blackwell Ramsey's poems have appeared in such journals and anthologies as the *Indiana Review*, *Southern Review*, *Prairie Schooner*, and *New Poems from the Third Coast: An Anthology of Michigan Poets*. She won the 2006 Marjorie J. Wilson Award from *Margie: The Journal for American Poetry* and her poem "Pickled Heads, St. Petersburg" was chosen for the 2009 edition of *Best American Poetry*. Ramsey's *A Mind Like This* is the 2011 recipient of the Prairie Schooner Book Prize in Poetry.

Katherine Vaz was a Briggs-Copeland Fellow in Fiction at Harvard University from 2003 to 2009 and a 2007 Fellow of the Radcliffe Institute for Advanced Study. She is the author of *Saudade*, selected for the Barnes & Noble Discover Great New Writers series, and *Mariana*, published in six languages and selected by the Library of Congress as one of the Top Thirty International Books of 1997. Her collection *Fado & Other Stories* won the 1997 Drue Heinz Literature Prize, and her short fiction has appeared in numerous magazines. She is the recipient of a National Endowment for the Arts Fellowship and is the first Portuguese American to have her work recorded for the archives in the Hispanic Division of the Library of Congress. Vaz's *Our Lady of the Artichokes and Other Portuguese-American Stories* is the 2007 winner of the Prairie Schooner Book Prize in Fiction.

Rynn Williams received her MA from New York University and her MFA from Warren Wilson. Her poems have been published in the *Nation*, *Massachusetts Review*, *Field*, *Agni Online*, *New York Quarterly*, *North American Review*, and *Prairie Schooner*. Williams is the 2004 winner of the Prairie Schooner Book Prize in Poetry. She passed away in 2009.

In the Prairie Schooner Book Prize in Poetry series

Cortney Davis, *Leopold's Maneuvers*

Rynn Williams, *Adonis Garage*

Kathleen Flenniken, *Famous*

Paul Guest, *Notes for My Body Double*

Mari L'Esperance, *The Darkened Temple*

Kara Candito, *Taste of Cherry*

Shane Book, *Ceiling of Sticks*

James Crews, *The Book of What Stays*

Susan Blackwell Ramsey, *A Mind Like This*

Orlando Ricardo Menes, *Fetish*

To order or obtain more information on
these or other University of Nebraska Press
titles, visit www.nebraskapress.unl.edu.

In the Prairie Schooner Book Prize in Fiction series

Last Call: Stories
By K. L. Cook

Carrying the Torch: Stories
By Brock Clarke

Nocturnal America
By John Keeble

The Alice Stories
By Jesse Lee Kercheval

Our Lady of the Artichokes and Other Portuguese-American Stories
By Katherine Vaz

Call Me Ahab: A Short Story Collection
By Anne Finger

Bliss and Other Short Stories
By Ted Gilley

Destroy All Monsters, and Other Stories
By Greg Hrbek

Little Sinners, and Other Stories
By Karen Brown

Domesticated Wild Things
By Xhenet Aliu

To order or obtain more information on
these or other University of Nebraska Press
titles, visit www.nebraskapress.unl.edu.